I0732195

Shine

www.powderriverpublishing.com

Dedication

This page is dedicated to my senior-year college roommate, and original editor of the book, Nic. Nic has been an amazing help throughout the entire process. During my senior year of college is when I really started fleshing out the story and the direction I wanted the book to head. It was thanks to Nic's creative ideas and being my sounding board that I was able to get the ball rolling further.

After I graduated college, Nic and I stayed in touch while I continued my efforts to finish the book. At the start of the year 2020, I finally got to the point where I felt the book was done, but I was not ready to submit it to a publisher because I felt it needed a lot of work. Nic came in and did my initial edits and helped me better formulate areas that I had left blank. It was thanks to Nic's help and support that in 2021 I am proud to say that I am able to publish this book.

Thank you so much for all your help and support. I could not have done this without you.

Published by:
Powder River Publishing LLC
147 N. Burritt Ave
Buffalo, Wyoming 82834

Copyright © 2021
ISBN: 978-1-7366659-0-9
Printed in the United States of America

Table of Contents

The First Night

The sound of hooves and rain beating along the cobbled road penetrated the night. It was pouring outside, so much so that the road itself was made into a river. Yet, the rider continued. The city was not much further up the road, and it only took her an hour more to reach it.

The city gate closed behind her as she passed through, allowed only by the fact they recognized the insignia on her cloak. An insignia that burned, even in the dark, as if it were a torch. A simple serpent with its fangs bared, a crown floating above it. It marked her as the royal witch, Rizza.

As Rizza reached the courtyard of the tavern inside the city, she let the horse ease to a halt near the stables. A boy raced to assist her, cowering under a meager blanket as he did so. Her body slid off the horse with ease as she flipped a coin to the stable hand. She left to allow the horse to be taken to the stables. Her boots did not make a sound and neither did her cloak, in spite of how heavy it was. Despite the mud puddles and thick rain, Rizza was silent.

The night air was made that much cooler by the rain and it made for a miserable night. Still, making it to the city tonight was far better than having to spend another day in a tent on the cold ground. The lightning cracked in the air over Rizza's head as she walked, her thoughts drifting. The horse probably enjoyed it more too, especially as it was led away to sleep comfortably in a stable rather than under the shelter of a tree. If the stable hand was of any use, he would dry the poor creature off before putting it to bed.

Her feet carried her into the tavern itself and up to the counter where the keeper stood cleaning a glass with a dusty rag. The thin clothe could not possibly have been any help in cleaning. Then again, the tavern was not of the best repute. It was in a poor part of town, but probably the only part of town that would serve someone of her distinct history. There was one other place she knew for a fact she could go, but she was not yet ready to visit. Time would tell when she was.

She kept her thought about the rag to herself, not wanting to already appear on the wrong side of the place and get herself thrown out of another establishment. Long ago, she had given up the idea she was able to dine in a place that was fitting for polite company. That idea was forfeited when she realized she was not fit to be polite company. It showed, having been thrown out of the palace on not one, but ten separate occasions. A soft grunt escaped her to get the keeper's attention, causing the man to raise an eyebrow.

He was stout with a long nose and thin lips that did not match his round chubby face in the least. His beady eyes looked at her warily but gave away nothing else. "Aye?"

"A room for the night." she said, her words barely audible, keeping her voice down as she spoke. She hated speaking, and the reason why showed well when the man responded. Instant attraction showed on his face as the spell that was her voice wrapped around him and charmed him in a way that only she could do naturally. Well, her or any other magic wielder, though others like her were few and far between, and none quite as powerful.

Of course, she could alter her voice, use magic, put a spell on it to negate the one that was there from birth. Yet, what would be the point? It was late, she was tired, and such trivial things were the last thing on her mind, even if she did cringe at his reaction. This was one of the many reasons she had secluded herself away from others.

A soft wince contorted her face, hidden by the heavy cloak. Humans were the weakest of creatures, drawn to her voice like bees to a honey pot. The keeper was no exception. The interest on his face and the way he seemed to be compelled to do whatever she asked stated as much.

Not a word was spoken by the man, but he still handed over the key. She slipped the coins required over to him from the counter. Even her hands were covered in fabric, thick gloves that were made of leather to combat the heavy rain. They were dyed a dark red, nearly the same color as blood when it ran free of the vein. It was almost like he did not even realize she needed to pay. As he took the coins his face filled with surprise. She did not stay long to question it, simply reading the location of the room from his memory before disappearing down the hall. Just as the images he provided her unwittingly accounted for, his little tavern was much larger than it appeared on the outside. The Tavern was longer than it was wide, which left her walking down a long, dimly lit hall. At the end, there was a dark set of oak stairs that led to the second floor, lit by a single lantern that made them more ominous than the hall itself. She could not complain, nor would she, it was the first time in a few weeks that she would have been given an actual bed. Plus, it was not like anyone else had her magical talent anyways. Unless they got a lucky stab in before she sensed them, she could easily deal with anyone who attacked her. A shady tavern was far better than the woods, even if it was inside the capital city of the kingdom.

The kingdom... Her thoughts drifted again as to why the hell she had been drawn from her mountain keep, being brought to the royal capital on a summons of little sense. She was a lot of things, but an errand girl was not one of them. Arguably the most powerful witch in the realm, sure, but not an errand girl. Worst of all, the message had been unclear.

Her gaze glanced over the dingy room. It was as poorly lit as the rest of the building, not that it mattered. After she shut the door, the fingers on her left hand deftly pulled the glove off her right. The freed hand lifted into the air and her fingers snapped. A small ball of blue flame ignited in her hand with a simple grumbled word. She had it move to the middle of the room. She could have lit the few candles that were there, like a normal person, but the witch light provided better lighting, cleaner lighting. Instead of bathing the room in a golden glow, she got a clear white light from it. It made all the imperfections that much more obvious to see.

The bed was covered in a ratted sheet that showed the poorly stuffed mattress under it.

Inside the Mattress there were holes leaking hay, probably caused by rodents, or worse, roaches.

If that were the case, then Rizza could only assume that the hay was also rotten. A soft frown creased her face at that thought. If there were bugs, there were probably bed bugs as well. The idea of waking up with hives all over her back from the little vermin that had bitten who knows how many patrons did not sit well with her.

Rizza slowly removed her hood, her gaze still locked on the less than adequate room.

Could it even be called a room? She was not entirely certain. It was more like a hovel. Pulling her hood down gave her a better view, though.

In public, she could not be bothered with such an act. She found it infinitely easier to keep her hood on and her head down low. Her voice was already bewitching enough, she did not need people staring at the markings on her skin that clearly denoted her a witch. They were soft patched spots that marked along her eye that made it look like someone had embedded silver into her skin.

They seemed to be dotting her face like the stars in the night sky. Her skin was pale as death, giving the markings a more eerie quality. These 'stars' lay under her fully purple gaze that held no pupil. She also had black hair that fell more like spikes than locks of hair ought to. The fact that her fingernails were long, pitch black, and sharp by natural design did not aid a welcoming vibe. No, she did not need more attention.

A familiar ache crept over her as she looked around the grubby and uninhabitable space; an ache to be home, away from all except those who dared ventured into her mountains looking for a remedy to this or that ailment. Home. A place far from here, at least a month's ride out from the capital city in good weather, just to arrive at the cursed capital city. This was not her home.

She was not born in the mountains. No, she had been gifted those mountains much later in life, when she pledged to serve the throne in times of dire need.. 'Gifted' the mountains when the king and queen could no longer handle her wanton ways of magic. 'Gifted' the mountains in a plea to have her play hermit so that she may stop proving everyone wrong, because no one liked it when

she was right. That thought alone displeased her, to have to come
to the capital city heightened it... but a pledge was a pledge. A
witch could not break their vows any more than a mortal could
escape death.

Her thoughts lingered on her 'job' as she walked further
into the room. She had not really been told what to expect, simply
that she was summoned and to appear in a month and one day later. It was a very mysterious summons, something that happened
often. Rizza couldn't help but notice the creak of the floorboards
as she moved. Much like the mattress, she assumed the wood
under her feet was probably rotted away. It was amazing it could
even hold up the furniture that sat in the room.

The Royals hardly ever called on her to come from her
home, but when they did, they knew they had best make her question what the hell was going on. If Rizza could refuse by letter,
she would. They always gave her one more day, just to be sure she
would be on time for the summons... not that she was ever, ever
late.

Finally, she began to do a simple dress down of the room.
Words in an ancient and very dead language flew to her mouth
as her fingers drifted through the air, preoccupying her thoughts
where they would otherwise stray towards the fact that she would
rather be anywhere else.

It was very likely that she didn't actually need to speak
to use her magic, her innate ability was such that it wasn't necessary, yet there was a calming quality at saying the things you
wanted done. It also added a more 'official' feeling to what she
was doing, as if her magic needed some sort of validation despite
how overwhelmingly endless it was.

Where she glanced and looked around, the room began to
change. Slowly, it became a place that was fit to be in. The mattress became one stuffed with feathers instead of rotted hay. The
pillows molded into ones that were feather down with rose petals, fit for a queen. She conjured, and the floor began to creak as
old dead wood grew into new. The candles grew back as the wax
reformed and the wick became reborn. Subtle changes turned
monumental, until the room she was standing in could be considered one of the best in town. The bed frame was replaced with an

elegant four-post frame when she was done, the rotten mattress and sheets replaced with a heavy soft comforter and a much softer mattress and sheets. The room was still the same size, but was visibly improved in quality as she had changed the composition of the furniture to something more elegant. It was simple work for someone like her, but still added to her exhaustion after a long day.

She moved to the chair in the corner of the room and pulled her cloak from her shoulders, hesitating as she stared at the sopping wet fabric in her hands. The water made the cloak at least ten if not fifteen pounds heavier, which would do no good if she tried to sit in it, even if she was already soaked. Looking around, she found the fireplace, and hung the cloak near it to dry. She placed the thing just close enough that the fire would dry it and not burn it once it was done. A hand ran through ebony black locks as she let out a very tired and weary sigh. The capital city. A glance out the window showed the dim-lit windows of other buildings throughout the place and far up on the hill, the palace. A place she would be venturing tomorrow.

She strode back to the chair. Again, the urge to sit was strong, but she forced herself to refrain from it. She was still standing in soaked clothing.

"Kit." The word was barely a whisper, but the little wisp appeared anyways. "Clothing." A soft command, not usually one she had to give as the companion usually knew without being asked.

The little ball of orange light bobbed in the air before a shimmer appeared in front of her. Dutifully she held out her hands and the garments were dropped into them. Her gaze looked down at what the wisp had given her, and she frowned before glancing up and glaring.

"Funny. Real clothing." The garments shimmered before being taken away to be replaced. Where the frilly silk nightgown had been in her hands was now a soft black wool one. A smile appeared on her face. That looked warm enough. Shrugging out of her wet clothing, she let Kit take the garments before sliding into

the nightgown. Between the warm fire and the way she had rear-
ranged the room, the place was beginning to feel more comfortable. Still, not home.

She shuffled over to the chair, finally able to relax as Kit
fluttered around her. Her gaze watched the playful wisp as he
danced about. At least... she assumed kit was a he. Mannerisms
spoke volumes, and he always seemed to want her in something
light and revealing. That, or her little wisp could be a very playful
creature who just wanted to help. Yet, she still felt he was a boy.
He danced around her head for some time. Usually, a time like this
was when she would talk to him as if she understood what he was
trying to say. For once though, she stayed silent.
Eventually, the wisp seemed to give up on their attempt at com-
munication, as she was simply too tired to follow, and disappeared. She remained in the chair for a while, simply letting her
muscles relax until her eyelids began to feel too heavy to lift. At
that point, she stood and moved to the bed.

A soft flick of her wrist and all the lights in the room went
out; she was left to her sleep.

The Palace

Rizza was expected to show up to the palace bright and early in the morning, the time most every other mortal got up, the time the gods were most happy: first light. Rizza, however, was no god, and no mortal. She hated the morning, and it showed on her face as she rode into the courtyard of the palace. Her expression, thankfully, was hidden behind her thick cloak as always when she climbed off the horse.

A servant rushed forward to take it from her as she stared up at the towering building that loomed before her. The Palace hands all wore pristine white livery and dared not even glance near her face. They were petrified of being noticed by her, so she did them the favor of pretending she did not notice as she looked at the towering fortress before her.

The Palace was nothing to shirk at. It was large with rising spires and grey stone that made it look more like a stronghold. Though, it was still beautiful.

She knew it was built in a way that surrounded an open-air garden in the center. The main building was square, with crafted scenery in the middle and branches to the East and South wing connecting it by long hallways. The route to the West wing, home to the Royal Family, was hidden and few knew of the entrance. Beyond that, the Wing could not be accessed from the outside, cut off by a set of walls on either side to the North and South respectively. Then, to the furthest western point, there was a cliff. Getting to the West Wing would take going from the castle into the gardens and finding a way inside... possibly by blowing a hole through the stone wall.

Rizza was one of those few who knew how to actually enter the place. Why it was a secret was beyond her, though. Anyone could easily blow the west wing up from the outside and simply be done with it, but if she pointed that out again, she was afraid she may lose her head this time.

She and the crown prince had fought many times over the layout of the castle and its safety. He claimed nothing could breach it, and she had proven with a few simple spells that someone like her easily could. He did not take well to having half of the west wing blown away, especially not with the crown princess, his fiancée, bathing in their suite when she did it.

The poor girl was exposed to most of the palace in that little stunt, and it was only because Rizza was the only witch of her caliber that she kept her head that time. It was then that they decided that they should change the security. Though they loathed the fact that Rizza was right, it didn't change the fact that she was, and so, two new fortified walls were added to the North and the South. These were the walls that now stood to block access from the outside to the Western wing.

That had also been when they had decided it would be a good thing to 'gift' her the mountains and get rid of her by doing her that kindness. The joke was on them; it was the best gift they could have ever given her. Rizza hated people, and, therefore, they were doing her a huge favor by sending her far away from them. It was a place to call her own that became a place of nightmares to others.

A long stare up at the building in front of her was earned after all her traveling. She rarely came to the capital city due to the fact that she tended to prove her point by using her magic. court nobles did not like that. They were all a bunch of pampered pups anyway. What would they know about mystic arts and defense when all they ever did was sit around and bicker as if they were not bickering? It was all extremely tedious, and she hated it.

Finally done gawking at the gaudy structure, Rizza began to climb the steps. It was evident from the second she entered the building that she stood out. Her cloak, while enchanted with all sorts of spells for protection, was not beautiful. It looked ratty and old, which didn't matter to her, but it earned her several glances. She, of course, was not wearing the cloak she had worn to ride into the city. The nobles didn't deserve to see that cloak, it was too nice. The cloak covered Rizza from head to toe and the hood of it cast her face in shade to the point where only the tip of her chin showed. This cloak was a dark, almost black, purple, unlike her flashy red one. It was indeed a very frightening outfit if one had spent their entire life in luxury, as many of the nobles walking by her had. It was why she dressed as she did.

Rizza also could not help but bring along a staff, just to add to the dramatic effect as she walked. She leaned heavily on the staff, and made it pound into the marble floor with each step just to draw attention and make everyone as uncomfortable as she was. A lot could be said about her, and one thing was for certain: Rizza was nothing if not dramatic. She liked being dramatic, it worked well for her.

Despite having not been in the palace for many years, she still knew where the dining hall was. She made her way there effortlessly. Once there, it was with great pleasure that she used a small gust of magical wind to blow the doors open for a grand entrance. She did not move from her withered-looking pose as she stood in the entrance, gaze scanning the different tables from where she stood.

The room had clearly been lively before Rizza had startled everyone. A small malicious smirk played along her face at that idea. Far be it from her to disturb the delicate sensibilities of the nobles. They all began whispering nervously as she resumed walking. The sound of the staff stabbed into the ground punctuated each step as she took it. She walked past several tables of curious onlookers before she was able to draw near to the dais that held the royal family's private table. It was set at the very back of the enormous room.

At the table sat the entire royal family save for the youngest of them. She assumed more had been added since her last visit, because she could see the Crown Prince and Princess had wedding rings on their fingers, finally.

Though that thought wasn't concrete... perhaps the two hadn't had luck in that department. Rizza remembered having to 'help' Drake's father with his ability to conceive. Perhaps Drake inherited the problem, but none of them knew she had helped, so they didn't know to ask. She didn't assume Drake would ask even if he did know, since he rather loathed to owe her anything.

It was so nice of them to invite her to the wedding. It even sounded bitter in her own mind. However, the crown prince was not
even looking at her. His head was firmly in his hands where he
seemed to be hiding a groan. Another smile flashed across her
face. He hated her so much. She had to give him one thing though,
he was good looking.

Soft brown hair ran down his shoulders and back in small
waves. The white and gold suit he wore greatly complimented his
fair but strong complexion and his build was nothing to shirk at,
either.

If she was so inclined, she could probably take a memory or
two from the crown princess of exactly how he looked under that
suit. Though, such uncouth activities were below her. She had
already done that years ago in her youth.

Beside him, the crown princess was also beyond beautiful. Her fair blonde, almost white, hair was a contrast to his soft
brown and her gentle blue eyes always seemed to be laughing.
She had soft features and a subtly curved figure that made her
gorgeous. Her skin was even fairer than her husband's, and it just
made them the most perfect couple in Rizza's eyes, not that she
would ever tell the arrogant jerk that.

Sitting at the center of the table, to the Crown Princess'
left, were the king and queen of the court. Rizza swept them a
bow, hardly paying attention to the other two princes and the
young princess on their other side. The king and queen shared
their son's complexion and hair color, though the king's hair was
slightly darker brown with wisps of gray in his hair and beard.
The frown on his face was permanently in place, but next to him,
his wife smiled happily at Rizza. Rizza had always liked the queen,
and it was only because of her that she had pledged her magic to
serve them. They were dressed in matching dark blue and black
garb, the royal colors of rulers in the kingdom.

As the room seemed to settle into silence again with the
echo of her staff fading off, Rizza gave a deep bow to the rulers of
the kingdom, again. The gesture was almost mocking in its overly
elaborate execution, and the silence only made it that much more
audible when the crown prince groaned. The irony was not lost
on the queen and Rizza knew it as the titter of laughter it incited

filled the hall.

Rizza did not like to bow or bend for anyone. She hated to admit that she owed anyone her services, her pride swollen and steadfast against it. In this life, she was quite full of herself and arrogant. Others needing her did nothing but aid that constant thought. Rizza was self-important and couldn't imagine a world where she wasn't the most important person.

"Your Majesties, I have traveled far, and am so glad to have been summoned from my quaint, isolated home, that has so few people nearby, to be here, in the capital city, with the rest of the sheep!" The voice that spoke was not her own, in fact, it was masculine in nature. A spell she had cast on her vocal cords masked her usual speaking voice, so as not to enchant anyone at the present company. Rizza enjoyed jokes like that, and she did not have to turn around to tell everyone at the tables was startled. They expected Rizza, so why was there a male voice attached to the small frame huddled in the unkempt and possibly dirty cloak? The whispers began just as Rizza expected.

Again, she heard the queen's delightful laughter at her little stunt, quickly accompanied by a groan from the crown prince. He caught on to her heavy sarcasm and was not happy. Oh, well. Rizza couldn't make everyone happy, and, frankly, being forced to be in the capital was something she did not want for herself. In fact, no one else wanted it for her, either, their reasons were as selfish as her own, if not more so.

"Rizza, please rise and lose that terrible voice." The queen's laughter rang through her voice as Rizza raised her head. The queen was someone of constant mirth. Where her family was like a gloomy cloud, the queen was a beacon of light. It always made Rizza feel good to be around the woman, especially when she laughed at Rizza's jokes bred out of contempt. She hated being in the palace, more so after basically being banished from it without the formality of having actually been banished.

A small smile played on her lips as she glanced at the royal family again. The crown prince's head was still buried in his hands, and next to him, his wife was giving him a compassionate look of sympathy as her fingers curled over the top of his in a loving caress. How sweet. The king, however, seemed to have a little less of a frown on his face, but maybe Rizza was just dreaming.

"My queen, I am sorry that I cannot lose my voice, as I do not wish to subject anyone to my natural one.... We all remember what a problem that can be." Rizza grinned as everyone in the room seemed to groan at the memory of them being made into dancing puppets the last time they had asked for her to speak in her normal voice.

The entire court had been made to act out an entire play, and by the end of it, everyone was naked. She was quite certain some people ended up in the wrong rooms that night. It had not been entirely her fault, though. Rizza had always cast her own magic on her natural voice to keep it from showing. She did not want to enchant the court. However, on a particularly alcohol-filled evening, they all demanded to know why she did that. When an explanation was not enough, they demanded a demonstration. It was not her fault they did not like what they got. There was something to be said for Rizza, she hated when people demanded she use her magic for stupid things. Punishment was in order. This was one of the many reasons she had been cast out of the palace.

"No, Rizza, that is alright. We shall accept your ridiculous voice.... Please don't drop it." The king spoke with an unamused tone of voice that seemed rushed, as if he could not get the words out fast enough.

He had been especially ornery that night. Some people just could not take a joke. Even though he spoke softly, his voice still seemed to boom throughout the room as it echoed off the marble-like a quiet, rumbling thunder. It was always amazing how he could extend such power in his voice without enchanting it in the least. Then again, her own enchanting voice was caused by the birth defect of being a witch.

"As you wish, your majesty." Rizza could not help the mirth that seemed to show even in her altered voice as she spoke. Silence fell on the room once more as everyone waited on the king to speak, as it was he who summoned her.

"Rizza." His first word was spoken softly, seemingly as if

he was pained to say it at all. The way he said her name always made her think of someone who was swallowing something vile, as if they did not want to take their medicine. A lot of people said her name like that, some things never changed.

"Rizza," he started again. "I am sure you are wondering why I have summoned you to the capital... especially given your wanton ways." His voice reflected the cringe he felt, but his face was still in that permanent frown. Did he just not know how to smile at all?

"In my defense, I did usually give you warning that some things were bad ideas, but you all had to argue and tell me 'no, Rizza, that's not the case'." Rizza mimicked their voices in a mocking way, and that got the queen to snort again in amusement.
Rizza always gave people a fair warning of what would happen. It was hardly Rizza's fault that instead of listening to her, they all decided to argue until she had to prove what she was saying, usually by using her magic. Though it would not be a far-fetched argument to say that in this life, Rizza was indeed very childish, spiteful and slightly unruly, even at the age of 23. She was always getting yelled at for blowing up this or that wing, or making so-and-so's hair fall out, or for making Lord Erlander purple for an entire month. He seriously had asked for that, in a way. Honestly, it was not like she enjoyed tormenting people... Okay, maybe she did, just a little.

"Rizza..." The king's voice held a warning tone to it, which made Rizza silently bow again as if offering for him to continue. "Right. Well, truth be told, and it pains me to say this, but we need you to marry..." His voice still had that booming echo that demanded respect, but the way he said the words made Rizza go still.

No, it was not the way he said the words, it was the words he spoke that made her go still. "You want... me... to get ... married?" The deep masculine voice that she had adopted was very hesitant as she spoke. Her entire frame was very still for the briefest of moments before she started laughing. The laughter filled the room like an echo chamber, and it took her several minutes to get things under control once more.

"Rizza..." The queen spoke this time, concern lacing her voice.

"Your highness! That is the best joke you have ever told! I have to admit that I did not even think you had a sense of humor!" Rizza was laughing, holding her sides with one hand as the other gripped her staff.

"Rizza, we aren't..."

"I mean, honestly, the way you always yelled at the crown prince and I when we were growing up made me think you were nothing but angry, but that is really funny!" Rizza continued, ignoring the attempted interruption on the queen's part.

"Rizza!" The king shouted her name as his fists slammed into the arms of his chair. That caused her to stop laughing. The room shook once more with the quiet, rolling boom of his voice, anger lacing it at her insolence. Rizza went completely silent as he spoke. "Rizza. We are not joking; you are to be wed at the end of the month."

Her entire body went rigid as the realization that it was not a cruel joke set in. They had decided ... to force her to marry. They had not asked her, not that they needed to, they simply decided it.

Rizza was stunned. She could think of no joke or anything that would ease this situation in her mind. The idea that they would force her to marry never occurred to her. Rizza had always assumed she would become the scary old witch in the mountains that kids told each other about to scare the crud out of each other. She never thought she would... Her world seemed to be spinning. Was the room spinning?

Rizza gripped her staff for balance as the world seemed to lurch. Was she fainting? Rizza did not faint... but that was a lot to take in. Married...

"To... To whom?" Her voice came out as a stutter. "Who am I marrying?" The shake in her voice was obvious.

Trepidation filled her, anxiety, fear, and most of all, betrayal.

How could they do this to her? Arranged marriages were obviously a thing, but she was the witch! She was not one of their children!

How could they arrange her marriage? Besides that, Rizza was, well, Rizza. She had spent years outside the palace.

Rizza was lifetimes old. In this life, though, she was childish. Those who knew of her in this life feared her, not because she was malevolent or cruel, but because her way of dealing with things and teaching lessons was less than desirable, and people wished they could, but simply could not forget. Rizza was not the kind of person anyone would want to marry, she was too immature and bratty, and she knew it. She knew it, and she liked it.

"You..." The king began to speak but was cut off by the sound of a chair scraping against the ground.

Her gaze darted up to the stand where the royal family was. The second eldest son was on his feet, a hand on his father's shoulder as he looked at him tenderly. It was only then that she noticed the thrum of magic that ran through him. Her pupils dilated at the sheer amount that radiated off him. He was almost as electrically charged with magic as... as she was. Her attention was wrapped around him.

"Perhaps... father... I should talk now..." The king nodded as he turned towards her.

Unlike the rest of his family, this prince had jet black hair. Yet, it did not end there, he also had jet black eyes, the whites and all. Rizza began to blink furiously.

How had she not noticed him before? He was... he was a Wizard. The claws, the flecks of gold on his pale skin... and judging by the magical power radiating off him, a very strong one.

How could this be? In his own right, he was handsome, but he was still very off-putting to her. As she watched his mouth move, she saw that his teeth, like her own, were also pointed as if someone had filed them into needles.

"Lady Rizza..." He began to speak again, and his voice also held that quiet thunder that his father had. "It is a pleasure to meet you... though we are not so different in age, we never met before now."

The prince's words rang true. She had never seen him.

Growing up in the palace with the scholars, she had never once seen the second prince. She had only ever spent time tormenting his older brother, the crown prince.

Her gaze darted towards the crown prince as the thought crossed her mind. He was smiling ear to ear. The cheeky bastard was getting a thrill out of her panic. Even if he could not see her reaction due to the shadows cast on her face from her cloak. He had been so tormented, not only today, but most of their early years, how could he not look for petty revenge? This was a bad joke.

"Prince..." Her mind drew a blank to his name. Who was he? The crown prince was prince Drake... his fiancée was princess Raelynn... the king and queen were Sven and Catherine... who were the other three royals? Rizza had never bothered to learn their names, she realized. They had not mattered to her because they served little more than bobbleheads in the kingdom, as they would never gain the throne. Rizza had never once encountered them, or thought of them as anything important, so she never bothered. Heat colored her face as the realization dawned on her.

Rizza was bad at court politics. In fact, she was downright terrible at them. Yet, the realization that she could not even remember the names of the royal family was embarrassing on a whole new level.

Everyone knew Rizza was not fit to be at court and this simply proved it. Perhaps that would let her go home though. She could dream. Her chin tucked as she cleared her throat at the realization, trying to hide her growing panic while most of the room watched with avid curiosity. They were waiting for the next bit of gossip.

"Pratt, my name is Pratt, Lady Rizza." His voice was smooth and calm. Despite her obvious blunder, he did not seem even slightly ruffled by it. If anything, he seemed extremely relaxed. The look on his face practically begged her to calm down. That mistake was still immense, and she would likely make many more before the day was done.

"Prince Pratt, then. I ..." Rizza cleared her throat, and the voice that she projected turned to that of a delicate female. The new voice got the crown prince to bark out a single 'ha' before going silent as he listened, a fist pressed to his mouth to keep himself mute. The rest of the room waited with bated breath as they watched the drama unfold before them.

"I have no idea what this is all about, but I cannot see how me marrying you and dragging you off to live in my mountains is a good idea," she finished. She ignored Drake's outburst.

Why would anyone want to live with her in her mountains anyway? They were her mountains, nice and warm during the summer and freezing in the winter. A prince living up there? He probably wouldn't even be able to chop his own wood, how absurd.

The prince chuckled at that, as did everyone else. As usual, there was some aspect of this business that Rizza was missing. Her eyes narrowed as she looked around the room. Why was everyone laughing at her? Clearly, they thought it was as funny as she did that a prince would try to live in the woods. Why else would they laugh? This entire thing was just nonsense.

"No... Lady Rizza..." The prince began to speak again but Rizza waved her hand.

"My name is Rizza. Drop the 'lady' business, you are not going to woo me by using it, so you may as well give up." She had never been called lady in her life.

Well, except when the nurse was scolding her in her youth. 'Young lady, stop that right now!' Ah... good times. However, this was not a good time, lady was not something someone called Rizza. 'Lady' was a title of the court reserved for the ladies of the court. She was not one, nor did she have the intention to become one.

"Alright... Rizza then." The prince seemed slightly upset by not using formalities but went on anyway. "Actually, Rizza, we would not live in the mountains... you would be required to move here, into the palace, with us."

The words drew another laugh from her. "Me? Move to the palace? Please tell me that is a joke. You did not give me an entire mountain range a month's ride from the capital for absolutely no reason."

She glanced at the crown prince again, he still seemed highly amused. The queen looked sad, and the king (as always) looked mad. Why was no one laughing? That was a joke, it had to be. Her living in the palace for sixteen years had been hell for everyone involved, especially her. They wanted her to live in it permanently? Were they all going mad? This wasn't her past life where she'd gotten along with everyone. This was her now.

Her gaze turned to the assembled nobles. Tables dotted the room here and there, and every one of them was full of people staring at her. Not a single person looked ready to laugh. Actually, several of them looked scared and more were whispering behind closed hands. None knew of this until today... so why?

Another thought struck her, and she jerked her head back to the prince known as Pratt. "You want me to marry him to strengthen his magic..." the dawning realization angered her. Rage ran through her, and every lamp in the place flickered out at the same time as a crack of thunder could be heard. Yet another laugh escaped her, but this one was without any mirth at all. There was no merriment to be heard, only dark laughter at her own expense.

Somehow, that looming detail had gone way over her head among everything else. She had spent so much time laughing at the joke idea that was her getting married she had almost missed why they wanted it. Anger flooded her.

"Rizza... please calm down... Yes, we want... they want... us to marry for the good of the kingdom, but it is also for your own good!" The prince seemed to have to shout over the noise the wind was suddenly making as it gusted outside. A storm was brewing as Rizza's temper grew. The trepidation in the entire royal family was clear as Pratt tried to placate her.

Rizza was the most powerful witch in the land. It was no secret that wizards were rare, but witches were rarer still. What was a secret, however, was what happened when a witch and a wizard were bound by a ceremony as strong as marriage. Their magic was enhanced. Individually, their magical power would grow for the both of them.

Judging by the strength of magic he held, he was probably the most powerful wizard in the realm, the reason people wanted her to marry him. The only more powerful wizard before him had been her. They wanted to make him that much more powerful. They were using her. Anger continued to flood through her.

She was about to unleash hell on everyone before she abruptly made the storm stop with a slam of her staff on the ground. Fear was etched in the lines of everyone's faces as Rizza did it. Rizza was not the witch you pissed off. Even if she answered to the king and queen, they still feared her. Rizza was the most powerful being to ever have walked the earth. There was nothing she had yet been barred from doing that was within the realm of possibilities.

"You want me to marry your son so he can be even more powerful. You are making me into a ... a... doll." Rizza basically spat the word out as she sneered behind her hood. Her fingers deftly picked the fabric off her face, so she could entrance them all with her appearance. Her fair skin was dotted with flecks of what looked like silver, her deep purple eyes, the jet-black spikes she called hair, and the sneer peeled back her lips to reveal her needle-like teeth. Where the prince somehow looked exotic and gorgeous, Rizza looked like a monster drawn from the depths of hell. A creature ready to steal every soul, eat babies and feed on the blood of the living.

A collective gasp escaped the nobles in the room as Rizza pulled her hood back. Of course they would gasp. Rizza kept the hood on to avoid getting stared at, because she knew she was not appealing.

Yet, this once, she needed that. She needed to remind everyone of why Rizza was not someone they wanted to marry their son off to, not someone they wanted in the palace, not someone they wanted to piss off -- which they already had.

"Rizza, dear, please." The queen interjected at that point. Her body swept from her chair at the high table to glide down the steps and approach Rizza. Rizza took an involuntary step back, causing the queen to pause.

The queen was someone Rizza usually was happy around. She was someone that made Rizza feel like she belonged, even though Rizza knew she did not. The queen had been the one to save her from certain death, and raised her alongside her eldest son as if she were her daughter. The queen had been the person Rizza had served loyally in her past life in this court.
Yet, today, Rizza felt so terribly betrayed she could hardly stand to look at her. Had they raised her in the hopes that this day would come? The idea of it made bile rise at the back of her throat, and made her stomach turn and knot.

"Rizza..." The queen tried again, a tentative hand still lingering in the air.
Rizza turned her back on the queen as she clutched herself to her staff, her frame quivering against it in anger. She was working hard to handle her temper. If she did not restrain it, her magic would lose control and possibly kill people. Anger flooded her, but she tamped down on it, bent on keeping it concealed to avoid harming anyone.

"Rizza... this is for you, as well. When we found out Prince Pratt had the ability to cast some of the strongest magic, we knew it would be a good match. You can come back to the kingdom and live with us again." The queen tried to sway her, and Rizza flinched as she did.

"So, I can be your little pet witch who fuels your son's magic..." The words were more bitter than she realized, and the queen visibly recoiled as the king slammed his fists back down into the table.

"I've had enough!" the king practically bellowed as he stood up and glared daggers at Rizza. "You swore an oath to serve us however we needed you. That oath binds you more than anyone else, as witches can't break oaths. I am calling on that oath, Rizza. At the end of the month, during the full moon, you will marry Pratt and the marriage will strengthen both of your magic." His voice brooked no-nonsense.

Rizza stood frozen for a very long time; she did not want to say anything. Rizza did not want to do anything either. In fact, she simply... did not want to exist. Betrayal washed over her in waves. How could they do this to her? They had not always gotten along, but Rizza had always been a loyal aid to the throne. She had always come when called... how could they use her like this?

The king called upon her oath, and it made her chest twist in pain more tightly for every second she did not answer. The mark on her skin glowed faintly under the cloak as she twisted around it, feeling it squeeze into her life force. Finally, she was short of breath and gasping for air. The oath she took was more binding than any mortal oath. It bound her body and soul to the king and queen of the kingdom.

She could do nothing to harm them and she could not defy them. If she did not answer the summons to the oath within the next few minutes, Rizza would lose consciousness and probably die. The worst part was... if she died that way, she would lose her magic, not only in this life, but the next, and every life after. She would not get to be a witch anymore, and it would probably be her final death. Granted, that was all speculation. She didn't actually know what would happen, because she had never taken a vow before. All she knew was the pain was excruciating, and not worth risking her magic.

"Yes... your majesty..." Rizza choked the words out as her fingers bit into the staff to keep herself upright. Sensing her distress, Kit appeared in a puff of magic and hovered around her until the pain eased away and the mark went back to being invisible even on her skin. With a shooing motion, she made the spirit flee.

The king did not wait for another minute after her fit of pain seemed to stop. He nodded and sat down once more. "Good. You may go rest in your room in the west wing." The west wing... she had a room in the west wing. Bile again rose in her throat, but she simply bowed and exited the room as quickly and quietly as she could.

Him telling her she 'could' go was as good as him telling her to get out. It was not something one ignored. The second she was out of it, she raced down the hall, it was not until she was in the secret passage of the west wing did her steps falter. Her breath came in ragged gasps as she fought to breathe. She was marrying into the royal family...

A guard showed her where her set of rooms were in the west wing, and it proved to be much larger than even her home in the mountains. Granted, it was a small cottage. This... this was a mansion in a castle. She had her own sitting room, office, bathing chamber with a full-fledged tub and a fireplace nearby, and bedroom. Rizza winced as she looked at the fancy decorating and cringed harder as she realized they had carted all her belongings to the palace. She really was going to live here... it pained her.

Breath

Rizza had not bothered to appear at lunch or dinner that day. In fact, she remained hidden away in her rooms for three days straight. The betrayal lay heavily on her shoulders and she did not want to face those at court who would mock her. She was not trained to put up with such blatant mockery. Her job had never required that she interact with the court. While she had been raised among them, she had not actually dealt with them. Court etiquette was left up to the crown prince's training while she spent more time studying old texts and tomes she had written for herself in previous lives.

Her fingers curled around her knees as a servant came in to take away the food she had barely touched from that morning. The sun was just beginning to peek over the hills as Rizza sat in the sill of her window. Of course, she had a room with a window. She was not the 'important' royalty; guarded by stone walls on all sides so no one could try and break in through the glass panes. No, Rizza was just the dummy they were using to enhance their son's magic. Again, that familiar ache of betrayal scorched a path through her body, leaving her feeling empty and weak. Worst of all, she could not even run away. Just the idea of it made the mark on her chest burn and left her panting for air.

Rizza had spent three full days locked away in her suite. She was refusing to meet with anyone, despite how many times people tried to draw her out. She did not want to see anyone. Moreover, she did not want to be near anyone. Still, she knew she needed to emerge at some point. If she did not emerge by choice, she had a feeling the dratted king would call upon the oath again to drag her out. The idea of it made her flinch as she unfurled herself from her perch near the window. Her feet touched the ground lightly, and her hand flicked out into the air.

She did not need to call Kit, as he was already waiting for her to summon him. He had been hovering over her almost nonstop since the royal decree, knowing she was upset. It was amusing that her most loyal ally was nothing more than a child's spirit, forever trapped and bound to her will for magical purposes... though she could not remember exactly how it happened. Kit just appeared to her one day. Ever since, he had found her each time she was reborn. He had been her willing companion in each life. No matter what form she took, or what name she had, Kit was always there.

As her hand stayed in the air, Kit provided her with clothing. She stared at it when he did, a frown of annoyance on her face. The look should have been enough to show how little she wanted to wear it.

He gave her a usual set of clothing, a normal black dress that was simple and form-fitting with stockings and undergarments. However, he also gave her a cloak. The cloak was not the one she usually had him conjure that left people thinking she was a dirty little rat. No, this cloak was one made of soft velvet and weighed heavily in her hands. It was also a rich blood red embroidered with simple stitches that depicted different magical runes and her emblem, a cloak she hardly ever wore. The cloak was almost as old as Kit himself, only brought out on very special occasions.

"Kit... normal clothing." She waited several tense seconds. He did not change the cloak. She glared at the wisp, who seemed to be mimicking shaking his head at her as his small ball of light bounced from one side to the next.

"Traitor." The bitter word was bit out as the little wisp disappeared, leaving her with her clothing for the day. She took in a deep breath and let it out as the anger flooded her. She could not be mad at Kit, he was just trying to make life easier for her. Yet, still, she was angry overall. The royals were forcing her to marry, and to their son, no less.

Quickly getting dressed, she glanced at herself in the bronze full-length mirror. Her reflection glowed back at her, making her look golden, and she snorted. The cloak did look good on her. She had obtained it many lifetimes ago, during one of her few lifetimes spent as a male. It was still so very strange that there was a male wizard who topped her magical ability as a male.

Sweeping the hood up and over her face, she left the room, which startled the attending servant. The man bowed as she left, clearly relieved she was gone. She had not been pleasant in her self-induced solitude.

The palace was quiet at that time of day, the nobles all off to breakfast in the main hall. Rizza hated early mornings so much. In fact, she would probably still be in bed until the sun was well into the sky, but had not been able to sleep. She was so stricken by the ugly truth that she was just a merry pawn in the royal family's chess game that she could not help but feel... well, used. It had kept her up each night, unable to sleep, and when she finally could, her dreams were anything but pleasant.

Sneaking from the hidden passageway, she emerged into the garden in the center of the palace. Due to the ornate design of the Palace, the garden was quite large, and it was easy for Rizza to find her hidden alcove. She had decided to come out of hiding, but she still remained in hiding. Frustration gnawed at her as she did so. She knew at some point she would have to let someone see she was out of her room, or perhaps that little servant by her door would inform them. Rizza could only hope, as the last thing she wanted to do was deal with people... especially Pratt.

No, she would comfort herself with her hideaway. The place was a corner of the garden that not many dared to venture. Unlike the rest of the garden, the lush vegetation never grew there anymore. All the plants were black or dead, not always both. Some of the black things that were there were alive and growing, and very, very poisonous. Surprisingly, when Rizza had accidentally created that corner of the garden, she had not been cast out of the palace. The queen had seen it for what it was, an accident. Rizza had not intended to charbroil the entire section; it had just happened when she spoke a wrong word. Ancient languages that no one else could speak got tricky at times, she had written things down for herself for a reason. Remembering her past lives was tricky without the physical evidence, she had to spend years remembering everything.

Her gaze flicked over to it as she noticed, or rather sensed, someone else was already in her spot. That alone drew her out of her dazed self-reflective state she fell into when alone, losing herself in her pasts. Worse yet, it was the prince. She could tell just by feeling the amount of magic radiating around the place. Aggravation spiked in her again. Why was he in her place? That was her place... or it had been six years ago. Part of her wanted to storm off, but that was her hiding spot, and she'd be damned if she let someone else take it from her, especially the spoiled prince who was using her.

Marching around the blackened hedges, she stepped into the center of the clearing that was the corner of the garden. It was hidden by a black dead tree and several varieties of poisonous bushes.

As she stepped around the corner and into the center, she noted him sitting under the blackened tree. He had not registered her presence yet, but was instead bent over some papers he was quietly working on. A pause, and he put the quill towards his mouth slightly in contemplation before jotting something else down. His eyelashes swept low over his cheekbones and despite his slumped state, he had a regal figure with a rather beautiful air about him. It was like watching a painting.

"The hell do you think you're doing?" Rizza could not hold the words back as her hands sat on her hips under the cloak. She was, as usual, covered head to toe. Beautiful or not, the man was in the way. She couldn't just sit still and daydream about a beautiful prince sweeping her off her feet. He wasn't doing that. He was using her.

His head jerked up as she spoke, and he stumbled to his feet, carefully setting aside his writing and ink well as he did so. "Rizza!" The word was shouted half joyously, and half-filled with surprise. He took a step towards her and her glare intensified, not that he could see it.

"The hell do you think you're doing? This is my spot. I burned it... by accident, so it's mine." Rizza did not let him near her. Instead, she was moving towards the opposite side of the small clearing, still glaring daggers at the prince. How her burning it had made it her spot probably did not make sense to others, but to her it was a personal spot, especially since the queen had left it burnt just for her. Though, Rizza wondered if that was more due to the fact that nothing could undo what she did than wanting to keep it for Rizza. Still, she wanted to think that the Queen hadn't bothered trying to fix it for her sake.

He did not seem at all put off by her anger. Instead, he continued to smile at her as if she were the best thing ever to happen to him. That did nothing to make her comfortable. In fact, it pissed her off more. What right did he have to be so happy when she was so miserable?

"You're out of your room! I tried several times to come see you, but you wouldn't have it... were you looking for me?" He ignored her words as he spoke his own. Yes, he had tried to see her. Ten times in fact. She did not want to see him. Especially not in her area. His ignoring her just pissed her off more. His stench would have clung to the room, his aura, his presence an unseen force that would have made her hate the space that much more. She had not wanted him there, not in one of the few places that she could call hers. Yet, here he was, in one of those places, doing that exact damnable thing.

"No, I was not looking for you. I wanted to be in my hiding spot. You just happened to have overtaken it. Get out. You don't belong here." She glared at him, sullen and agitated. Her fingers were curled into fists and still balled on her hips. The words 'get out' were imbued with magic as she dropped the spell contorting her voice. He did not budge.

Of course, he did not budge. Why would he budge? That would be too easy. She scoffed at him and the glare on her face deepened. He looked genuinely puzzled, but something about him made her want to be mean to him.

"Your spot? Because you burned it? Rizza... I have been coming here for years, since long after you left." His words were filled with confusion as he stood there. He seemed almost hurt by her accusation, more so when she tried to force him to leave with her magic. A sneer perked across her lips in the dark.

"My spot. I have been coming here since well before it was burned on accident. Just because you took it while I was gone does not mean you can keep it." Rizza hated that his magical stench was filling her spot. A spot that had previously never been inhabited by anyone else. They had all been too scared to go near it, mostly due to Rizza's wanton ways and the fact that she had also accidentally put the poisonous plants in it.

"Rizza... why don't we share it? I rather like this spot, too... it's so different from the rest of the palace... sort of.... well, like me." The look he gave her was pained as he said it. That caused Rizza to pause slightly. Why did he look so upset at being different? He was still revealed to the public, still part of the royal family. No one could insult him to his face... unlike Rizza.

"Different? You? You fit in perfectly with the rest of the court. So polite, upright, and two-faced. How could you possibly feel left out?" Rizza jabbed at him. So what if on the outside he looked like her? No one treated him like a nightmare.

"Well. I learned to adapt. That doesn't change the fact that I'm different, and I rather like this spot. I don't want to leave." Pratt had paused for a moment before voicing his thoughts. He hadn't wanted to disperse from there so easily himself.

"No. I created this spot for my solitude. Though, on your way out, be sure to inform your father I'm out of my room. If he calls on the oath again, I'm going to be pissed." Her words were a grumble as she pointed towards the entrance to the little alcove.

She would not comply with the spoiled prince. Since he was getting something from her she could not refuse, he was going to give up her spot as his hiding spot. This was hers long before it was his, and no amount of emotional bull was going to change that.

The prince paused for a second, clearly wanting to argue with her more, before he let out a sigh and gave a nod. Gathering his things, he quickly left the alcove, which left Rizza in peace. Good. She needed peace.

Kit appeared near her shoulder, and started bobbing in the air, almost as if he were angry at her. Ducking towards her, he pulled on her cloak as if he meant to shake her. She scowled at him.

"I was not too harsh to him. He is creepy. Look at his black hair and black gaze, not to mention that set of teeth. Anyone would be mean to him." Rizza was being an intense hypocrite. The pause in Kit's movements said as much before he began to bob up and down again angrily.

Rizza let out a sigh of aggravation and brushed her hand through the air and through his little flickering light. The action caused it to extinguish and made him vanish as she did so. He appeared again only to bob twice and leave. The gesture was enough. He did not have to say the two words, but they still hung in the air in his wake. He was pissed off at her and she knew it. However, at that moment, Rizza did not care.

How many times had people said those exact words as Rizza had run away crying? Words she had just used on the prince. How many people had been extremely demeaning to her growing up just because her hair looked more like quills and her skin looked slightly off? How many people had run screaming when she had ridden into town, causing her to pull up her hood just to be able to be in public?

Every time she tried to smile, a little child screamed and had nightmares for life. Every time the parents wanted to convince their child to behave, they said, 'be good and don't do this or that, because Rizza will come for you.' Every time... this life had not been so long, but so long were the stories already, the legends, the lies, the things that made Rizza the one who went bump in the night even though all she ever did was try to help people. Yet here she was, trying to be helpful and having it used against her.

Rizza's hand gripped her cloak as the memories washed over her, the familiar ache of loneliness filled her. Yes, Rizza was abnormal... a freak, even. She had been told so all her life. Even Elves did not look as strange as she did with their small spots of animalistic patterns and colors. No, Rizza was by far the scariest thing to go bump in the night.

Putting those thoughts away, she glanced around her area. Rizza wasn't one to stew in self-pity, other than those three days of self-loathing and abhorring having to deal with this ridiculous charade.

Pratt's magic still clung to the air, and she quickly began to sweep her own over it to get rid of its stench. Her fingers had to pause by one of the plants as his smell seemed to linger there the most. Why was that the spot that his stench clung to? Rizza frowned, but as the scent washed away, so did her interest.

Her area was finally back to her own again. No more scent of the prince at all. Granted, his magic wasn't so much a scent as it was a feeling in the air. Still, it was a stench in her eyes, something rank and foul that coated the area in a vile way. Its absence was an improvement, and with that accomplished, Rizza sat down under the nook of the tree, the same place he had been sitting before she evicted him. Her cloak was tightly wrapped around her as she started to shuffle through all her lives, something she did often to remind herself of all she knew.

Despite Rizza's insignificant 21 years in this life, she was almost a thousand years old in all. That, of course, only counted the years she had spent walking the earth, not just stuck in limbo waiting for a new vessel that could handle her magic.

The first time Rizza had been born to the earth, it had been on a poor, desolate farm. She had been killed almost immediately when they saw her deformities. That happened a lot in the earlier years when no one understood what it meant to be a witch.

Then, as Rizza got the chance to get older, and explore her powers, she started to craft her magic and learn what she was. Those had still been dark times, back when she was very weak. So much time, at least fifteen -- if not twenty -- lives were spent learning a vast majority of her magical capabilities, abilities that put her where she was now.

Most witches did not get as many lives as her. Why the creator had left her to be the one with so many lives, Rizza did not know. All she knew was that her lives were not up, nor would they be any time soon. Whether Rizza would continue to be born again and again until the end of time was yet to be seen. The only thing that remained the same throughout each life was its conclusion. She always ended it alone.

Rizza had spent all her lives alone. That was nothing new to her. In fact, it almost seemed comforting to know the end of her tale. Whether it was tragic or not, all her lives ended with her by herself somewhere. Granted, sometimes she was reborn as someone with tact and was actually missed when she died.

That made her think of her life before this one... she had been missed then. Rizza frowned at the memory. That was why the queen took her in and raised her when she was born again; Rizza had served as the queen's right hand. She had always been there for the queen, watched the queen grow up as a princess, saved her life even. She had been there when the queen and king had gotten married... and sired their firstborn, the crown prince. Then, she was murdered. Rizza still did not know who had killed her. She had never asked if the murderer had been found, a bit too close for comfort in this life. Perhaps that was what she should do at the castle, solve her own murder.

It was a thought that had crossed her mind even before she was summoned. Some sort of loss at being banished from the kingdom at the time had only shown when she realized she probably wouldn't get an answer. Part of her wondered if anyone had bothered to look into it at all.

Rizza drew herself out of her memories after a time. It was around lunch when she did, the sun sitting in the middle of the sky. Her gaze went to it. She supposed she should probably join everyone in the grand hall, eat with them and make merry or something. Rizza cringed at the idea, but she dragged herself to her feet. Some food would do her good, and maybe she could learn to get along with people, or just find a better way to avoid them all.

Lunch

The banquet hall was packed when she arrived. This time, she did not have the staff with her to make an elaborate entrance. Instead, she made her way in silently. Despite doing so, heads still shot up as she entered. A soft sigh escaped her lips. Yes, she was drawing attention even when she did not want to.

Her gaze swept the banquet hall for a place to sit. She finally found an empty corner and table... memories flashed through her. That table used to be covered in people who all ate with her. A small smile played along her lips as she remembered her life before this one, not that it mattered much. The people in the banquet hall now all feared or hated her... usually both. There were still some of the people she used to sit with in this room, glances thrown her way as they remembered the old her. Yet, all that remained of that version was the magic. The kindness, the laughter, and the joy were all gone. Rizza was now the spoiled child that no one wanted anything to do with. She was even female now. No longer the sweet, compassionate man she was previously.

Rizza's feet carried her over to that part of the hall silently. A servant came over and brought her some food: chicken that was practically falling off the bone, a fresh loaf of bread, some type of green vegetable, and a cup of red wine. The servants at least knew her taste, even if no one else did. A small smile went towards the servant, who did not see it. Instead, she offered up a gold coin. The servant's eyes basically turned to saucers as they saw it, but they took it and bowed, thanking Rizza immensely before scurrying off. She was not stingy with her wealth. Most of her gold stayed locked away with Kit, and she had been compiling it for many, many lives. She had more than one person could spend in a life, no matter how hard they tried... it was not like she would ever go without. In each life, she had earned a stipend that had been a little too generous, and now, she had more than she knew what to do with. It was enough to start her own kingdom, she imagined… at least monetarily. Who would follow a witch into a kingdom, though? Plus, where would she get the land? Ha.

Despite how packed the hall was, none of the royal family had arrived yet. In fact, it would be some time before they arrived, as being fashionably late seemed to be their favorite thing to be. Like everyone else in the banquet hall, Rizza waited patiently for the royal highnesses to grace them with their presence. No one touched their food, despite its growing cold. It was customary to wait until the royals arrived, and Rizza yawned as she waited.

That, of course, drew attention. Everyone loved a good chance to gawk at her teeth, but, sucks to be them, she had them safely hidden away behind her usual cloak. It was not so usual. Rizza did not like wearing her red one. Kit's insistence on it baffled and aggravated her still. Why did it matter which cloak she wore?

After a decent amount of time, the Royal family finally joined them. It was probably only a few minutes, but Rizza had found that in this life, she detested waiting for anyone. She was by far the most powerful being in the world. It probably wasn't nice, but she was egotistical. Waiting on others was beneath her. She had started nibbling on her food despite the clear distress of those around her before they had even walked into the hall. What was the royal family going to do if she ate without them, behead her? Ha, fat chance. They wanted her to strengthen their son's magic. As if she would die before that happened… or after. They needed her alive for that to happen, and if they killed her, who knew how long it would be before she would be reborn again?

The king and queen were the first to enter. Slowly after them came the crown prince and princess. Each in turn looked around the room, and their gazes all seemed to linger in one corner: Rizza's. They always looked towards Rizza, but more so now that she was dressed in red. Well, that, and she finally bothered to appear in public. As the second the four of them sat down, Rizza began to eat with a bit more gusto, ignoring everyone else who entered.

A long time passed with her delightfully gorging herself on

the food, and hopefully not making a fool of herself as she used her needle-like teeth to pick flesh from bone. It was so good to be able to eat good food again. Hunting in the forest was all well and good, but she could not use her magic because it always left the meat tasting so ... warped. No, she had to hunt by natural means. It took forever that way, and after all that, the gamey taste was not to her liking. She liked the castle-raised hens that they fed everyone here. It cost a fortune to do so, but Rizza thought it was worth it.

About halfway through her meal, Rizza heard the scrape of a chair near the dais where the royal family resided, and her head tilted up, along with everyone else's. The king was standing on his feet with his glass in hand.

"I believe a toast is in order... to Rizza, for accepting her marriage to the second prince. Hear hear!" The king then turned his glass towards her, and rose it in his hand. Those around dutifully followed with 'hear hear' of their own, ones they did not mean.

Rizza was also expected to raise her glass to that, and disgust washed over her at the ridiculous tradition, but she raised the glass for them anyways. The cheers were fake, the royal family was fake, this was all fake, and she hated it. Finishing her meal, she went to stand. However, as she did, the second prince entered the room. A groan escaped her. She was so close to being able to simply leave... so close, and yet so far.

The man entered the room, and his gaze landed on her, as well. It was as if some natural force had a beacon over her head screaming 'look this way' for him. It was awful, and, like always, he lit up like a Christmas tree full of candles. He always seemed so happy to see her, but she could not help but call his bluff. No one was happy to see Rizza, ever. Rizza was not the kind one would give an 'oh yay you're here' to. It was more like an 'Oh no... you're here' kind of thing. Rizza had never once in this life received a warm invitation. Sure, in past lives she had, but not this one.

His feet carried him straight to her, and everyone watched as he did so due to the fact that his walk was not elegant, more rapid and giddy like a schoolboy. Avid curiosity and the beginnings of new court gossip were on the tips of their tongues as they all strained their ears. A smug smirk played across Rizza's face as she flexed her fingers in a semi-circle through the air. Immediate confusion fell on the waiting crowd as they realized they could not hear. Trying to sound things out for themselves was funny because Rizza could hear them just fine. The prince took no notice of the chaos Rizza had caused, only watched her as he approached... so obnoxious.

"Rizza, you came to lunch!" His words were like an excited puppy, the same as his face before he frowned. His voice was all too loud, piercing her ears with the volume. "But... Why are you sitting alone? You're my affiliate, you should be on the dais with the rest of the family." He went to reach for her arm to take her there, but Rizza pulled away immediately. No expression showed on her face, but she was very, very unhappy.

"Just because your family is using me to their own ends, it does not mean we have to be nice to each other. Once we are bound together by marriage, your powers will increase, and I can go back to my happy mountains and avoid you." Her words were curt and cold and seemed to cut him to the core. For a second, she thought he may cry as she stood up.

Rizza did not do well with waterworks. She did not want anything to do with him especially, that would be the last thing she needed. Moving around him and the table, she tossed her napkin on it.

"Good day, Prince Pratt." The words were not so much a courtesy as a curse at him before she left the hall. Rizza hated to be made the pawn, and even more so the idea that he dared think her foolish enough to believe he genuinely cared about her. That was just too much, that joke was going way too far.

Though, there was one thing that Rizza could not figure out. How had the prince gotten magic? Usually, one parent or the other had to have some trait for it, and neither of the parents this time did. Rizza knew because she had screened them both before the first prince had been born, so how had the second prince come to have magic? It was beyond curious. Perhaps she had missed something.

Moving through the empty halls of the palace, Rizza looked around it. It had been seven years since she had really looked at the palace. Seven years... she had been fifteen when they had made her move into town, sixteen when they kicked her out of the capital in general. Now, she was walking back through the palace only because they needed her. Of course, no one ever wanted Rizza. They simply had to accept she existed, because no one could ever do what Rizza did. Just great.

The grand hallways were made even grander by the stained glass windows that lined them. Carefully painted art of the different past rulers lined the hall until the most recent pair. After that, the windows were simple panes of glass that let light in, but they all seemed to have window cushions where one could enjoy a book or a glass of wine and some grapes and enjoy the view. The view, of course, being that of the central garden. Currently, different nobles were inhabiting the scenic area, sheltered from the rest of the peasants. A courtesy really, because who wants to mingle with their subjects? Certainly not the social elite. They may hear the complaints against them or something.

Leaning against one of the cushions, Rizza took a seat. Her gaze was locked on the nobles below who seemed to be going about their daily routines. A duchess was painting a picture while a duke fawned over her. A lady and a lord were strolling together. Two children looked like they were fighting. One pulled the other's hair while the other tried to get back her doll... wait... why was everyone a couple?

Looking around, all she saw were couples. No one was alone, or with the same sex... wait no. There were two women... making out. Rizza frowned lightly. What was this, a playground for the lovesick? She had not cast a spell, perhaps the prince did. When Rizza went to disenchant the garden, however, she found no magic infused in it or any of the people. What the hell? No one was that lovey-dovey for absolutely no reason. Somehow, that pissed her off worse than anything else she had to deal with. She was in a terrible mood, but, of course, the rest of the court was having spring romance. Disgusting.

Moving from her perch, she groaned. Everyone else got to be together because of love, but she was engaged to a prince who knew her reputation, not her. That was delightful. Of course, that irony would fall on her. Granted, she did not ever intend to marry, or fall in love, or deal with people in general, but still. One would think they would at least give Rizza the right to choose, but no. She was going to be forced into marriage because she had not already taken a husband at 21 years of age. Who wanted to marry that young, anyway? Rizza was a witch; she had all the time in the world. If not in this life, she could find one in the next. In some of her lives, she had gotten married. Why did she need to make it every life? The idea of immortality really did not stick with the non-immortal. Why was the one person in court who had to face an arranged marriage here? Wasn't that lopsided? It seemed the others were falling in love or already in love.

Rizza moved through the castle, away from the window. Yet, no matter where she went, she saw love. People were trading poetry, girls were giggling and talking about their suitors, and everyone was merry. Everyone was happy, and in blossoming or continuing romances.

It was during her groaning that she heard someone clear their throat behind her. Turning around she saw a face she wasn't expecting to be behind her, Drake. He cut an imposing figure as he stood in the hall. No one who passed by the two of them stopped to chat and it left Rizza and Drake to stare at each other.

"Your highness." Rizza broke the silence first. She didn't bother trying to curtsy, rather standing tall as she could next to his imposing height. He'd actually grown up well since they'd last seen each other. His build had filled out more and his shoulders seemed broader somehow. He definitely looked like the athletic prince he was. She had a feeling he still did training with the knights.

"Wow, a formal greeting if I've ever heard one from you, Rizza." Drake seemed amused by the idea. His hands were behind his back as he stood there.

"Here to gloat?" She asked, not bothering to hold the pain she felt back. She could see the laughter in Drake's eyes without even trying to.

"A little. I also thought it would be nice to check in on my old friend." His smile formed on his face. He moved his hands from behind his back and moved to sit on the sill of the window nearby. Seeing what she did on the castle grounds he cringed. "Ah. I see why you looked so constipated when I walked up." He noted.

Rizza snorted. "I did not look constipated." She argued out of instinct. Some sense of familiarity was drawn from her when she heard his words.

"You so did." He replied earnestly. They turned to stare at each other before Rizza stuck her tongue out. He laughed.

"Some things never change, do they?" He asked after a moment. The smile on his face held a sense of longing for the past. When they were kids they bickered a lot but it never stopped them from spending moments like these together. As many bad memories of the prince that Rizza had, she had that many more good ones.

"No, some things don't. You're still a know it all goody two shoes." She added. Her own smile and mood-lifting a bit.

"Am I?" He asked earnestly. He thought of all the torment she'd put him through and he frowned almost immediately. "And you're still childish." He commented.

"Sure sure. How is your fiance?" Rizza knew what he'd think of if she asked and she saw the way he scowled at her. She merely smiled at him in return.

"She is great. It's nice having someone to rely on. You really should just accept this marriage and try to find happiness." Drake spoke flatly. He was worried. They had grown up together and yes, she had tormented him, but she was still his friend. Drake stared at her. He was also worried about that brother of his. The stubborn boy had agreed to the marriage so readily but everyone in the kingdom knew how Rizza was.

"Oh? But, I don't love your little brother. Nor do I care for you much if I'm being honest. Why should I take your advice?" Rizza raised her eyebrow in question to him. Her eyes narrowed slightly. It was clear she was going to be stubborn, using her childish nature to try and drive him away so he would drop the subject.

Drake always rose to the occasion with Rizza. He let out a sigh of annoyance as she seemed to become belligerent when he brought up his brother. "You can grow to love him. It's not the end of the world. Honestly, you are such a brat. Think of someone outside yourself for once." Drake chided her.

Rizza snorted. "I think we are done here. Good day, your highness." She had almost felt like they were back to how they used to be, quietly getting along. He had to ruin it by trying to reason with her about the marriage. She didn't want to fight with him. They had quarreled so much in the past but it was always playful. She was afraid that if they were to fight now, similar to the fight they'd had when she blew up the west wing, she'd end up hating him. This wouldn't be a fight that ended well.

She took one last look at the stupid lovesick fools before turning away. She had had enough of being in the castle. Not listening as Drake called out to her to try and hold her back she left. Her feet carried her to the stable, she wanted to get out of the castle for a bit. Maybe seeing the common folk would make her feel better.

Wrong

Rizza rode into the city on a horse that was nondescript. It did not have fancy bridles or anything on it, but her cloak gave her away for what she was. Technically, Rizza was nobility. Not in the way that she had a title and all that, but she did control an entire mountain range, and nothing happened there without her knowing. It was the kind of place that struck fear into other people's hearts. For her, it was delightful, it was home. Rizza was happy to be home and relaxed, this was just stressful, but because she had that mountain range, she had a title. Countess... or duchess... or... Rizza really couldn't remember. The cloak on her back was a sure giveaway that she came from the nobility, though.

Rizza rode down the tightly-packed streets of the city. The horse she was on was barely managing not to trample anyone under hoof. Meanwhile, Rizza couldn't help but notice the way she was getting stared at. However, they weren't looks of fear that marked their faces. They were different looks, looks of curiosity. Some people looked over, intending to be mad at the rude person riding a horse through a crowded street, but when they saw Rizza they blanched. None dared to oppose the royalty. It seemed the royals just didn't want to mingle because of contamination. None of the peasants seemed inclined to mingle, or even malign her. No one knew it was Rizza who rode atop the horse. She did not wear the cloak all that much to make it her 'signature' unless it was in lore or some other type of thing. It made it easier to be a nondescript noble. The cloak she had just happened to be of fine material. The peasants wanted to know the noble atop the horse, however. Her face not being shown made them all very curious. That much was clear by the eager looks in her direction. She wondered how they would feel if they realized the person they ogled with a mix of fear and curiosity was the nightmare they put their children to bed with stories of.

Rizza hated the stares. No matter the reason behind them,

she could not handle them. The fact that she was getting stared at was tolerable only because she didn't want to be in the castle. Rizza's fingers tightened on the reins of the horse causing it to stir slightly but keep moving forward.

Rizza was in a mood. She could tell she was in a mood. The mood she was in was a dark one, a childish one. She wanted so badly to be mad. She wanted to pitch a fit and throw herself on the ground and then make everyone do as she said... but she couldn't. Her vow to the royal family made it impossible to break. Such was life when you made a vow. She hated herself for making it, for thinking it would never bite her in the ass. She hoped her future selves would never be so stupid.

Trying to pull her mind free of her dark and demented thoughts, she looked around the town. Taverns dotted almost every street, along with inns and other such things. There was even an open-air market where people were selling their goods, and having a nice time chatting. Something that looked like a festival was happening in the square. That caught Rizza's interest. What fun could be had if not in a festival?

Settling on that to remove her mind from wayward thoughts, Rizza slid off the saddle of the horse and took the reins to guide it through the thick crowd. Whatever was going on was drawing a lot of attention, and the atmosphere made Rizza happy. Vendors were selling their wares, children were running around wonton without their parents, adults were dancing in the street and playing music, and everything seemed to be just for fun.

As Rizza joined the crowd, she could feel her good mood returning. Everywhere she went, there were smiling faces and people greeting her without knowing her. Rizza was not much for crowds, but this one was a lot of fun. No one cared that she seemed of noble birth. They all just seemed so happy. It was... refreshing. The side streets had been so crowded... was it because of this?

Slipping between some people, Rizza looked over some jewelry on a counter before moving on. The horse was following dutifully behind, but soon people grew agitated that it was there.

The poor creature was too big.

"Ma'am, I can take that horse for you 'til you're done! Just three silvers!" A young man cried out to her with a wave of his arms. He seemed generally enthusiastic about all of this, and it made her smile all the more. Walking over to him, she dropped three silver coins into his hand. He seemed happy enough, and more than excited to work despite being surrounded by happy festival-goers. He was about her height with sandy brown hair, big brown eyes, and freckles spattered all over his face. The grin on his face was also missing a couple of teeth, definitely still a child. A good boy at that, he was probably helping his father and mother work the stables.

"Tell me, what is this festival they are holding? It is ever so delightful but... I am not familiar, as I'm not from here." Rizza's words came out in a gentle singsong voice that belonged to a woman much prettier than she. The voice was lyrical enough that the boy perked up upon hearing it.

"Why, Miss, this is the Mid summer's festival! All the crops are really good this year, and everyone is getting ready to bring them in, so we are having a grand party before the hard work starts, of course!" The boy was practically yelling, but it was charming, rather than agitating. He was so excited just to be there that Rizza could not help but also become so. Bouncing slightly on the balls of her feet, Rizza dropped a gold coin into his hand as a smile fell over her face. The boy's eyes turned as round as saucers at the sight of the gold coin. Most common people didn't see too many of them, especially not at his age.

"Make sure to keep up the good work! I'm sure your parents are very glad to have your help, and I sure enjoyed talking to you! Have a good festival, and thanks for the information!" Rizza practically skipped away as she continued to observe the crowd from under her cloak.

The boy waved her off. She could feel his joy radiating from him in waves as he bounced around and cheered to himself at his fortune. It wasn't every day a noble was so generous with their wealth, and he probably felt like he'd struck the lottery.

Yes, Midsummer's festival, that was an interesting time. The farmers were probably all very excited to get the tax season over and done with, and enjoy a long winter with the family. Granted, winters down in this part of the country were not nearly as bad as the ones in her mountains, but they were still rather fierce, in their own way. Due to the city being on a plane surrounded by trees, there was little blocking the wind from ripping everyone to shreds and sinking the chilly winter air into all parts of them. That was not the only dreaded thing about winter here. The stone buildings did little to stop the ice on the streets, either. It turned into an over-glorified skating rink all through the city. The guards had to pick the streets each winter to keep the cobbles from freezing too much. It did little to help, and their hands were usually frozen solid by the time they were done.

However, today was nice. After the rain upon entering the city originally, Rizza was enjoying the heat that the day had to offer her. How could she not, with so many kind people around her? She gladly strolled around the market, watching everyone as they passed. The stalls were busy and the people were happy.

Carnival people were dancing through the crowd, street performers were everywhere, and vendors were selling cute trinkets: little hand-crafted things that kids would love, or a person trying to woo another would enjoy as a gift. The festival was busy, and the vendors were making a good bit of coin selling things today. It was wonderful to explore through.

Until her feet got too tired to carry her any further, Rizza wandered. At that point, Rizza chose a small perch on a fence between some booths to sit down and relax. It was not the most comfortable perch, but she could see a lot of people from where she sat, and it made watching them all the more enjoyable.

Her gaze went around the different stalls, vendors, and people, and she smiled. There were couples here and there dotting the place, but most were just out with their friends having fun, and that was what Rizza liked. An old ache sparked inside of her at the idea of friends. In her past lives she had had several... but not in this one. In this one, she was alone. No one liked her eccentricities, and it made it hard to make friends. Moreover, her strange appearance was only common among witches and wizards, and those were few and far between. Since she began this life, she had not met a single witch, and the only wizard... her mood soured some as she thought of the over-inflated prince who stroked his own ego. Granted, she had not actually seen him doing so, but he was a prince, and his brother did it, so why wouldn't he?

"Come one! Come all! These jewels are the finest in the land!" A vendor near where she was sitting was shouting about his wares and drawing people in. However, most ignored him because his wares were ridiculously overpriced. Though, as she watched, one couple did approach.

These two wore fine clothing, and were clearly nobles of some kind. If Rizza remembered right, the male was a Duke of something or other. He seemed to be trying to woo the lady as she looked at the jewels, but, suddenly, a frown appeared on his face.

"My good man, how could any of these be considered good? The flaws are evident, why, just look at them!" he barked at the vendor as he held one up to the light.

Rizza remembered him now, he was pompous and mean. His family owned their own gem mine, and he was rather good at spotting imperfections in them. However, that did not mean he had any right to be rude to the vendor.

The man in question was chubby, with a simple tunic and round cheeks. His hair was pulled back into a ponytail, and he was trying frantically to look good, but it mostly just made him look off somehow.

Rizza's head tilted as she watched him frantically deny the other man's claims as he argued about price and such. One would think the vendor was a crook, trying to swipe money from everyone in every way he could. A quick review of the 'gems' with magic revealed he was. They were just very well-designed, shaped glass. However, it was because they were well designed that Rizza took interest. Why would a man go out of his way to sell obvious fakes at such a high cost? A small smirk played along her lips. She wanted to find out. The man clearly had something going on.

"If you don't want to buy it, noble Sir, then don't buy it, but don't defame me just because you are stingy with your wealth!" the merchant argued. His face looked genuinely enraged at being slandered. He was quite the actor.

"Defame you? What good does defaming a peasant do me? You are beneath me, and I am merely keeping you in place. I should have you arrested for your lies," the man spat back. The gem in his hand was carelessly tossed back onto the table, a sneer on his face as he looked at the merchant.

Her head tilted to the side some as she slid off the fence she'd been perched on. Others around her may try to pretend like they weren't listening avidly to the heated debate between merchant and pompous fop, but Rizza was not most people. No, she walked across the open space of the street to the other side and leaned against the post that was holding up the awning the merchant was under. That earned her curious glances from both the merchant and the fop, but she simply stood and continued to watch.

The stand was not as good as others. The wood it was made out of was cheap, and the fabrics surrounding it were most definitely wool and simple things that were easily purchased for a cheap price. The poor merchant's own clothing was rather shabby, and his wares were not so much proudly displayed as recklessly, as if he did not care if they were stolen. He wasn't really selling the whole 'they're real I swear' bit. Everything about the man reeked of desperation. It wouldn't be hard to tell he was a scam artist by the way he looked. His acting was good, but his showmanship was incredibly lacking.

"Now, listen here. I am not paying you 30 gold for something that is clearly not even worth 1 gold. You will take my three Silver, or you can leave town. I can make sure of that." The noble was clearly trying to pull rank and Rizza snorted softly at that.

That made others look toward her again. The merchant was going to formulate a reply before he glanced over at her. "May I help you, stranger?" The man was clearly hoping there was a new customer, or at least someone on his side. He also looked a bit fidgety. Should she play with him, scare him more than he already was?

Rizza waved her hand off at him, causing him to frown at her. The fop at that point began to glare at her. "Do I need to call the constable?"

That made Rizza snort again, earning her a hand-on-the-hip, sass master stare that she doubted anyone but a noble could pull off. Still, it was funny.

"Sorry, youngin' I just needed something to lean on... these old bones don't work like they used to." She enchanted her voice to sound like a cragged old man and even went the extra step to glamour her hand, so it looked wrinkled and sun spotted as she waved it in the air to shoo the arguing gentlemen.

The noble snorted at her, and seemed to lean away as he leered. He clearly was that much unhappier with her being there-after 'finding out' she was old. What a loser. He clearly had a phobia of the elderly, or at least an aversion to them.

"Perhaps you would find a better place to stand, beggar. I will give you a shilling to leave." A shilling, the man offered. Rizza withheld the snort. As if that could buy anyone anything. A shilling. What the hell? What a grungy jerk, she knew he had money, and he hoarded it like it was going out of style. Beyond that, her cloak was anything but what a beggar would wear. On a normal day, it was easy to mistake her for a beggar. Yet the fine material she wore should have been a dead giveaway. The fop really was looking for trouble without using his brain.

While lost in thought about the stupidity of the noble, she suddenly found a glass of water presented to her. Not long after, she was also given a small crate where she may sit. The merchant was much more kind. Her eyebrow rose under her hood as she took the glass. A soft and caring smile was on the man's face as he 'helped' her sit down. Well, that was an interesting twist, indeed. She had expected him to be as off-putting as the noble. He was, after all, trying to scam people for coins. Yet, he showed kindness.

"Thank ye, young man," she said in the same craggy voice as earlier. Seeming satisfied at having helped Rizza, the merchant went back to glaring at the noble.

"Those are real gems, I tell you, and if you don't want to buy one at the price that is set, which is half of what they would cost elsewhere, then you can just walk away, Sir. I don't need you clogging up my stand." The merchant swiped the ring the noble had been ogling back for good measure. Somehow, he seemed almost brave, but the quiver of his legs behind the table gave him away to Rizza as she sipped on the water.

Her face contorted in disgust as she tasted what was in the cup. It tasted of algae and fungi growing in it. The poor man probably didn't have good water judging by its gross taste. Carefully setting the cup on the ground, she waved her hand over it, so it was refreshed. She did it low, so none could see her action and give up her game. That was another telltale sign, though. How did one not get good drinking water in such an abundantly rich city? This place had lakes and rivers and streams all around it... how curious.

The noble barked out a laugh, catching Rizza's attention. She had missed part of their squabbling, but the Noble suddenly reached across the table to grab the merchant by the shirt and haul him forward, practically dragging him onto the table to snarl in his face.

"I will call the constable, and then we will see exactly how real these 'gems' are. Trying to fool people in the capital city may just get you banned! GUARDS!" the noble yelled, causing the merchant to blanch. Well, that was not very nice.

Rizza chewed on the inside of her cheek for a moment before springing to her feet and snapping her fingers. That got their attention, and both glanced at her.

"Enough of that now. What makes you claim this man's jewels are not real? Come now, let's hear it." The old man's voice was back, and she moved her head as if she were looking between the two, knowing her hood did not exactly give for good facial expressions.

She could hear pounding feet behind her. Metal on cobble made for a defining sound, and it was what the guards of the city wore. The clank of armor was obvious, and she knew the guards would be coming at any moment.

"Why, look at these gems, old man. Even a sodden old coot like you could tell that they are flawed glass and nothing more." The noble not only insulted the merchant's wares but also Rizza... how incredibly rude, and very stupid. Who dared to insult Rizza? That was the last straw.
Rizza wanted to play with him all the more for that. She could not help it, jerks like him deserved to get their butts handed to them once in a great while. That time was soon to come.

"Why, I do not see what you're talking about, young man. " Rizza purposefully grabbed the ring he had been holding and held it up to the light. A little bit of glamour and the thing looked like the real topaz it was supposed to be fronted as. "It looks plenty real to me. How can you tell it's not real, show me?"

The noble sneered and snatched the ring from her, holding it up to the light. This effectively made the Merchant fall back behind his stand as he was freed. Rizza gave him a small thumbs-up behind her back making him very confused, oh well.

"Now, look here. When I hold it up to the light just right there is a flaw right...." The man seemed to frown as he looked all over. The flaw he had seen was seemingly gone. Good thing, too, because right then, the city guards showed up. The man sneered, and looked at Rizza. "You did something didn't you?"

Rizza put her wrinkled hand to her chest to show affront as she gasped audibly.

"I am just a weary old man. What could I possibly have done youngin'? All I did was question why you are bullying this poor merchant, even being violent to get the price lowered! You nobles always think you can just do as you please la-di-da and no one will be upset! Well, Sir, I see no flaw there! You admitted it, too, so pay that man his money and be on your way! Wouldn't want these city guards getting mad at you, now would you?" Rizza squinted at him. Her hand pointing shakily at the Noble she was accusing of highway robbery. This was truly a fun day for her.

Rizza could see her words had an effect. The guards around seemed to grumble and agree that the nobles often were misusing their powers and it was not fair. He would gain no allies there, and the man seemed to notice that too. Disturbing the peace wasn't something one wanted to be accused of. If they were, they may just get into trouble. Looking utterly affronted, he quickly pulled out the money and put it on the counter, hastily stuffing the ring in his pocket as he sneered.

"Good day, your highness," Rizza said theatrically, even throwing in a touch of a bow as he stormed off. That seemed to calm things down quite a bit. Everyone in the market went back to what they were doing, and the guards stalked off rather gloomily as they had probably been hoping for something to do, some reason to rough people up that day.

That left her alone with the merchant. The man stood there, stunned, looking at the pile of gold before looking over at Rizza. "How did you do that...?" His words were barely a whisper.

"What are you talking about, young man? It is not hard to stand up to nobles. Why, if I had my cane, I would have cracked him right over the noggin. Knocked some sense into him, I would have." Rizza shook her fist in the air and gripped her back as if she were old. Why was playing an old man so much fun? Rizza loved acting. It was entertaining to pretend to be someone other than herself. She was still the same personality, more or less, but more likable because none knew she was a witch.

"No... you ... you made it real... you made the ... the glass really a topaz..." The man stared at her, befuddled, and Rizza raised a hand to her lips to hush him. He seemed utterly troubled, but she wasn't going to give his secret away.

"None of that, now, you don't want those guards to over-hear you're selling fake things. That would just be bad for business. I didn't make it real. I just made everyone think it was real, and I'll keep doing it if you keep your lip zipped." Rizza smiled happily as the man stared at her.

He seemed to debate about something in his head for a few

minutes before bobbing his head like a moron as he agreed to her. That settled it. She would help him out.

The rest of the day, Rizza spent the time sitting next to his stall making his diamonds, rubies, emeralds, and all his other 'gems' look realistic enough to get bought at the high as hell price he was selling them for. By the time they closed up shop for the day, he was rich, and his store of fake gems was empty. The best part was the smile on the man's face.

The Merchant

The streets were dark by the time the merchant and Rizza packed everything up. Silly grins were resting on both of their faces, and why would they not be? They had scammed practically everyone in the city. Granted, the glamour would wear off; but not for several months, and that would give them plenty of time to forget who they bought the fake jewels from. People in this city were so easy to fool.

Rizza slid down onto the crate she had been sitting on when she had originally gotten to the festival to watch as the man tried to fool the fop. Now, she was tired, and the place to rest was very much welcome. Compared to before, she felt a lot older, but it was worth it. All Rizza had to do was use magic here and there to make people believe what they saw.

Rizza watched as the man fumbled around in the dark corner of his collapsed booth before pulling out a jug of water. She assumed it was the same stuff he had tried to give her earlier that day. It was nasty stuff. With a flick of her wrist, the jug was taken care of. The water inside was no longer stale or rancid like it had been when he had offered it to her the first time, now it was clean.

As the man brought it to his lips, his eyes widened, and he immediately turned to stare at her. The look on his face was priceless, especially after the day they'd spent together.

"You did it again." His words were soft. He had been giving her funny looks all day. It seemed his curiosity was finally getting the best of him now that all the people were gone. There was no one left to listen to his questions. Only her.

"Aye. Don't you owe me dinner or something for all that hard work?" Rizza changed the subject as smoothly as could be. Her gaze went over the man's face as she waited patiently for him to decide. It was not hard to see him struggling to come to terms with the idea that she had not answered him, but instead asked him a different question.

Common courtesy won out, however, and he did not bring it up again. He gave a soft nod, and put the water in the belt of his robe. A smile spread on Rizza's face. Not too bad, she spent a little money to stable her horse... shit, the horse. Rizza ran a hand down her face before holding up a finger.

"Walk with me, young man, I know a good place, but first, I need to send my horseback to where it came from." The man looked confused, but followed along behind Rizza. He had never seen her with a horse, so when did a horse become part of the evening's agenda? He pushed the thought from his mind and dismissed it as an idea that she had stabled it or something before joining the festivities.

Sometime during the day, she had acquired a walking stick. She hardly paid any mind to how it happened. Probably someone felt bad for 'little old' her. Nonetheless, it added to her disguise until she decided to lose it. At that exact moment, she did not feel like losing it.

It took them less time to get to where the stable was than it had for Rizza to go from the stable to his stand, but that was probably due to the lack of people. It was hard to squeeze through the crowd when she was so small, but this? This was easy, when no one was around to hassle her or call her names for her small stature. Yes, this was an easy walk that took no time at all. Neither of them was winded by the time they reached the small stables. Now that it was not surrounded by all kinds of things, Rizza could see that it was nothing fancy at all, just a little shack with a post for one single horse: hers. Why was there only one post? That was so out of place. As she walked towards the animal, the boy from earlier came running out to stop her.

"Thief, THIEF!" The boy shouted at the top of his lungs causing Rizza to pause in her steps before tilting her head. She watched patiently as the boy moved between her and her horse. That was more puzzling, he seemed like a good child earlier that day. Perhaps he had a change of heart and thought to rob her.

"Excuse me young man, but that is my horse." Rizza's voice

had taken on the feminine appeal from earlier and that made the merchant jump. The boy seemed to blush but continued to glare at her as his arms stretched wide to fend her off from taking her own horse. How amusing.

"I do not know what you are talking about. This is my family's horse; we have owned it for..."

"Cut the crap, son, this old man h-... I thought they were an old man... but just now..." The merchant seemed confused as he walked over to his son, his bag of gold weighing heavily on his shoulders. It was only after his father spoke that the boy piped down. His own confusion showing on his face at his father's broken speech.

"Anyway, we owe this stranger a favor. Now, go wash up. Now that I know their horse is safe, we are all going out to dinner. We made quite a bit of money today, your mom may get that help she needs, after all." The man smiled happily before glancing warily over at Rizza again. "The hut is small... could you...?"

"No problem." Rizza's voice seemed to shift again, this time to a different masculine voice which made both of her companions raise their eyebrows. She realized, while pulling her little stunts, that she did not know either of their names. Curious. She would have to learn them. However, at that moment. her stomach grumbled and holding them up to ask silly questions was... well, silly.

Rizza waited patiently outside as the two went into their hut to go do whatever it was they needed to do. Part of Rizza figured the two would try to make off like bandits, but something about the sound of the boy's mother being sick made Rizza think otherwise. One would not want to piss off the witch, which she assumed, if they had any brains, they had already guessed she was. The man didn't seem completely dull, and the boy sure made an effective con artist.

Rizza was right to have a little faith in the pair. As they came out, they looked a little less scraggy than before. The man had clearly put on his best tunic and the boy the same, though neither looked particularly amazing. Still, as far as commoners went, it was rather dashing, she had to admit. It was also flattering that they would bother to dress up for her. Rizza smiled lightly, and let the pair join her as she began to walk to where she wanted to go.

It had been some time since Rizza got the chance to go to Old Ale's tavern. The last time she had been there, the tavern owner, Mars, had been harping at her about using magic while drunk. Honestly, some people did not know how to have fun.

Still, the old woman was rather amazing in her own right. Large and jolly, and always ready to knock heads together if people got out of hand. She was not the kind of woman you said no to lightly when she asked you to do something, and even more so when she told you to do something. Mars had a very strong air about her, which is what made her tavern the best tavern around. It was too bad it was in the roughest part of the city.

Rizza and the two fellows did not talk much as they walked there, which was all well and good for Rizza. She did not like chit-chat conversations that just seemed to fill the air. It was easier to be lost in her own head than to deal with other people's constant yammering for attention. Rizza was content with her oh-so-quiet demeanor that did not lend anything to helping people figure her out. One minute she would be completely quiet, and then she would wind up like a squirrel and just run for hours. Rizza never really noticed the running for hours part. That sounded awful, who had that kind of energy?

After what seemed like hardly enough time to blink, Rizza was at the door of her favorite tavern. She had to stand in awe of it for a moment. The place was the same it had been when she left, the timber that supported the frame was still showing, the carefully edited woodwork on the upper floor, and the mud-brick on the lower that created the walls. It made for a beautifully welcoming vibe. The best part was that Mars never replaced the sign Rizza had accidentally burned. She felt she may cry, with how touching the memory of the woman was.

Quickly bouncing through the door, Rizza grinned as she smelled meat cooking, as well as booze and sweat. It seemed like a fight was happening, with Mars right in the middle playing referee. The woman always let things play out until it went too far, at which point, she would put an end to everyone's nonsense, but letting people get out their frustrations was better. Rizza clapped, delighted as one man threw the other into the wall and started hammering his face with his fists. She did not know why the fight started, only that it was entertaining. Jumping up onto a table, Rizza let out a holler of delight.

"Get him! Kick his teeth in! WATCH THAT HOOK!" Her fists went up mimicking the fight with absolute joy. Behind her, she noticed her companions lingering in the door, clearly debating on running away. Rizza hopped from the table and ran back over to them. Before they could turn to run, Rizza was pushing them by the smalls of their backs into the room and to a corner table that had a good view of the action.

"You two act like you have never seen a fight before. Loosen up. I promise it does not get that bloody with Mars watching the place. Plus, Mars makes a dang good steak, when she is in the mood." Rizza grinned happily.

"You're sure none of us are about to hit the butchering block for being here? This area is not exactly..." The older man began to stammer. The man seemed to be down on his luck with money, but didn't seem to like this part of town.

"Well reputed. I know, I know, but I promise, you're safe with me. Nothing could happen to you as long as I..." Her words were cut off almost as quickly as she had cut her companion off.

"RIZZA! AMY! FLASKARDA! HOW DARE YOU WALK INTO MY TAVERN!" Mars's voice shouted over the din of the room, causing the entire place to go dead quiet. Each part of Rizza's full name was enunciated clearly as Mars yelled. Rizza grinned excitedly as she pretended to cower in a corner. This was the part Rizza loved.

"Mars! It has been too..." She began to stammer meekly, though the grin on her face gave away her joy.

Her words were cut off as the much larger woman stomped over to her. Her arms were almost as buff as any strong man's, her chest twice as big, and her hips big enough to really do damage if she put them to sitting on someone. Best of all, her dark brown eyes glowed with a type of livelihood that Rizza just adored, the kind that says she'll fight you if she needs to, but would rather just eat, Rizza's favorite pastime.

"Don't you dare come in here and tell me 'how long it's been' and start with all that mushy crap, you useless little witch, you! You dare disappear for six years, then show your face without so much as a how do you do?!" Mars's hands were on her hips. She stood at the table with her fists clenched, with her eyes glaring daggers at Rizza like she was earnestly debating murdering her.

Everyone else in the room seemed petrified, the merchant and son included. Though, they also looked ready to bolt for the door if the immense woman blocking them would give them the chance. Everyone was holding their breath for a very long, uncomfortable time as they looked between Rizza and Mars. They were expecting some sort of fight to ensue. Not expecting the women to actually be friends of any kind.

"Oh..." Rizza said the word slowly, before hurling herself across the table at Mars. Before the larger woman could complain, Rizza was wrapped around her neck in a tight hug as she laughed lightly. "I missed you, too, Mars! Silly royal family banning me to the mountains, what fun is that?!" Rizza giggled. She felt a hug that could almost crush her squeeze around her small frame.

That was quickly followed up by a tremendous laugh from Mars. The woman spun her around before setting her down to sit on the edge of the table. The much broader woman still looked pissed, just a little less murderous, when Rizza looked at her again. Crossing her ankles she leaned back against the counter lightly. "Tell me, now, what gave me away? I was trying so hard to be sneaky, too." Rizza grinned despite knowing her friend could not see it.

"What gave you away? You're kidding right? Look at that bright-ass red cloak. Who do you think you are? Some fairy tale hero about to fight a wolf?" Mars flicked the hood before scowling at Rizza again. "Speaking of the cursed thing, you know the rule in my tavern." She, again, placed her hands on her hips in a matronly, 'I'm pissed at you' manner.

Rizza let out a whine as she did so. Her feet kicked in the empty air as she bounced herself on the table, not unlike a child would do in the throes of a tantrum.

"I DON'T WANNA TAKE IT OFFFFFF. THEY'LL ALL RUN AWAY AGAINNNN." Rizza whined at the top of her lungs as she threw herself back down on the table and sulked, arms folded across her chest.

By now, everyone in the tavern was highly confused. The merchant and the son were not sure if they wanted to laugh or cry at the way Rizza and Mars were acting. No one really seemed to know how to act when the little witch got to be near her best friend. However, this was how things were meant to be. Rizza was not just going to give in to every idea most people had. That would be oh so very boring, and so very not worth her time.

"Rizza Amy. Do not make me snatch that cursed thing off your head. You are not a child. This is my tavern, and everyone in here can bed their mules for all I care about what they think of you." Mars did not back down one bit.

She did not care for Rizza's tantrums or the way she tried to get her way with magic. Rizza was not allowed to have her way in Mars's tavern, and it was absolutely delightful. She was able to bully everyone else into getting what she wanted, just not Mars.

"Fine, fine." Rizza laughed and she sat up again. Her hood fell away as she did so, revealing her odd features, which made almost everyone in the room gasp. About half of them shot to their feet and mumbled 'witch' under their breaths.

Rizza blinked several times, stunned, before a very shaky hand ran up to her hair to pull a strand towards her eyes. She let out a shriek of horror and bolted to her feet as if possessed. That made everyone in the room freeze in terror. The shriek was shrill enough to make any grown man feel the chill run down their spine. Fear showed deeply on Rizza's face as she looked at Mars. "WHY DID YOU NEVER TELL ME I WAS A WITCH?! WHAT KIND OF FRIEND ARE YOU?!" Rizza began fake crying into her hands as she flopped back on the table again. Her dramatics were top-notch. Her acting was terrible, though. The entire place was ready to burn her alive for making fun of them once they came to their senses that she was still putting on a show.

"A WITCH! I'M CURSED!" She cried harder.

Mars let that continue for a short while, which was making everyone uncomfortable before she let out a snort and started walking away. "So, you want your usual steak and potatoes with ale, then?" Her words were tossed over her shoulder as she walked away. There was no recognition of the drama Rizza tried her best to act out, Mars was too used to it.

Rizza's head immediately popped back up with a pointed-toothed grin on her face as she flopped back to sit down in the chair she had previously sprung from. "Yes, please, and for these two, as well, please!"

Rizza shouted the words towards the kitchen. Everyone continued to stare at her. Rizza looked around with a goofy grin on her face, and waved at the still-staring people. However, everyone looked away when she looked at them. It was depressing, really. No matter how silly she acted, people still feared her.
"Nice to meet you all, my name is Rizza!" She laughed lightly. She did not take it to heart, their fear. It was common for simple folk to fear her. It was nothing new. Humans always seemed to fear what they could not understand.

It was only after everyone had seemingly gone back to their business that she once more looked towards her companions in full. They were completely blanched of color and looking like they had seen the devil himself as they stared at her. Though the nice thing was, they were looking at her.

Most people blanched, but they didn't meet her gaze when they did. Instead, they looked away and freaked out like... well, like she was a demon, honestly. That was always the worst problem, people always seemed to think the worst of Rizza, though she never actually did anything wrong... okay, sometimes she did do something wrong.

"You have questions." Rizza's smile slipped from her face. She seemed to grow serious. Her fingers folded together, and she set her hands on the top of the table. Her gaze went from the father to the son and back again before landing on the father. Her head nodded lightly, as if to give him the go-ahead.

"Y-Y... I mean to say... That is..." He stuttered over his words and Rizza could not help but smile lightly. "You're Rizza... the... The royal wi-witch, the..."

"The most powerful being in all the lands, the girl who has walked a hundred lives and knows all the secrets of every corner of the world, the one who can be a great asset to a kingdom or bring about its destruction, the woman of untold stories, the thing of nightmares, of horror stories you tell your children to keep them in line. Yes, yes. That is me, nice to meet you." Rizza smiled lightly as she looked at the man. She cut him off and said it herself because she knew there were more ungracious ways to recall her fame and glory. He seemed to go even paler. How was that even physically possible? "Oh, come on. We got along just fine when you thought I was a craggily old man; how can this possibly scare you?"

The boy seemed to flinch at that, but the man just let out a startled laugh before a hand went to his head. "Did I make friends with the demented witch?"

The words were out and stinging before he could take them back. Her mouth fell open before she pouted. "Demented? That is not a very nice word... I am very sane, thank you very much. In fact, I think the queen had me tested at one point, no one could find a single thing wrong with my mentality. It must be all the lives I've lived." She scratched the bridge of her nose slightly. She didn't want to feel hurt, but felt it nonetheless. 'Demented', they called her. That was such a harsh word.

Rizza tried cracking a joke, but both the father and son sank into their chairs. Rizza gave them a chance to calm down as she sat patiently, cleaning her nails and waiting for her food. It was still very uncomfortable to be without her hood. She wanted it badly, but if she put it back on again, then Mars was going to yell at her, and that was no fun at all. Rizza did not like when Mars yelled. She was loud and scary, like a bull on steroids.

Before too long, the boy seemed to let his curious nature override his fear and he sat up with gleaming questions sparkling in his eyes. How did questions sparkle in one's eyes? Rizza did not know, but it was clear what was happening with the boy.

"So... that story of you blowing up the west wing of the palace when you got into an argument with the crown prince..." He began to question her.

"Completely true. In fact, that got me thrown out of the palace and pissed off the queen and king to no end. I was fifteen, and frankly, the crown prince told me no one could, so, I proved him wrong." Rizza smirked. She was so glad someone found that as entertaining as she did. The boy's face lit up with delight at the realization that she would talk to him so openly, and it also made the tension she didn't know she felt fade.

"What about the one where you turned the Duchess of Dunthorpe bright blue for an entire month?" The boy's eyes lit up more as he began to ask her about her stories. It seemed this one was more excited by the idea of magic instead of terrified, which excited Rizza in turn.

"Also true, though slightly under-exaggerated. It was for a year. She started painting her skin white again, just to make herself look normal. She dared insult my enjoyment of blueberries, so I turned her into one. It's not my fault she can't take a joke." Rizza and the boy both laughed as Rizza said it.

Mars came over and plopped the ale Rizza had asked for in front of them. Her gaze leveled on Mars. "Do not go convincing this boy to join in your shenanigans. I already had to replace that sign the first time you destroyed it. Don't you dare finish off what's left of this one." Mars grumbled as she walked away again.

That sent the boy and Rizza into a new fit of laughter. The boy's eyes were alighting with delight. "What did you do to the sign?"

That sent Rizza into a whole new line of storytelling and explaining. Some pompous noble had wandered into the tavern to see why Rizza the great wanted to hang out in such a dingy place. He dared insult it, and Rizza got too upset, and too drunk. The man and her had gotten into a long duel over who was better that ended when Mars's sign caught fire and Rizza got thumped hard for it. Mars had not spoken to Rizza for a month after that. It took bribery of the best butcher in town as a connection to get her to calm down. Even that was more for Rizza than Mars, though. Rizza really loved a good steak.

By the time their food arrived, the son and Rizza had become fast friends. However, the dad was still keeping a calm distance, which she did take notice of. Though she held her tongue about it until their food was well into their stomachs, and they were relaxing once more.

"Did I not tell you that Mars makes the best steak in the kingdom? That woman has the magic touch." Rizza smiled happily as she used a toothpick to pry meat from her teeth. A soft frown took over her face, however, as the merchant stared at her. "What?" Rizza was highly confused before the man tossed down a bag of coins.

"For you to leave me and my family alone... and never speak of what we did today again... Your horse will be sent to the palace." The man's words were cold before he stood from his chair and stared at his son. "Nathan, we are leaving."

"But, Pa..."

"NOW." With that, the man gripped his son's arm and jerked him up. Before Rizza could even blink, they were gone and out the door. What a cranky merchant. To think Rizza had helped him, even. Part of her felt hurt at that, she and his son were having a good talk. However, she could not blame him. Rizza knew people had a hard time stomaching who she was. Not only that, but she had befriended him by helping him scam people. It wasn't like she didn't know what he was like.

With a soft sigh, she reclined in her seat further. It was very late into the night, and it had been a very long day. She was too tired to be upset at anyone. However, the smell of fresh cider caught her nose as Mars dropped it down in front of Rizza. A smile spread over her face again. She looked up at Mars, who was now sitting across from her.

"I'm taking the gold, because we both know you don't need

it, and you owe me after disappearing without a word." Her words were cold, but there was a kindness in her eyes as she pushed the drink to Rizza. Mars was true to her word and took the bag of gold before slipping it under her apron. Rizza didn't protest a bit.

Rizza sat up in her seat to take the offered drink and take a sip, grateful to have it after the day she had. Some people could not take a joke, and that was just painful. More often, people could not handle her at all, and that was worse. Rizza did not realize she was sad until she found herself staring down into her mug. "Mars... I'm getting married..." Rizza choked slightly as she said the words. Bile rose in her throat. Her coming to the tavern had two meanings. She had not simply wanted to see her friend, she wanted to tell her, to get some kind of comfort... comfort she could not find in the palace full of nobles.

Mars stilled, clearly deciding if she wanted to yell at Rizza or not. But the look on Rizza's face must have stopped her, because, instead, she simply reached out and took Rizza's hand between both of hers.

"My dear girl... any man that marries you has got to be batshit crazy." Her words were certainly mean, but not untruthful. They stared at each other for a long, tense moment before laughing.

Rizza had to take a moment to breathe before she could explain further. It was good to have someone who could bring you away from your sorrows so easily. "It's the second son of the royal family... he is a wizard, Mars... a wizard and..."

"WHAT THE HELL, RIZZA?!" The words came from the door as it slammed open. Rizza and Mars both jerked as they saw the royal family crest on two guards as they entered first. However, quickly on their heels was... the prince. Son of a... Could she not have one thing?

"And... has really, weirdly good timing." Rizza finished. Her eyebrows drawing together as she watched the procession disturb the rather rough atmosphere. Everyone had settled back into their routine after the initial shock of seeing Rizza for the first time in six years. Now, everyone was on edge again because of the damn prince.

Rizza pulled her hood back over her face, quickly concealing herself as she sulked in her seat. That man had to ruin everything. He looked furious as he glared pointedly at Rizza, as well as her friend.

Mars glared at the man. She seemed to come to a sudden realization as he came storming into her tavern. Yet, even she dare not offend the royal family. Her tavern could easily be blacklisted from the city and she could be banned.

"We have been searching the city for you! Ever since we found out you left, we... WE WERE FRANTIC! And yet here you are, drinking... what is this? Cider? Inside a rundown tavern in the worst part of the city?!" the prince shouted at her, wagging a finger as if he were her father and in charge of her or something. Rizza let out a snort as she took a sip of Cider.

"I am the single most powerful being in all the land. What the hell did you think was going to happen to me, I'd get attacked by a bunny and die?" Rizza snorted again as she watched Mars move to intercept him.

"This him?" Mars asked calmly, staring down at the prince, arms folded over her chest as if to dare him to try something. She knew it was. Rizza knew better., but Rizza also knew Mars wouldn't actually do much. He, to his credit, glared back at her earnestly where most men would pale and faint.

"Yup. That would be Prince 'charming'." Rizza said sarcastically, finishing off the ale.

"Move, this instant, or I'll see to it that you are..." Rizza stepped from behind Mars after she finished her ale. Lightly patting her on the arm as she walked towards the prince. She knew the second he walked through the door that she was not going to get a moment of peace. He always had to come along and rain on any parade she had.

"It was great seeing you. I got this," she said to Mars softly before turning back to the prince. "Let me make one thing clear here, prince Pratt. You threaten Mars again, and there won't be enough of you left for them to hold a funeral. Do I make myself clear?" For once, Rizza did not have her voice enchanted to sound different, her voice was very much her own. Anger was also very audibly laced through it. How dare he come into her place of refuge and threaten her only friend in the world? The nerve. The room was dead silent, no one dared talk as the two stared daggers at each other. Though, some were seriously amazed at seeing Rizza actually infuriated. It took a lot to get her to that state.

The prince stared at her for several long seconds. He was clearly at a loss for what to say, before he gave a simple but curt nod and turned away.

Sometimes, it was not the fight that was best, it was backing down. He probably did not want to try and challenge her magic, no one did. It would probably level half the city to beat him, but she would damn well would. He paused at the door before turning back. His expression was a lot gentler than what it had been before he almost stormed off. Rizza stared at him.

"Will you come back to the palace with me, Rizza?" His words were a lot softer, a lot meeker as he spoke that time. He was clearly upset with her, but he also did not want to draw any more anger from her.

"May as well, the place that had my horse sent it back to the palace already," Rizza grumbled as she walked out the door. She did not wait for him or his guards to join her. Moving to the door, and past the prince, she made her exit. No fun could be had with him around anyways. She also didn't want his scent stuck in yet another place she frequented, or to see him attack Mars, either.

Her hand rose into the air to flip off Mars, as a customary goodbye between them, before she exited the building. She did not have to look behind her to know the crude gesture was returned in kind. Mars never changed. It would be a shame to live the next life without her.

Back to the Grind

Rizza let out a sigh as she sat in the palace again. She was trapped here; after her disappearing act, everyone had become panicked and the king had forbidden her from leaving. The nerve of some people... as if a trip into town was really all that bad. Why couldn't she leave? That did not even make sense. No place had been blown up, no one had been injured. The most that had happened was one whiney prince wasn't able to find his fiancée to fake-win her heart and make her fall madly in love with him like the rest of the cursed palace seemed to be. Who the heck did he think he was anyway?

He was not even the first-born prince. No, he was the second, yet he was strutting around like he was king of the world... as if someone like him deserved her attention. Now she was stuck in the palace. It had been two days since her 'incident'. Time was dragging on slowly, each day seemed more painful than the last, and meals were unbearable. She was being forced to dine with the royal family, and all sorts of hell broke loose when that happened. She and the crown prince just did not get along as of late. They could not avoid arguing about the marriage, and it seemed neither of them intended to try. The Queen had to separate them on no less than three occasions already.

Rizza was currently hiding in a window seat in the library with a book in her lap, one of her many tomes that told stories of her lives. This life had been filled with a grand adventure of piracy. She vaguely remembered it. Though, the memories were so buried that it would probably be a while before she could remember the details as well as she had written them. Her fingers traced the page she had open. Her thumb pressed into the well-worn fabric of the page. The paper had turned yellow from the years sitting on the shelves, but each tome was stored well. Each was easy to read without damaging still, after all these years. The ink saturated the fabric, and looked as good as the day she wrote it.

Each life she led was completely different from the last. Each life she led held its own joys and sorrows. The interesting thing was, as much as each kingdom fought, they all had agreed to one thing (mostly by force): Rizza was to be left the tomes containing her memories whenever she was reborn, no matter where. The kingdom that she was born into also received her tomes and records. That was something she had told them they all must do... or something about one curse or another. That was in one of the tomes, but, honestly, it was too much effort to remember every little detail. No kingdom had dared to break that rule, so it was perfectly fine by her. Who needed to remember something when no one else bothered to question it?

The sun was bright outside. It was oddly ironic, because in all kinds of stories when the hero was upset, the clouds were in the sky and everything was bleak and dull. So, why was that not the case for her? Was she not the hero? Was she not balancing the world? Why was she being forced to marry... The words bit into her again at the idea. Forced to marry... yes. She was a puppet in the kingdom's chess game. Delightful.

A sigh escaped her again. She did not know how many sighs had left her, but just that day alone, it had been many. What was she going to do with her life? The idea of leaving her sunlit perch was too much. Perhaps it would be easier to just... end this life and start the next... However, she did not have her recently-recorded tombs here. They were all written and filed away someplace safe and away from prying hands. Granted, no one could really change what she wrote. The language she wrote in was completely dead. No one knew it but her. Every life, it was the one thing she always remembered, the dead language from so long ago. By now, things were so different that no one would be able to read the tomes she wrote but her. That made things safe, she supposed, if a bit more boring.

How much more interesting would it be if someone did try to change her memories to suit them? How much more interesting would it be if, say, someone tried to control her by warping her until she could not remember herself? Then, at the last second, her true memories would prevail, and she would conquer the evildoer. The images filtered through her mind: Rizza saving the day, the brave hero, all hail Rizza.

Her finger waved through the air like a mini sword before she feigned stabbing an invisible enemy through the heart with a soft laugh. All of the reading about her pirate self must have been getting to her. The idea of stabbing someone seemed somehow appealing to her. Was she losing her marbles? Probably. That wasn't her problem, though. The crown prince and Princess could deal with that when she became part of their family. They could suck on that lemon cake.

Lemon cake... Why was she thinking of lemon cake? That idea was amazing. Her nose twitched slightly, and she realized why. She could smell it. It was fresh. Someone had baked a lemon cake. Rizza's legs uncurled from the window, and she plopped down onto the ground. Before she could really think about it, Rizza was heading towards the scent. She let her nose lead her. The way she walked almost looked like she was floating in a very comical way.
It was not in the library; the librarians would have a fit of anyone getting butter crumbs on the delicate pages of the books. No, this was from someplace else.

Rizza followed her nose down the hall and to the left until she found... the prince. A sigh escaped her as she looked at him. He was standing by an open window with a mitten on his hand... and a lemon cake in it, freshly baked.
A grin was on his face, as, clearly, whatever trick he was pulling had seemed to work. Anger welled in her. Not only for his trick, but also because now she could not have the lemon cake without giving into him. That was just cruel. Playing on her love of sweets was a nasty trick. Even she did not stoop that low... at least, not in this life.

"Princess Rizza... You looked sad and mother said you liked this cake... so I made you one..." The prince's words made her frown even more. He... made her a lemon cake?

He did not have it made, he said he made it. With his own hands? Rizza glanced down, and, sure enough, his fingers that were not covered by the oven mitt were covered in burns, and there was also a matching one glaringly red on his cheek. How the heck did he burn himself on his cheek? Wait... why did Rizza care? Rizza did not care. Letting out a snort, she folded her arms over her chest without replying.

After several long and uncomfortable seconds, she could see the prince's confidence waver. He moved to set the still-hot cake on a table he had prepared with a fork and a plate. The man was wise, he did not have one there for himself. That did not earn him extra credit, though. Everyone in the palace knew Rizza liked two things: a well-seasoned steak, and sweets. He would do well to try harder if he wanted to win her affection this time, or next time, or any time. He was not smooth, and it was beyond obvious what he was doing.

"Rizza ... I... you looked tense, so... I thought you may like some cake... and... maybe we could talk?" The prince looked slightly hopeful. It was almost a delight to crush his hopes. No... not almost, it was a delight.

Rizza snorted and glared at him from behind her hood. "Prince Pratt, I think we have done all the talking we need to do. You are to have my hand in marriage, and get everything you have ever dreamed of, all the power a wizard like you could want, leached from me." Rizza's words were biting and cold. Her voice held no sympathy, and the wilted look he gave her brought her nothing but joy.

Why should he be happy when she was miserable? Why was he allowed to have what he wanted, but she was forced to put up with this degrading 'I swear I love you' bull? Rizza wished he'd play the bad guy role properly, instead of pretending to be the victim. He was the one forcing this on her, not the other way around. Why did she always come out looking like the bad guy?

Rizza pulled the cake away from him. Her fingers deftly snatched the fork away as she took a step back before he could stop her. Despite her hatred for him, she loved the cake. Her mouth watered as she took the first bite. It was slightly dry, but the effort was there, and it was the cook's frosting. She had missed the cook's frosting, he did it perfectly. She savored the bite, keeping from moaning as he prattled on. Ha, Pratt prattled.

She amused herself.

"Rizza I... that was my father's idea... I want to marry for love..." The prince seemed almost defeated in the way he said it, as if he had to defend himself. His words made it sound as if he'd been forced into this too. Even though his actions spoke a different tune altogether. If Rizza was a kind person, which she was not, if she held sympathy, then the way he looked so broken when he spoke may have affected her, but Rizza was no fool, and court nobles were damn good actors.

"No... you don't. Put up your lies in front of all these court snobs, do as you will, but don't you dare....." Rizza was about to yell, fork pointed at him flippantly and at the ready to stab, as well, when they heard the sound of running footsteps. She would have to forgo her happy, pirate-induced dream of running him through with the fork he had given her, as they were soon joined by a guard.

She and the prince turned at the same time to see a guard heavily clad in armor running towards them. The man must have been running all over the palace, judging from the way his cheeks puffed up with a bright shade of red, and sweat beaded along his skin. When he reached them, he practically fell over, trying to catch his breath, wheezing, out of air. All Rizza could think was how little training palace guards must get, to be that out of shape. However, the man obviously needed something, so she waited next to the obnoxious prince to see what it was the man wanted. The cake was about a quarter of the way gone by this point. Little yellow crumbs dotted her face.

It was a few minutes before the man could breathe again, but the pain and fear on his face were evident as he said the words. "Lady Rizza... P-...Prince Pratt... the crown P-P-P-Prince and P-P-P-P-Princess ... THEY'VE BEEN POISONED!" His words were choked out as he tried not to sob. The man was clearly at his own breaking point.

Even Rizza's cold, dead blood ran rigid at that. Without another word, Rizza bolted down the hall. She did not check to see if the dip prince was following, or if the under-exercised guard did.

The only sound louder than her footsteps was the pan and cake hitting the floor with a loud clatter against the marble. It mattered not. The crown prince was more important than a sweet... she would never tell him that, though.

Who could have poisoned them? Why would someone poison them? Sure, the prince was an arrogant jerk, but no one really knew that but her. She was the only one he was arrogant and mean to. Why would someone poison him?

Rizza did not stop running until she was in the corridor of the royal wing that led to the prince's chambers. A guard tried to bar her entry, but she immediately flung him out of the way with a burst of magic.

"Do not DARE tell the one person who can try and help not to help! Honestly, how dumb can you be?" The words flew from her mouth as another burst of magic sent the doors flying open, almost hard enough to break them, as well. That was not her concern.

In the room were two physicians, they were old and wrinkled from many years spent serving in the palace. Rizza knew them well. The old woman and old man had always been kind to her, except when she messed with someone and hurt them with her magic. A lot of people got sent their way because of her. Actually, originally, it was just him, but, because of her, they had to hire a new physician for the court. Good times. Not the point.

The room also held the king, queen, and the other royals who were huddling nervously in a corner as the physicians worked. Their faces were strained. Pain clearly laced their expressions as they glanced up and saw Rizza. They were scared, not only of her for once, but also for the crown prince and princess.

The pair lay in their bed. The bedside table held only the candle holder with a lit candle and a bottle of wine. They clearly had been intending a romantic evening. Small petals from flowers dotted the floor and watermarks from behind the screen indicated there may have been a bath. Two wine glasses were discarded on the floor, broken. Rizza took the scene in quickly, but paid little heed to it. What happened before they were poisoned didn't matter as much as the fact that they were poisoned.

Her gaze left the family to turn back to the physicians. A tight, thin line of the mouth and a small shake of their head was all Rizza needed. The Royal family began to bawl at the same time Rizza stumbled over to the bed. In it lay both the crown prince... and princess... dead. Rizza could do a lot of amazing magic... but she could not raise the dead. The poison had been very fast-acting.

Rizza looked over the corpses of the two. They had blackened fingers and bluish-black lips as if they had drowned or frozen. When Rizza carefully examined their skin, it was clammy and cold. There was blood on the sheets around them as if they'd been coughing it up.

Pain laced Rizza's expression as she looked upon the dead figure of the man that had once been her only brother... her family... at least, in this life. Her fingers trembled as they reached out to lightly touch his cheek. Yet, a hiss escaped her, and she pulled back. Where her fingers had touched his skin, bright red welts were forming on hers.

Her jaw opened slightly before she turned on the royal family. Her hand rose into the air, causing them all to choke on their sobs as they saw the marks on her skin. The question she asked next was filled with accusation, the hurt, and the betrayal she felt, at seeing the welts. She knew the welts well, only caused by a reaction to a certain thing: her.

Tensions rose in the room as the pain from losing the loved ones mixed with fear at Rizza's realization.

"Tell me... if I were to try laying hands on any of you... would this happen?" Rizza's words were barely a whisper.

"Rizza... dear, you don't understand, we..." The queen began to try and placate her.

"Would... this... happen?" Rizza's words came out in a thunderous tone despite her lack of yelling.

"Yes... It would happen if you tried to touch any of us." The king's voice came out strong, but the look on his face held panic. It took a lot for the king to look scared, but he did. He still defended his family, though, his form moving in front of them as if to shield them from Rizza's wrath.

Rizza could not begin to describe the emotion she felt. They were not her family. They were not her friends. They were her dictators, and that was evident in the fact that they had coated themselves in a holy magic like any moron commoner could do with a little holy water. The family must have done it religiously, to have as strong an effect as it did, to make her skin blister that fast. Rizza sneered while looking down at her hand. A wet spot appeared on the palm of it, and another. Rizza realized she was crying.

Rizza was upset, and overwhelmed. She was not one to cry, she would not normally cry, yet... She was stunned. She would probably feel the emotions soon, the tightness in her chest, the sorrow and anxiety. However, it was not there yet. Right now, it was only the tears giving her away. Damn them.

At that moment, prince Pratt pushed into the room. His face was ashen, like the rest of the family, and they all began to cry again. Rizza could not contain the rage she felt. If she stayed with the family another minute, she would end up killing some-one, and she knew it. There were enough deaths. However, she needed something first.

Her fingers snaked out to the crown prince again. Taking his wrist in one hand, she ignored the blisters that formed and cut his wrist with one sharp claw. Blood pooled on top of his skin and she swiped a finger across it before drawing it to her mouth to taste it.

No sooner had it touched her tongue than she was spitting it out again. Acid... it was like acid. They had been drinking holy water, not just using a basic purifying ritual. A small barking laugh escaped her. Rizza could not believe it. Worst of all, even with the small taste, Rizza knew what kind of poison it was. Irre-delum.

"Your fear... your beguiling fear set them up for this! You are the ones that killed them!" Rizza's laugh became hysterical as everyone in the room blanched. She was infuriated to the point of insane laughter. Hurt beyond words at their mistrust in her. That mistrust had killed the crown prince. Rizza couldn't bring herself to acknowledge the overwhelming feeling of guilt that knowledge brought her. If she had been more pleasant to be around, they wouldn't have been scared of her. She knew that, but could not face it at that moment, so she turned on them instead.

"It was your need to defend yourself against me, whom you had banished. That substance was harmless... unless mixed with holy water." Rizza's laughter turned into wracking sobs. She could not believe the lengths people would go to. No, this was not the time to feel sorry for herself. The idiot had caused his own death, and his wife's, as well, all because of what she was.

Rizza could finally feel it. the soul-crushing contraction of her chest from the amount of pain she felt, the loss that threatened to drive her into endless sorrow. The prince was dead.

It was her fault her rival was dead. It was her fault he would never have kids. He would have ruled the kingdom, having to deal with calling on her and begging like a brat. She had been looking forward to those days. Now they were all gone... all because she had scared people. Because she was a monster in this life, the prince was dead. Pain coursed through Rizza's chest as she felt like it was being torn in two. Her fingers pressed tightly into her cloak as she bent over, keening in sobs.

If she had not been such a conceited jerk in this life, they would not have feared her, would not have set up his death so brilliantly. He died because of her. The pain was drowning her. Tears flowed from her eyes in waves that burned down her cheeks.

A hand on her shoulder drew her attention, and when she glanced up... she saw prince Pratt. He was in tears like everyone else. He was mourning like everyone else... but he was also touching her. Her fingers snaked out to touch his face... Nothing, not a thing.

Rizza realized... he was the only one of the family that had not drank... well, technically, he couldn't drink it any more than she could. That proved nothing. The pain returned. She had almost hoped, before remembering he was also like her.

A flash of rage ran through her as something crossed her mind. Her fingers pulled away from him and she pointed at him with a claw. A snarl built on her lips. "You did this. You killed your brother!"

She shouted the words in his face, making everyone stare at her, again. The prince did not only look startled, he looked genuinely hurt that she was accusing him.

"How could I have p-...poisoned my brother? He was my hero, Rizza! How dare you accuse me of that! I was with you when this happened!" Pratt's voice rang out through the room. He looked utterly pissed and desolate at the same time. Pratt had pulled his hand away from the air. Jerking it back as if he had been stung by her accusation.

Tears streamed down his face, but he cried often. He always played the victim. Rizza was not buying into it. Racking sobs filled his chest, causing his family to huddle around him.

"You did it. I know you did. I don't know how, yet, but I will prove it. I am not marrying the murderer of Drake!" Rizza yelled at him. Her fingers curled into her palms, cutting them deeply as they did so, but Rizza hardly noticed. Rage was filling her again, more so, the empty feeling that sat in her chest was getting completely consumed by it.

The king squared off against her. His gaze was filled with anger and despair. His son died, and Rizza was accusing his second son of being the culprit. She knew why he was mad. Yet, she was madder, still. She had to be, or sorrow would consume her.

"Pratt would never harm his brother, Rizza! Silence your tongue before I have it removed!" His words were a roar, filled with pain and rage. He stood up for Pratt, and the entire family turned to glare at her as one. She was alone in this. They did not believe her. Why would they?

"He did, I..." Rizza began to talk.

"HOW?! You have no Proof, Rizza! He even said he was with you! How could you blame him for his brother's death! This is no joke!" the king snapped at her again.

"We have put up with your insolence and bratty behavior

for long enough! Even now, when my son lay dead, the heir to my throne, you still make jokes! Have you no compassion?!" His face was turning redder with every word that he spat at her.

Rizza's face drained of any color it may have had as she watched him. "I was not..."

"DO NOT FEED ME YOUR LIES! WE BANISHED YOU FOR THIS EXACT REASON! YOU ALWAYS HATED DRAKE, AND THE SECOND YOU COME BACK, HE IS DEAD! YOU ARE THE PRIME SUSPECT, SO IF I WERE YOU, I WOULD STOP TALKING AND POINTING FINGERS!" The king's words were laced with venom and hate.

Pain struck any anger she had left. He... he thought she did this? Sure, she and the prince did not always get along... but, the idea of killing him... Rizza's lower lip quivered at the mere idea of it. How could she kill the crown prince?

Her gaze went to the rest of the room. No one looked at her. The queen's face was eerily calm. Rizza was too distraught to care why. All was clear, though. They all assumed it was her. No one, not a single person, trusted her.

Rizza did not stay in the room to find out how they blamed her for that. She fled. Her feet carried her out of the west wing and down the hall. She fled from the castle, not bothering to stop to get a horse. Her feet carried her all the way to the city's edge... but she could not leave. Her gaze looked longingly down the road. The road that led home... but she was getting married in two weeks... she couldn't leave.

A scream tore from her lips, a scream that held all the pain, rage, and frustration she felt, along with all the sorrow and betrayal. That scream sounded not unlike a wounded animal that was drawing its last breath. Rizza screamed, and as she did, the streets began to empty, people began to hide for fear of whatever was making that sound. The sky darkened, and rain began to pour, then sleet, then hail. It was the rain that should have been there in the first place, the rain that should have been there in the library. Yet, it was Rizza's explosion of emotion and lack of control of her magic when it happened that caused the weather to change now. She was no hero.

The ground shook with a resounding earthquake from her loss of control. She could not handle this. She was a monster, and her only 'friend' in the palace was dead because of it.

The guilt and the pain weighed Rizza down. She couldn't think. The shriek tore through the air in her lungs. It burned away at her core and ripped up her vocal cords. Nothing could eliminate the pain she felt. Nothing could score the memory of the accusing looks from her mind. She had murdered him. That thought played over and over in her head.

Rizza screamed until her lungs burned and her throat itched. She screamed until she could not scream anymore, until she could not make a single sound. Then, she blacked out.

Waking Up

Rizza woke up near the gate of the city, the same place she had collapsed the night before. Sitting up sent a jolt of pain down her spine. Her hands went to the middle right side of her back as she let out a groan. She glanced down at the ground she'd been laying on, and found that there was a rock where her back had been. No wonder it hurt.

Memories fluttered back to her, pain in each one: the conversation with Pratt, the news of the poisoning, finding out Drake and his wife were dead, that the royal family had zero faith in her, and then, finally, being the prime suspect in the murder. What a wonderful day. That was right, she'd been accused of murder... and no one believed her that the hoity-toity prince did it.

Moreover, through the throb of her head, she remembered who she was accused of murdering. The betrayal of finding holy water in his blood and finding out the source of his death all came flooding back to her: the king's yelling, the brat's denial of it. Tears began to flow anew down her cheeks. She wiped them away. It was a telling sign that she had been left outside to get soaked by the rain that had come through with no one to bring her in. They did not want her back. They did not want her in the first place. No one wanted her in this life, they needed her... two things that were very different, like vegetables or medicine. No one wants to eat them, but you must, or you die.

The idea made Rizza snort. Maybe it was time she gave them their medicine. The thought alone eased some of her pain. No one ever trusted her in this life because of how childish she was. Nevermind the fact that she was the most powerful, and longest-lived, being in the world that anyone knew of.

Her gaze was on her hand during all her rumination. A bruise was there. How? She pulled up her sleeves and realized there were golf ball-sized bruises all up her body. She had made it hail... not just rain. . The ungodly scream she made came back to her, as well. She had terrified the city... and passed out.

She must have lost control of her magic when she did, so

not only was she left out in a rainstorm, she was left out in a hail-
storm. The city was probably petrified of the abnormal weather
patterns. It wasn't really a shock anymore as to why no one came
and got her. Even she wouldn't have come to get her after causing
that big of a mess... talk about being over-dramatic. That was just
great.

She went back to the medicine idea, not wanting to linger
on that pain. The idea made her smile. She would be giving people medicine; the thing they seemed to want so bad. Rizza's mood
was terrible. Her beautiful red cloak was soaked through, and
she could feel cold seeping into every part of her body... that was
probably why she had woken up before the sun. Her gaze went
around. It wasn't a shock that the citizens didn't try to help her,
but why hadn't the city guard? Were they all cowards now, too?
That would be something to report to the king later, if he wasn't
still cross with her. Hell, she wouldn't be surprised if he accused
her of 'fleeing the scene of the crime.' Especially after labeling her
the prime suspect.

Rizza slid the cloak from her shoulders, and snapped her
fingers. Immediately, Kit appeared to help her. The cloak was
gone in an instant, and fresh clothing appeared, hovering in the
air in front of her. Rizza slid into an alley and slipped them on before smoothing her hands down the front. She wore a classic dress
with a set of stockings and boots. Her hair was tied up carefully
behind her head in a jet black ribbon, and, overall, she looked like
a very dark, gothic doll in a red dress.

There was no cloak, hood, or hat to hide her looks for once.
She was tired of hiding, tired of cowering from the people that
should be thanking her for all the things she did for them, tired of
playing the ignorant child, when she had lived many times more
than they all had. It was time for Rizza to be Rizza. It was time
to remind the kingdom why they did not upset Rizza to this extent. However, pain still tore through her chest, her breath was
still labored, and it was like a weight was now on her shoulders.
They had blamed her for his death, when they were the ones
spoon-feeding him holy water.

Rizza marched from the alley, and those who were around and awake would gasp as they saw her pass by and scurry away from her. All ran when they saw her: the witch, Rizza, the legend, and she was in the capital city. Of course she was, that was no news. The news was the fact that Rizza was in the capital city without a hood. Rizza never went anywhere without her hood. In this life, or any other, she had always seemed to have it. It had been written in the very first journal she had to read each time. Life was easier with her hood. Keep the hood on. The first tome outlined that, and how to enchant her voice so she didn't enchant others. That was always a delight. She would just have to see how the royal family would deal with her not hiding her face anymore. Pity on the fool who messed with the most powerful being in the known world, especially when they were 'oh so generous' to help serve the royal family.

Rizza spent a good amount of time walking back towards the palace. She had to, the capital city was huge, and she had made it all the way to the gate before she had collapsed. Two hours of walking, and she was not there yet, but the sun was up, at least. Rizza had to be two-thirds of the way through the city, and was getting into the better parts of it, as well.

The only problem with walking so long was the fact that, after a while, one tends to lose their motivation for vengeance. It was all well and good to think about wanting to seek retribution on a kingdom that was ungrateful, but in reality, she just wanted to go back and find out who murdered Drake. More so, who murdered her in a past life. Two things to sort out. The third, if she had to name it, was getting a marriage called off. Fourth, if she really wanted to think about it was resting. The bruises on her body were aching something fierce at this point and she was exhausted.

About the point when she was entering the 'rich' district, something happened. Of course something happened, god forbid anyone see an ominous pissed-off witch and realize they should probably leave her alone. No, nothing was ever that easy.

As Rizza stepped towards a side street that would be a

quick cut towards the palace gates, she found her exit blocked by a set of rather impressively large men with pitchforks and ropes. As she looked up the street, she saw yet another set, with similar items, and grim expressions. Oh dear, it was the angry mob scene. Cliché.

Rizza let out an annoyed sigh as they began to stalk towards her. She let them get within twenty feet of her before her hand rose in the air. That made them all pause. Immediately, they started eyeing her warily, and she waited until she was sure they were all about to move again before she spoke.

"Wait. You're supposed to do the whole 'you're not welcome here. We're going to teach you a lesson, witch. Monster! Freak! Loser! YOU DON'T BELONG!' accusatory thingy you guys seem to love so much. Honestly, if you're going to do this, do it right, or I just can't get into it." Rizza's words were pouty as she dropped her hand again. She was pissed off, and still making jokes. Was that how she handled life? Joking about it? Maybe that was why no one took her seriously until it was too late. Morons.

It quickly occurred to them that she had raised her hand to ask permission to speak, as a child would do for their tutor. She wasn't raising her hand to cast any magic, and when she did speak, she was just taunting them. She didn't take them seriously at all.

Anger seemed to stir further into the mob as she spoke. The words sank in, and more anger brewed. She had told them how to try and 'take care' of her. They were supposed to be scary; she was supposed to be scared. Obviously, they did not expect her to expect that, and want to groan at the pure ignorance and annoyance of it. It was not their fault, really; they were new to this.

"Shut it, witch. When we are done, it won't matter what we said." That seemed to get a hearty chuckle from the rest of the group as they started pacing towards her again.

"Well... at least that was something." Rizza said with a docile demeanor. The group advanced on her, and she couldn't help but shake her head. These were not your typical villains, or simpletons. Weren't the stories told about such scenes usually...

grander?

Rizza let out a soft 'puh – puh – puh' to get them to falter. This time, her finger was in the air and nothing else. Her eyes lingered on the one that seemed to be the leader, and she smiled lightly.

"I honestly think you should reconsider. You may think you're being smart, but I'm really, really mad right now. Using magic when mad can get... dangerous. Not for me, of course. If I die, I'll just come back again in a new life, but you guys... well... Can't say as I've ever seen an afterlife in my time in the inter-im. In fact, when I'm not walking the earth, everything is rather black for me. Or, maybe, I have my memory wiped. Either way, I don't think you live after you die... so... I wouldn't. I really, really wouldn't if I were you." Her words were soft and cheery, but the threat was clear enough. She was giving them fair warning, and it was the only one she'd give them.

She was not offering any type of kindness to those who dared get in her way now. Her rage was still fresh, and the fact that she was remaining composed at all was rather fascinating to her.

In fact, she was quite happy to try and kill them all should they try and kill her. She had spent so many years playing the victim. She had lost so many lives because someone decided she no longer needed to walk the earth, and she did not think it fair to use her powers to stop their ideas. After all, she got a ton of lives, and they got one. It would be cruel of her to take their one chance away from them when she would just come back.

Rizza was always trying to be the better person, and no one ever saw it. It was something she always tried to do, no matter how growly she got in each life. However, right now, that did not matter. The big picture did not matter. What mattered was prov-ing that asinine prince to be the killer, and she could not do that if she was dead. Those who wanted her dead, injured, or otherwise inconvenienced would simply have to go.

The group snarled at her... that was a new thing even for an angry mob. Who snarls? Most cuss, use violence, throw things, yada yada, usual barbarian behavior. Had society digressed to the point of animalistic tendencies such as snarling? That was just sad... and Rizza's thing. They were stealing her thing. She pouted slightly at that. Their frames advanced on her, and she had to let out a sigh. She gave them fair warning.

Right as Rizza was about to raise her hand and end the fight with a simple removal of air from the area, they could hear the sound of hooves on the stone street. Not that that was unusual when it was just one set of hooves, the issue was that it was... four, in a group, even. Rizza's eyebrow rose as they all seemed to turn as a collective to see what the noise was about. Why were there four riders together? For that matter, why were they riding down such a barren street? Rizza paused with her arm in the air, fingers bent slightly towards her palm, and her thumb pulled toward it, as well, as if she were literally going to pull the air from the area. Her gaze went to the group of steeds as they rode up.

It was easy enough to figure out when the beloved prince appeared... this time, with two palace guards and an empty horse. His expression looked drawn thin and grim from staying up late, and the bags under his eyes attested to it. Rizza assumed he had not slept, though why was beyond her. His plan was going perfectly... oh, except the part where the king would probably find a way to pin the murder on her, so she would be executed, and there went his one chance at advancing his powers to their full potential. Hmm... maybe she should let them think it was her. The idea gave her sudden, morbid glee. If it was his fault, he got screwed, and if it was her fault, he still got screwed... how delightful.

As the prince's gaze landed on her, the look on his face seemed to worsen. It mildly shocked Rizza that it was even possible for the usually cheery, fake-as-heck prince to look so grim. The sight of the prince made the angry group of men scatter to the winds. She doubted that mattered, though, because the look on the prince's face clearly said he was there for her.

Her hand fell down to her side once more. With the pests gone, there was no need to murder. Which, she supposed, saved her some explaining to the king, and that would keep her head from getting sliced off for at least a little longer. Rational thought kicked in just enough for her to remember that maybe murdering citizens was bad.

Pratt looked drawn thin, and the way he looked at her was like a predator watching its prey. He did not look in the least bit happy to see her, and, further than that, he looked completely done. Still, the set of his shoulders relaxed some once the bandits had run. A sign of relief, at least. Had he been looking for her? That would be silly, considering anyone in town could have told him where she was. It wasn't like she was subtle about being emotionally devastated last night.

"Rizza, you're coming back to the palace." His words were devoid of emotion, empty and soulless, almost as if he were sad. Though, the look on his face held more anger than anything else. Perhaps he was still butthurt that she knew it was him who pulled all this. That had to be it. She needed to figure out how he did it, though.

The thought occurred to her, and she ended up ignoring him to instead sit down on the street and begin to think. She often behaved this way, partially because she had oppositional defiant disorder. How dare he tell her what to do. No, that wouldn't do. Even if she had intended to return to the palace now, she just wanted to be a pain, so thinking about how he was a murderer sated her need to do just that.

She had, indeed, been on her way back to the palace, but the sudden urge to figure out how this oaf of a man had outsmarted her made her pause. It could not wait. How would the prince have done it?

Obviously, he had planned to drive her out of hiding with the cake as a way of making sure he had a witness to his location when the crown prince got poisoned. He had probably hired some servant, or maybe several, to help. Though, finding out which ones would be difficult, as most of the servants in the palace were well-trained. They didn't easily divulge their masters' plans. It also helped them, and hindered her, that they were usually well paid, and had worked in the palace since birth.

Rizza's anger seemed to become a distant throbbing in the

back of her mind. How had the prince gotten the poison into the crown prince's food? The most likely vessel for irredelum was food, as could easily be hidden under the spices and go undetected. Not only that, it would not be hard to make it react with the holy water, but if one was careless, they could have killed the entire royal family.

No, this was done carefully... not just carefully, but deliberately. It would have taken some careful planning. Who knows how many security revisions they made because Rizza pointed out that what they had was not enough, and even proved it on several occasions. Perhaps the cook had aided him. That would be a pity, really. She liked the cook.

If careful planning was something Pratt was good at, Rizza may not be his match in this life. She was too impulsive and impatient. Even while thinking about how he did these things, she was confusing herself. Yet, she felt like she had to try. She may not be a very good detective, but she had to give it the best shot she could. No one else had seemed to believe her that Drake was murdered, and even if they had, they weren't investigating, as far as she knew.

Her train of thought was interrupted at the sound of someone dismounting their horse. Rizza's gaze lifted from her thoughtful position of staring at the stone under her. The prince was the one who dismounted. His body was wracked with tension as he did it, but still, he held himself ramrod straight as if he had something uncomfortable in his clothing. The man was impeccable at trying to save face, even if his face looked like someone recently risen from the grave.

He walked over to her, and towered over her, glaring, as she did not seem inclined to budge from her position.

"I said, 'we are going back to the palace, Rizza.'" His words, again, were cold and emotionless, though he held his hand out to help her up... as if she would take it. It was only then that Rizza realized he'd called out to her several times.

"Did you say that? I'm sorry. I was too busy thinking about how you managed to pull it off." Rizza waved a hand in the air with a dismissive motion before she pulled it to her jaw to rub at it in thought.

"Pull what off, Rizza?" His voice dropped to a whisper, his dark expression only adding to the tension in the air. The other two riders were clearly nervous, and the horses were borderline spooked. To anyone else, that would seem intimidating, but someone like him did not scare her in the least. To her, it just sounded exhausted. He had been up all night. Though, she could not fathom why. The thought that he could actually be mourning the loss of his beloved elder brother didn't even cross her mind. Even she had slept some.

No one truly scared Rizza... not really; the worse they could do is make her restart all over again. Meanwhile, she could end them permanently. A cocky attitude came in strongly knowing you would not truly stay dead, not for that long, anyway.

"Well, the murder, of course. What else would I be discussing? What else would make you stay up all night to pretend like you are upset?" Rizza glanced up at him again. Was he really so dense that she had to spell these things out for him? Maybe his sleep-deprived brain needed a little jostling to get going. Rizza almost felt bad for him, having all that potential and no idea how to use it.

The prince did not reply right away. His fingers curled into fists at his side before one of his balled fists was pulled towards his mouth. Rizza watched as he paced away from her, tenser than he had been before. As he reached a building his fist was suddenly slammed into the wall. Sparks flew across the hardened mud, causing it to crack and fall away, leaving a hole where his hand had been.

The guards and their horses were petrified at this point. The guards were sweating buckets, the horses seemed to dance in place, antsy with nerves. It took effort on the guards' parts to control their own horses, as well as the two others. Yes, that was something interesting, indeed. Rizza did not flinch, though. Her gaze went to the wall, and, as it did, the wall began to be fixed.

That action made the prince's gaze jerk to the spot he had busted before jerking back to her. A sneer went across his face as he marched back towards her. His arm swung across his body and up towards the sky getting ready to backhand her before he froze. The look on her face must have made him do so, because she held no expression. It was devoid of all emotion as he looked to strike her. His outbursts were not fazing her, all they were doing was making her see him more and more like how she assumed him to be: a monster.

Part of her wished he would finish the action, wished he would give her that last little inclination to hate him. As it stood, she hated him profusely, but had no grounds to. This would give her the last little bit. Her chin tilted up as if daring him to do it. She wanted him to prove her right, to prove he was nothing more than a really good actor on any given day of the week, that he wasn't this nice guy that he pretended so desperately to be... but the blow never came.

Changing his mind in the last second, the prince reached down and gripped Rizza by the top of her arm, hauling her to her feet easily. A snort escaped her, causing him to glare again, but she did not say a word. He was a coward, and she knew it. He would not do anything to risk pissing his father off or proving her right about him.

Rizza silently questioned herself on why she was being so passive suddenly. It would not be hard to remove his hand from her, in fact, it would be painfully easy. People like him were easy to deal with. Yet, she did not, she was letting it happen as he lifted her onto the horse, as the guards escorted them back towards the palace. She stared blankly out at the city as they rode.

Back, Again

As it was expected, the king was not happy on her return. She got a dressing-down on how improper her attitude was, which led to a full-on fight about how it was not her fault. Then, he went on to talk about how his brave son was damned to have to marry her and he was upset about it. He blamed everything on her, of course, and even complained about the way the village reacted to her scream of pain. It concluded with her being confined to her rooms until she could learn to 'act her age'. How would he know how someone her age acted? She was centuries older than he would ever be. One-life-people really did not have the same concept of time that she had. It was pathetic.

Beyond that, the entire conversation was just ridiculous. How could he say his son was damned to marry her, and not call it off? If he knew he was torturing his precious son, why do it? Not only that, but the man was now next in line for the throne, since he was now the oldest. They couldn't seriously still consider her a proper bride.

That left Rizza pacing around in her room. She had nothing better to do. There were plenty of books for her to read, but her mind was racing too much to read them. Every time she tried to open a book, all she ended up doing was trying to reread the same page over and over again. The words would not stick.

As it was, anger was still a constant in her stomach. She felt this overwhelming urge to do something... and, for once, also felt extremely powerless to do it. She could conjure all kinds of magic, was not scared of death, was the fiercest creature in the realm... yet she could not solve a simple murder.

It was the murder of one of the only people brave enough to face off against her without backing down, and alone, at that. She did not want to admit it, but she was probably also extremely sad to have lost one of her only true friends. Even if he did not know it, she felt that way about him. Maybe she was also sad that he did not know she felt that way.

When a sharp knock echoed through the wood of the door, Rizza was forced to forgo her self-hatred born of being useless to glance at the reception area. Her gaze darted towards it as the attending servant answered. The guest was none other than the prince... there was a shock. Rizza heard his voice before she saw the annoying man. The servant would bar him entry, if he could.

Rizza sat down in a chair as the maid let the prince in, without so much as a 'by your leave' from Rizza. Her middle finger rose to her eyebrow to itch it. She tried to hide the annoyance she felt at having the reason for his father's and her fight walk right into her room. Her legs crossed at the ankles as she sat back in her chair. Kit immediately appeared, but Rizza waved the hand she had up through him, banishing him away. She did not miss the glint of interest in the prince's eye at seeing her little wisp friend.

"His name is Kit, and no, you will never have one." Her words were cold as ice as she glared at him. She did not even bother trying to hide the natural haunted sound that was her normal voice. The way it sounded like it was coming from an abyss and not her, especially when she did not hide the enchanting way it seemed to draw people in.

She waited for a reaction from him, any sign that the voice had an effect on him. He stared around the room as he waited for the servant to leave. Even after she had departed, he still seemed to be waiting. His gaze went everywhere around the room, but avoided where she sat. Clearly, her voice held no appeal to him, and, evidently, he was going to stand there like a fool until she asked what he wanted.

She hadn't expected her voice to work on him, he was a wizard, after all. It was still a bummer, though. As for what he wanted, she did not care. For him, it was probably a huge step forward. For her, it was just an annoyance that needed to go away.

He would not get what he wanted from her. Rizza flicked her fingers at a book on the bookshelf, and it fluttered into the air before landing in her hands. Pulling out the bookmark from where she had placed it six years ago, Rizza began to read. It was an old book, one she had read maybe a dozen or so times in this life, a simple book about a kingdom at war, and the challenges it faced. The strategies in it were brilliant, and she could not help admiring the way the king's admiral took charge when the king had been wounded. That had been back in a time when kings still fought on their own battlefields instead of sending soldiers to do it for them, back when there was integrity, and people did not force the witch to become engaged to a murderer.

The mental reminder she gave herself did nothing to help her concentrate on reading her book. In fact, as she reached the bottom of the page, she realized she had not even read the page. She stifled the urge to groan before beginning over again.

With the king injured and no place to run, I was trapped. My men were losing food and motivation. The battle was clearly going to end, but I had to push on. If we lost here, we would lose the war. We had been outmaneuvered at every turn. There wasn't much I could do to stop it, but I had to try. Not only the lives of my men and my king were on my shoulders, but also those of my family and my country. I was not going to go out a coward. I did not want to end my life that way. I had to protect my kingdom, my king, my family, and my men....

The compatriotic way that the man wrote about his exploits made Rizza's heartache each time. He had people he cared about, loved ones he had to defend. The same thing remained in all her lives no matter what: Rizza was alone in the end. No fake marriage in this life would change a thing. Moreover, it would probably make the loneliness that much worse. Was that why she was pushing against it so hard?

Of course, that was why she pushed against it so hard. There had been times in different lives where she had loved a mortal here or there. In the end, though, after they died, that person was gone, and she was left to live again... alone... again. It was the worst nightmare, to connect to someone then have them vanish. Yet, what about the prince? Would it be that bad?

Rizza paused her reading as she thought about that. Would it? The idea made her glance up at the man in front of her, still avoiding looking at her. A second thought made her decide, no, she was just being wishful. Nothing was that easy. She had tested such things in previous lives. Marriage, love, romance. Just because he was a wizard, and that was new, it did not mean it would end differently. She would be reborn, and he would be left as a memory.

Beyond that, she simply abhorred Pratt. Whatever made her dislike this prince and the idea of marriage was deeply rooted, and obviously right, because she did not get premonitions about people on a whim. This was something much, much more ominous.

They resided in the room in complete silence for what must have been half of an hour before Rizza caved. Aggravation and a growing headache caused her to groan in defeat, and it did not help that her mind kept wandering back to him, either.

"FINE!" she snapped. That made the prince look at her. A brief look of triumph crossed his exhaustion-riddled face before it was masked. "What do you want, your highness?"

Rizza refused to use his name. Though she used his title it was not out of respect for him. She did not care for him nor did she care why he was in her room. She just wanted him out of her room and preferably out of her life. That second one would have to wait until she proved him guilty without a shadow of a doubt.

The look on his face briefly changed to one of triumph once again before it smoothed. "I want you to attend dinner with me." His words were completely calm and cool as he looked at her.

Her eyebrow rose, waiting for the punchline to the joke. When none came, she shook her head and waved a hand dismissively at him. "Didn't you hear your daddy? I'm grounded. Go away." Rizza gave him a brief sneer before turning back to her book. She was acting very bratty and childish at that moment. Even she knew that, but she could not help it. The look of amusement he gave her only made her want to do it more. How dare he be amused when she was pissed off.

"The king has granted me permission to have dinner with you, alone. You should not be so quick to turn down this kind offer, Rizza," Pratt shot back at her. He was pushy, very pushy.

"Kind. That is an interesting choice of words, Prince. I'll repeat my earlier statement: go away." Rizza's gaze rose to look at him again. Dissatisfaction plain as day on her face.

Pratt's gaze stayed calm as he watched her reject him again before he laughed lightly. "You won't even try to keep up appearances, will you? You know, they all think you did it, the poisoning. I'm the only one defending you, and here you are, thinking I did it. Rizza, when will you give up? You're going to be my wife very soon. On that day, don't you think it will be easier to say the vows if you have learned to tolerate me? Have dinner with me." His words were compelling. The way he spoke, what he said. It was all so enchanting, as if he were intentionally putting a spell on his voice. His voice was probably like hers, and his words weren't actually that convincing. He was defending her. Of course he was. If she died, his magic stayed as it was. Why wouldn't he defend her? As for the marriage... he wanted that, not her.

She was hoping for a new excuse to turn him down, but, as it stood, it was rude to continue. She wanted to, more than anything, but Rizza knew the court rules and bull well. While court politics and niceties were not her thing, she did know the ins and outs of them. If she had not, it would have been hard to have to spend years at court.

If Rizza turned Pratt away a third time, she would put that much more blame on herself. They probably would not allow her outside of her rooms to investigate to prove Pratt committed the murder. Not only that, but the king would probably also demand to yell at her again for impropriety or something stupid of the like, as if she actually cared about court customs.

Even though he probably would not try to frame her for this, she still could not let him get away with the murder. No matter how innocent he played, no matter what the others thought, Rizza could not bring herself to see him as innocent. Something in her told her he did it. He had to have. The scheming way he was forcing her to marry him only added to her suspicions.

No, she needed her freedom to conduct the investigation. She would get this engagement removed, get him banished, and bring justice to the crown prince all in one go. Then, she could probably go home.

Rizza's jaw worked before she glanced away from him. "Fine. I will eat dinner with you," She did not have to look at him to know the look of triumph was back on his face. He was such a pain. "BUT... I will not talk to you." She amended quickly. Joy was not something she wanted him to feel.

"I'm glad to hear that, Lady Rizza. Please, put on something nice. I will see you in an hour, in my private dining room." His words were merry again as he spoke. He clearly did not mind her outward rejection of conversation with him. He probably thought he had won some prize by-... Private chamber?

She flashed him a glare as he turned to leave her chambers. He wanted her to eat with him. Not only that, he wanted her to eat with him alone in his own room. The idea of it... the terrible idea of it was enough to make Rizza fume. How dare he assume that was a good place for them to dine?

The fact that they would be eating together, alone, in his private quarters, would make the rest of the court appear like they were getting along well. Just the idea that there would be rumors of what they did together infuriated her. He was a pompous fool if he thought she did not see exactly what he was doing. This game was childish, and she hated it so very much. However...

Rizza wanted so much to be mad at the idea that he would pull this stunt. She wanted to be pissed. Yet, it worked well in her favor. If she went to dinner with him, in his private rooms, then it would, indeed, look like they were getting along. It would make everyone around Rizza forget that Rizza had accused him of committing the murder. That would draw attention away from her where it was not needed. Then, Rizza could conduct her investigation in peace. All she had to do... was play nice with the criminal.

A soft groan escaped her. It seemed so simple in her head. Rizza preferred straightforward and easy, not scheming, but this did not seem too hard, until she reminded herself that she had to play nice with Pratt. It made everything that much more difficult than before. It made everything hard to deal with.

Rizza flopped around in her chair, refusing to move from it for a good long while as she pouted. She was centuries old. She was the single oldest being known to exist, and here she was, pouting like a child... again. She folded her knees up to her chest, and hugged them while resting her head on them. She let out another groan. She would continue to pout. She hated this, hated him, hated court.

"I want my mountains," she grumbled aloud. Her thoughts were echoed by her voice no sooner than she thought it. She was being childish, she knew she was, but she could not help it. Pouting was easier than dealing with her reality, the reality that literally nothing was going her way. Why have cosmic power if one didn't know how to utilize it to her best advantage?

Rizza did not want to play nice with the prince. Kit appeared near her, and his aura bobbed around in the air as he scolded her. She could tell it was scolding, because he only bobbed that furiously and jerky when he was pissed off at her. Well, he could be pissed off. She was pissed off, too.

"Yeah, yeah, yeah. Stop being selfish and go to dinner. I get it already, knock it off. Get me something formal to wear to this stupid thing. I want to look good if I have to be presentable." Her words were a grumble as she slipped away from Kit. Her feet carried her off to her private bathing chamber.

The maids were in attendance when she went to bathe, which creeped Rizza out. They seemed to be excited about the idea of her going to dinner with the man she was to marry. Her, on the other hand? She was not thrilled about it at all. She was more put out by the idea than anything. She was also quick to kick the maids out. She didn't need servants to bathe.

With that thought in mind, she climbed into the tub, and proceeded to scrub herself down. Rizza hated dirt anyway, and wearing clothing when one felt dirty did nothing to abate the feeling. It felt like wrapping dirt in grime, and it was just gross. Cleaning made Rizza calm down enough to actually force a smile as Kit appeared with her clothing.

It was a soft, yet elegant gown of deep cobalt blue to accompany her purple eyes. Rizza knew why Kit chose the dress; the heart-shaped, low neckline made it easy to see the features of Rizza she would rather keep to herself. While Rizza did not have much of a bust, there was enough there to still be pleasing in the dress. It also flared out around her hips, giving the illusion to anyone looking at her that she had them to begin with. Overall, it was a rather beautiful dress. There were no shoulders, but there were sleeves that clung to her upper arms and grew looser as they reached her wrists until she had draping ends that extended much longer than needed for her hand to fit through it. It was elegantly cut, and not too revealing. Rizza rather liked Kit's pick for once.

She gave him an approving nod as he gave her a pair of black boots to go with, and she slipped them on with ease. Allowing the little wisp his fun, she let him do her hair. When he was done, her spiky hair almost looked good. Her hair had been drawn up, and the way it feathered out of the pins Kit had used, it looked like she had a porcupine at the top of her head. It still looked oddly beautiful. He gave her some dark kind of makeup at the top of her eyes and out the corners that extended in a flare to extend the edge of her eye and make them look that much darker. Rizza was actually quite impressed.

Her gaze went to the little wisp as her eyebrow rose. "Since when did you start doing makeup, and learning all these interesting new tools, Kit?" Rizza's words were calm, but there was clearly mockery in her voice.

Kit's little aura bobbed around in the air lazily. She could almost hear the childish voice going 'oh, well, you know... here and there.' It made her smile. Kit had a way of expressing himself, even without being able to express himself. It was nice. Considering the small wisp was the only friend she had through all her lives, she rather enjoyed his company.

With her hair, makeup, and outfit prepared, Rizza had no more reason to dawdle in her room. The idea of joining the fop for dinner was a headache and a half just thinking about it, but Rizza tried to look at the positives as she left her room.

Worst. Job. Ever.

When Rizza entered the hall of her chambers, she realized there was a guard waiting for her. He was decked out in the typical palace livery: a sash across his silver metal chest plate that had the palace guard's insignia stitched into it in a golden thread. A simple design really, probably easy to fake. It was a wonder no one had tried to assassinate the royal family yet. It would be a piece of cake... oh, wait... Rizza frowned softly.

Deciding she did not want to be depressed, she scoffed and glanced up at the guard. "What's this, then?" she asked the guard, the ire in her voice very apparent.

The man's face was hidden by the helmet he wore, only a slit for his eyes to peer through. "The king has requested I escort you to the crown Prince's chambers for dinner," the guard said. His words sounded of false bravado and many hours of rehearsal in the mirror. He was trying to keep his voice monotonous, but she could hear the slight tremble in it that gave him away as he spoke. Rizza was small, her frame petite, and the small body only appeared that much smaller next to the guard's larger frame. Yet, to him, she was terrifying.

The man was terrified of her, though, that was sort of normal. Dealing with her was almost like dealing with a scorpion: the smaller the scorpion, the larger the chance the poison will kill you. Likewise, the smaller the witch, the deadlier... or something like that.

"The Crown Prince? Bugger on that title. If you start calling him that, then people may start calling me..." Rizza trailed off, not wanting to finish the sentence but the guard did it for her.

"The Crown Princess? Well, technically, you are..." he said. The discomfort in his voice was plain. He seemed to grip his halberd a little more firmly, as if it would somehow protect him from her.

"You sound ridiculous," Rizza grumbled under her breath. She did not like the idea of being the crown princess, what the hell kind of role was that for a witch? She was fit to be a pirate, sure; it was a given that she had been a knight at one point... hell, she had even been a beggar and a noble in previous lives, but a ruling monarch? Had the world gone mad? Maybe it would make sense for her to be a monarch about three or four hundred years ago, when the monarchs that were in power were nothing more than the militia's bobbleheads, and Rizza still had not fully figured out her powers, but now? In a life where Rizza was no less than childish, bratty, completely irresponsible, and irrevocably reckless?

"Even I find the idea of me as a ruling monarch completely irresponsible." Rizza said out loud, echoing her own thought process. Then she gazed up at him. "You should form a coup."

"A what?" the man stuttered.

"A coup," Rizza repeated. "You know, a coup d'état, a rebellion, a commoner's allegiance, a rise up, a stand against, a fight for your rights, a forward assault against the tyrannical monarchy?" She was hoping he'd understand at least one of the alternatives. Did the palace guards not get any sort of educational training? That would be a pity.

"I know what it is, Ma'am... I just..." He trailed off this time. He was probably uncomfortable with the topic, but Rizza hardly noticed as she walked through the halls.

"That's what I would do if I were you. Me in charge..." She scoffed again at the idea. Whoever thought that was a genius plan deserved to be fired... from a cannon... off a ship... into the ocean. See she was better suited as a pirate. Oh, or keel-hauled!. Rizza grinned at the idea of the gruesome death.

"Wha-...WHAT?!" The guard sputtered as he walked after her. He seemed totally lost.

"What, what? I said, 'that's what I would do in your position'. How long have you worked here?" The realization she had never met him before struck her.

"A year... why?" he responded after a moment of hesitation. Rizza had been right. He was new.

"Ah, so you do not know what happened in these walls,

and to them, when last I lived here, do you?" She asked calmly, though the amusement in her voice was barely hidden. He was someone new to pick on... train... help?... something like that. One of those things would prove true, maybe two if she was lucky.

Rizza looked around the hallways they were walking through. There were grand marble arches, and rugs on the marble floor. Here and there, a statue would accent the area or a torch would light the way. Rizza had literally no idea where she was at, or where Pratt's room was.

"Well... not firsthand, no... but I have heard some of the most outrageous stories," the guard admitted. He could not be older than twenty, but Rizza would guess he was probably only eighteen or so. He was young, spry, easy to manipulate, and scared of Rizza: her favorite combination.

"All are probably true. Can't say for certain, as I have not heard them all," Rizza paused. "But that is exactly my point," She continued on, spinning to face him as she did so. He had to stop in his tracks, or he would have slammed into her as she pointed a finger up to his covered face. "I can't be trusted in a position of power. I'm reckless, dangerous, even." Even under his metal armor, Rizza could tell the man was quivering. His hands gripped his halberd tightly as she got closer. "So, you see, I'd rebel if I were you. It's sheer madness to have me in a position of power." With her rant over, she dropped her finger. She thought she made her point quite eloquently.

The man seemed ready to wet himself though, poor guy. "But... none could-... could fight you," he said meekly. "You are the most powerful being..."

"In all the lands, and no matter how I'm killed, or what they do, I always come back. I'm akin to a god," she finished for him, shutting him up as she did so, and waved a dismissive hand in the air. "I know, I know, but still, it is madness. I mean, hell, you're so scared of me I bet you drank some holy water before meeting me to take me to Pratt. I bet you even doused your armor, did you not?" Rizza inquired, eyes peering up at him as if she were almost going to judge him for it. The way she squinted and pursed her lips was akin to an old lady ready to give a good scolding.

"I... that is..." even with the helmet, and his size being greater than hers, causing her to look up at him, he acted like a mouse caught by a lion. He stuttered so beautifully.

She finally let him stop squirming with a small laugh. "Even the royal family does that. Do not fear me being upset about it... it's not like I was close to you. It's a smart thing to do, in any case. Not fool-proof, but smart nonetheless. Even I don't know what I'll do next sometimes..." Rizza said caustically. He seemed to relax a tad, but was still extremely terrified. She began looking around again. The halls all looked virtually the same. They were at a six-way intersection.

"Where are we?" She finally gave up her pretense of knowing the way. The look on her face was that of chagrin as he realized she did not have a single clue, and had not had a single clue as to where they were going this entire time.

The halls were scarcely decorated here and there was mild dust around the area as if there were months where it went without cleaning. Rizza frowned. Something about the area seemed familiar but she did not know what. As she looked up she realized she was standing in front of a tightly closed door. However, it looked like it had not been opened in a long time. It clearly was not the right door.

"You don't know where you're going?" he asked. His voice held a mild surprise. He had been following her along so realizing that she hadn't a clue where they went was rather... he felt dumb.

"Of course not, I didn't even know the bloody prince's name until my most recent visit to the capital. How would I know where his room is, and what sort of guard lets their captive lead the way anyway?" Rizza chided him, her tone harsh. Yet, she was not serious. Making this man fidget was just one of the perks of dealing with all of this.

"I... Oh, for heaven sakes." It seemed the boy was not totally lacking in wit. He seemed to have caught on that she was having a go at him.

The guard looked around, and then led her back down the hall they had come from. They had gone in the wrong direction for quite some time. Rizza figured it was because she kept him talking that he had not noticed it. They did not talk the rest of the way; he was still scared and now also mildly put out.

When Pratt opened the door to his chambers, he first glanced at the guard. A look of concern crossed his face before he finally looked at Rizza. They were seriously late and he knew it had something to do with her. To her disapproval, he did not tell her how pretty she was, and here Kit had done so much to make her look cute. He raised an eyebrow in question towards her. "What did you do to him?" His tone of voice tinged accusatory, as if she had attacked his guard.

Rizza shrugged off his question while she stepped past him, ducking under his arm to enter the room. "Nothing. I simply told him he should start a coup. I mean, honestly, me as the crown princess. That is just irresponsible," she said while looking around the entrance room.

"I would never..." the guard began to sputter, but Pratt did not give him time, probably because he knew the guard had been had. The door shut on the poor boy's face as Pratt let out a sigh.

The room they were in was a large greeting room with rows of bookshelves. In the center, there was a table, probably set up for dinner. Her guess was based on the tablecloth, two chairs, and the lit candles that were on it. She did not see the rest of his chambers, nor did she care to... some detective she was.

"I can't leave you alone for five minutes without someone new getting terrorized. Lovely," he grumbled as he joined her in the room. He offered to take her cloak with a move of his hand, but she only stared at his outstretched hand until it went away.

"No one asked you to watch me," she replied torridly. She had a hard time keeping her emotions in check, which is probably why she never knew what she would do. How could one predict themselves when they could not even control their emotions?

"Well... we are to be married," he sharply reminded her, seemingly just as annoyed with the idea of her being his responsibility as she was. She refused to look at him. His argument was worn out and boring, and his point was hollow at best, so there was no point in arguing back.

"I am aware," she said briskly. After a moment, she sat down in one of the provided chairs. The table was set, but the food was not yet there.

"Hard to have dinner with no food," she noted. "Unless we are doing make-believe, like the ruse of us getting along and all. If that is the case, could we not have done so in my room? It has more pillows." The way she spoke did not aid the idea that they were adults, and not two children stuck together in a room.

"The food is on its way, Rizza. I thought this way, we could talk." His calm and collected air was back, trying to make peace. Rizza liked the idea of being a squabbling child, though, too much to give it up. She glanced at him before her gaze wandered around the room to his books. All sorts of titles roamed the walls, and all of them were leather-bound and very rare, costly items.

"Quite the collection," she said, absent-mindedly.

"I have been at it for a while," he replied. He joined her in sitting at the table. It seemed he had given up on trying to make her uncomfortable enough to behave.

"So, you do other things besides plotting the downfall of the entire kingdom, then? I guess even a madman needs a hobby." Her words were thrown out casually, but the biting sting would hit, she knew it. She did not have to look back at him to know he'd be affected by her words.

As if to prove it, he let out a lengthy sigh. Clearly, he was not amused by her off-handed accusations, yet she was not joking at all.

He stared at her. She finally stared back, after a time. He let the silence linger between them, probably hoping she would break it again. There was no tension though, just still air between them, dead air, even.

"Why? Why do you think I killed my brother and his wife, Rizza? I idolized him. He was my hero." Pratt finally broke the silence. The pain in his voice was clear, but what good was a criminal mastermind if they could not act?

"Because no one else stands to gain a damn thing with him dead," She said softly. "No one but you." Her words and expression were as cold as ice.

"How am I the only one?" Pratt shot back, a flare of anger seeding into his voice. "Our enemies could have wanted him dead, it's not like rival kingdoms don't sow discontent all the time. Plus, you could have wanted more power. Perhaps he had knocked someone's wife up. How should I know what got him killed?" Pratt's possible examples were worse with each new idea that popped into his head.

"How would the enemies benefit? From what I hear, you're more intelligent and cunning than your brother. As for me wanting power, that is bullshit. If I wanted power, I would not be as opposed to this marriage as I am. It pisses me off to be used for your games. The last one... I don't think I should even dignify. To insinuate that he would be anything but faithful is monstrous, even for you." Her words were barely a whisper as she spoke, the effect akin to that of a razor blade through the air to cut at heart strings.

Pratt stared at her. The hatred and anger burning in his gaze was evident, but he didn't retort. He had none, she had points that he could not refute. He was angry her logic made sense more than anything else and having to sit here and put up with it was excruciating. He rang the bell to demand their dinner be brought faster.

They lapsed back into silence. A servant knocking and bringing them the food saved them from further conversation. Rizza highly doubted that it would have been pleasant had they continued to talk. Silence was best. After dinner, Rizza went back to her room, still grounded.

An Unlikely Ally

The next few nights were similarly toned to the first; Pratt and Rizza continued to have dinner, and Rizza kept dressing up for it to maintain the appearance that they were getting along. Yet, when alone together, they never talked. Rizza ate the dinner in silence, and to make it seem as if they enjoyed each other's company they sat in his room... in silence.

They began to read from the mountains of books that Pratt had available. Rizza did not begrudge him a lot, but she did begrudge him his book collection. It was probably one of the more beneficial trade-offs of her having to go to dinner with him so often.

Though Rizza did not like her time with Pratt, she did enjoy the time walking there. The guard that was assigned to escort her remained the same through all her visits. This gave her the ability to get to know the man as a person, not just as a guard terrified of her very existence.

Rizza soon learned that his name was Lance, and that he was, indeed, eighteen years old. Not only that, but he was a second son. That should have been obvious to Rizza, as most second-born sons ended up in the military, since the firstborn were the ones to inherit the family business. Naturally, this meant that Lance had an older brother, but he also had three younger sisters who he apparently loved dearly.

Rizza found out that Lance's father was a tailor, and his mother was a seamstress that helped him out in their shop each day. The older brother was learning the father's trade, while the little sisters were learning their mother's. It was a delightful and quaint family. With so many kids, they had lots of helping hands. It seemed nice.

"So, you are the only one not at home, then?" Rizza asked during one of their walks together. They always wandered first before Rizza let Lance lead them in the right direction. She had learned of Pratt's location in the royal chambers, but it was still fun to feign being lost. Lancenever stopped her, and assumed it was because he was actually beginning to like her... or something.

"I am. Pa said having two boys in the house was asking for trouble, so, when I turned sixteen, I enlisted, trained for a year, then came to the palace. I've been here since," Lance said. His words were filled with contentment. Over the past few days, Rizza had noticed he had grown to ease, and even began showing his emotions.

He had been ill at ease with her at first. The jokes of over-throwing the kingdom did not sit well, but once he got accustomed to Rizza's sense of humor, he seemed to relax. Not many understood that Rizza liked jokes, however, Lance seemed to catch on quickly. It was fresh, new, and delightful. Rizza wondered if she had made a friend.

Nodding softly, Rizza placed her hands behind her back. His story was a common one among the guards. The second son was usually displaced from the family, though not forgotten. They made great soldiers, and even more so because they served in honor of their family as well as their king. Another time they had spent time talking about her, he had finally gotten up the courage to ask her some questions of his own.

"So, have you really lived many times? Like... many lives?" Lance inquired. He was finally getting to a point where fear was not ruling his tongue. That was a question she had not often been asked. In fact, no one bothered to ask. It was common speculation, and up until now, Rizza assumed it was common knowledge, though, there was one theory floating around that it was just a big conspiracy to keep the single, powerful witch happy in each lifetime. It remained a rumor, never mind the fact that she always seemed to look identical to the last. Male forms always looked the same and so did her female.

"I have. In one life, I was the Grand Duchess, Lisette," Rizza said, a smile on her face as she thought about that lifetime.

The guard seemed giddy with excitement, he had clearly liked learning. "Really? Was she not the duchess from the western kingdom with many torrid love affairs? She even had one with a prince from this kingdom, right?" he asked. There was giddy excitement in his voice. For a guard, he sure loved to gossip.

"Oh, that is rubbish," Rizza said in a half dismissive tone. Lance seemed disheartened until she continued. "Rupert and I were just friends. I think... I don't remember anything sordid." Rizza waved off his glee with a small smile of her own. He was so easily encouraged into enjoying her games.

After that, though, Lance seemed to be a lot more comfortable with her. He had admitted to being terrified of her when they first met. Lance still found himself wary, but he was beginning to relax around her. Lance was probably her first friend in this lifetime, and it made her happy. He was a good kid.

"Tell me something, Lance," Rizza said on their final walk to Pratt's room. Rizza was to be ungrounded tomorrow.

"What can I help you with, Rizza?" Lance said curiously. They had discussed all manner of things... even the murder. Lance understood why she was wary of Pratt. It was nice to have an ally on her side in this world, because gosh knew the royal family was not on her side in the least.

"Would you be put out if I made you my personal guard? I have enjoyed your company the last few days, and no one in this palace seems to enjoy my humor. You are honestly the only one who isn't terrified of me," she said with a soft pout, her gaze looking over at him.

"Rizza," he said in a stern voice. "I am beyond terrified of you. I don't know what you are talking about. After all, you are evil," he said as conspiratorially as he could. She laughed with him.

"I'll take that as a yes to be my guard. Oh, delightful. You can help me figure out how Pratt did his awful deeds. We only have three days left to figure it out. After that, he gains more power... granted I can still stop him, but you know how vexing that is," Rizza said. She had explained a clear majority of her problems to Lance, since he was so easy to talk to. It was a good thing, too, because the boy understood her well.

Lance pursed his lips calmly, and did not argue with her. She knew he was still uncomfortable with the way she insisted that it was Pratt who had murdered the lovely couple. Yet, she would not drop the argument. Pratt was at fault, she just had to somehow prove it.

She gazed at Lance for a second, until Pratt opened the door. Once more, she was cloistered into his room... for the last time. It was the same as always: they sat in dead silence while they ate, they read some books, he did some work, then, she left. Yet, even that was enough to spread the gossip that they liked each other. They always left with smiles on their faces to convince any passersby that they were on good terms.

The Engagement

The next morning, Rizza stretched as she woke up. She was off house arrest, free to roam around without the escort of a guard. Promptly, she got dressed, and went to breakfast in the main hall.

Naturally, this action alone would put others on edge, especially since Rizza hated getting up in the morning. As she entered the dining hall, she could tell the mood was somber. Everyone quietly gossiped, but even that stopped as she entered.

Everyone was still dressed in black. She could tell all but a very few of the entire kingdom's court was present this morning, and they all looked gloomy and sad. That was right, the prince's funeral was only yesterday. Rizza had not been allowed to attend. Of course, that did not mean she had forgotten.

Rizza had stared down at the funeral from her room, the window providing a view of the procession in the center garden. She had wept silently, but all that was done now. Today was the final day of the mourning period for the people to grieve for their prince, and Rizza would not interrupt. After all, she, too, was dressed in nothing but black.

Her cloak draped over her shoulders to hide her face, as usual. Yet, instead of the bright red she usually wore, it was pitch black, so black one might even think they could see the void in it, gloomy and unsettling.

However, in stark contrast to everyone's mood, the sun was bright, and the birds were singing outside the floor-to-ceiling windows. The glass danced with light against its painted frames. It was almost funny. Still, the silence made it creepy, somehow. Rizza felt as if she was looking at dead people who were only pretending to be alive.

Any other time, she would have made a joke. Yet, not wanting to get thrown back into her room and locked away with no chance of being able to figure out Pratt's evil plan, Rizza kept herself silent.

Her gaze wandered past the court nobles to the dais where
the royal family sat. The king was glaring at the door where Rizza
was. He was waiting for her to be obnoxious, almost as if he was
daring her to. She remained silent. To his right, where the crown
Prince and Princess had once sat, there were two empty chairs...
covered in black silk.

Rizza's heart clenched in pain. She did not dare comment
on it. She did not dare admit that she cared about the stupid
crown prince, whom she had bullied in youth. She did not admit
that he was like a brother to her. That would be folly.
Yet, it hurt. It would always hurt to see the place where he right-
fully belonged, and know he would never sit there again, to one
day see the king parish, and know that his rightful heir was no
longer there to take his place. Rizza was used to natural death,
but premature death stung.

If Rizza could not stop it, it would also hurt that Pratt, his
traitor of a brother, would then steal the throne, uncontested
due to his heinous act. Rizza wanted to cry from that knowledge
alone, though she could not. She had a goal.

With her back straight, and her chin tucked in slight sub-
mission to the throne, she walked into the dining hall. Her entrance was not loud or extreme. Her steps were soft and silent on
the marble floor as she moved. If anything, she was normal... for
once. Rizza was not eerily quiet, she was about the appropriate
level of noise, not bidding her clothing into silence so the fabric
rustled as she walked.

As Rizza drew closer to the dais, she could tell that the
king's eyes, as well as the young princes' and princesses', were
all red-rimmed. They had been crying. Yet, not surprisingly, Pratt
had not. His eyes were slightly puffy from lack of sleep, but not
red. He had not cried over the loss of his older brother who he
claimed to idolize so much. He was such a typical liar.

Rizza's gaze lingered on his, and as he watched her, she
watched him. She did note, though, that the queen also had not
cried, which was rather shocking to her. She had always doted on

Prince Henry. Why would she not cry over the loss of her favored son?

"Rizza... nice of you to join us this morning." The king's voice cut her train of thought short. She ducked her head into a soft bow.

"I hope your time these last few days was well-spent." He added. His words had a double meaning. He did not care what she did, just that she learned not to argue with him, and not to call his new heir the murderer anymore. Though he was the murderer, she just would not say it to the king's face.

"Yes, your highness. My time was well-spent. Prince Pratt kept me company the entire time." No one but her would be able to see the way the prince's lips thinned at her comment. Both of them had been tortured by that little venture.
The king gave a joyless smile as he gestured to the empty seat next to Pratt. Immediately, Rizza bowed, and moved to join them on the dais. Never in her life did she think she'd ever eat from this position. She instantly hated it.

How could one get away with anything while sitting up in front of an audience, all waiting and watching to see what you would do? That was just absolutely no fun. Rizza wanted to be in the shadows, to be the one they never expected, but regretted ignoring when it was too late. That was her favorite spot to be in. Rizza fidgeted uncomfortably as she slowly began to eat.

Though she did not look over, she could feel Pratt's gaze burning a hole into the side of her head. She did not once look at him, her head stayed ducked, and her hood stayed on as she ate. Silence reigned over the hall for a very uncomfortably half an hour before the king spoke again.

"Today... I would like to announce the official engagement celebration of Pratt, my dear, beloved son, and now heir to my throne, and Rizza, the royal witch." The king's voice echoed through the halls as he stood up. Everyone offered three cheers of congratulations, but all Rizza felt was bile in her throat.

"Tomorrow," the king continued, causing the commotion to die down so he could speak. "Or, rather, tomorrow night, we shall hold an official ball. Please dress in your best. I look forward to celebrating with you all," the king said diplomatically. It sounded like a speech that he had to spit out, lest it choke him. Still, he got through it before retreating from the hall.

The room began to buzz with excitement. They had been expecting a dance, so they were ready. Gowns and suits had been ordered weeks ago. They had just been waiting for the official announcement from the king. Courts were like that, always ready to party and spend their people's money.

Rizza stood the second he was gone, and began heading back to her own room. Disgust and trepidation washed over her. Why did he have to make them have a ball... especially when the wedding was two days later. Crud... Rizza had only two more days to figure out how Pratt had committed the murder, and still, she had come up with literally nothing. She was the worst detective ever.

Detective work;
Mischief afoot

As Rizza fled from the banquet hall, she found her feet carrying her towards the gardens. Just because she was let out of her room did not mean she could leave the palace grounds so easily. Rizza had a feeling that if she tried, she would be stopped at the gate. So, instead of trying, she went to the quietest place in the castle to think. She needed to figure out how Pratt did it, and fast.

She was literally the worst detective there was. Almost a month had passed, and she was still at square one. So many people made detective work look easy. If magic could solve this issue, it would be easy, but holy water always made for a dampening of that sort of cheating.

Rizza stepped into the garden, and almost immediately began to pace. There had to be something, anything, that she could use to prove it.

The past few weeks ran through her head. Rizza had an exceptional memory, making it incredibly easy for her to recall information and even analyze a scene in detail. She cycled through the key points of each day in her mind.

To start, she arrived at the palace first thing in the morning, bright and early. Nothing was strange there other than how Rizza acted. The queen had been cheery, happy to see her, the king was done with her already, the crown prince had been the same, the crown princess was amused, and the masses were terrified.

Pratt had quickly injected himself into the conversation when the king had given his decree for marriage, and up until that point, she had not noticed him.

Rizza ran her hands over her face in frustration, angry that she had not ever noticed him before. He was a powerful wizard, it was ridiculous, and she felt dumb.

She had to move past it. She had to remember what the

hell happened next, not dwell on her failures. Before the murder, Pratt had met with her, offering her cake as a peace treaty. He had a convenient alibi, since he had been with her. It was still annoying.

Rizza stopped her pacing, the concentration evident on her face. "The family had been ingesting holy water, so I could not touch them... annoying..." she grumbled to herself.

Why would they do that? Of course, she had to assume it was because she was chaotic. She could not compel them if they drank it. It was a trust issue; they had no faith in her. Though, that fact alone made it easier for the assassin to poison the prince and princess.

Rizza could guess that only the royal family and a select few others could have possibly known the fact that the royals drank holy water. Pratt knew, since he was a royal. Still, Pratt could not ingest it for the same reason she could not ingest it. It would cause him to burn and blister, just like it did to her.

Pratt had to know that Holy water mixed with Irredelum was deadly to others. Of course, most did not drink Irredelum, unless they had a cold, as it eased sore throats due to its natural sugars.

Prince Drake did not look like he had a cold, though, nor did the princess. He and the princess had seemed perfectly healthy, so why would they ingest the medicine? They wouldn't.

This was driving Rizza up a wall. How could this happen? Was it truly her fault? Pain seeped into her consciousness as she thought about it. If she had not terrorized the family when she was growing up, would they have drunk the holy water? Was it her fault that there was such an easy way to kill the prince and princess?

Rizza tried to remember something, anything, in the room that would give her a clue. There had been a subtle romantic at-mosphere in the room, overshadowed with death. There had been rose petals and candles. However, there hadn't been food. There had been, among the things in the room, wine. Rizza's eyes lit up a bit, but she had to think. Rizza tried to remember the label on the bottle that was on the table.

After a moment of thought, she had a realization. Rizza bolted from her sanctuary. It seemed so obvious now that she thought about it. Everything seemed so much clearer. Maybe she could not prove it was Pratt who did it... but... maybe she could at least figure out how it was done. Someone had used terribly bad wine.

Rizza ran towards the kitchen. Upon her entrance, the entire staff froze and blanched, scared witless of her. The place was massive. It held multiple stoves and many chefs and servants running here and there to help out and get meals prepped for the entire castle. It really was a grand undertaking to run such an operation, and Rizza could only imagine the amount of money they spent on food each month to keep this place running. However, she paid them no mind as she went directly to the manager of the staff.

"In the wine stock, do you keep any wines that use irredelum as an additive?" Her question was so direct and pointed that the man before her was shocked. He hadn't even had a chance to really process that she was there before he was being questioned by her. He had a plain figure, nothing really standing out about him other than the bright blue collar of his shirt, marking him as the manager of the kitchen staff.

In the castle, there were vast amounts of servants. Since they all had different jobs, there were those with management positions, a hierarchy that helped keep order. Each Manager got their own color of collar to mark their department. It also made them easy to identify.

"Well... yes... Prince Pratt enjoys the smooth taste, so we have always had it on hand..." the man stammered; he was scared witless of the girl in front of him. He had to take a moment to even reply he was so badly startled.

Rizza grinned, happy to have a clue. "And, by chance, did a bottle get taken out by him a couple of weeks ago, specifically, the day the crown prince and princess were poisoned?" Her words remained direct. She was overly excited about this breakthrough in her cold case.

Granted, anyone else would have put this together days ago, but Rizza was rather slow. Why would the prince and princess drink the wine that she remembered being in their room when it could kill them? That was, unless they did not realize it was not the right wine. Drake was always careless; he probably trusted his servant to bring the right one and did not check the label. If true, that oversight cost him his life.

"Also, did the crown prince ask for wine that day?" Rizza pressed another question forward. By this point the entire kitchen's processes had been brought to a halt as everyone stared at Rizza. They had no idea why she was questioning the manager about such things... but it seemed important and servants loved to gossip.

"W-...well... yes. Prince Pratt asked for a bottle, but he came down later mad beyond belief, because it was not delivered to him. Actually... the crown princess asked for a bottle, as well, and the bottle prince Pratt got had been that one. " The poor manager looked ready to faint, his already pale face looking that much paler from his fear.

Rizza was amazed no one else had put that together yet. The fact that no one had questioned about the wine before her gave her some hope that she wasn't the most useless in murder investigations. However, now was not the time to pat oneself on the back.

Rizza understood. Everyone feared her. "So, they were switched..." she mumbled to herself. She looked at him again. "Which servants were in charge of collecting and delivering the bottles to their respective places?" Rizza continued.

"Th-... the crown princess's personal handmaid and prince Pratt's personal attendant, I suppose... " He could not figure out why Rizza cared so much about wine suddenly, she had never cared for it before. Yet, he was also unaware of the holy water, which had been the catalyst of Drake's death.

"Thank you." Rizza tossed him a pouch of gold coins before leaving as quickly as she came. The man was left feeling as if a tornado had blown through his kitchen. She was there, caused chaos and panic, and then gone. He stared at the pouch of gold in his hands, wondering if he should even accept it, or if he should just tell the king. After a while, he decided to accept it. Seeing his staff still gawking he quickly shooed them to their tasks.

Shortly after leaving the kitchen, Rizza headed towards the servant's quarters. Since this was the palace, even the servants had decent beds and private rooms. Honestly, the king and queen were good to their servants.

Rizza moved to the lounge area of the quarters. It had soft couches, and a few tables to play various games on. Not a bad resting place, if a servant ever actually got time off in a place this large. At the end of the room was a desk with a man sitting behind it. He also had a collar on his shirt, this one red, indicating that he was the manager of the servants.

Rizza could see the man stiffen as she approached. This man, unlike the one in the kitchen, was portly, with a squashed pug face and a stout nose. He had large eyes, and lips that looked like he had been stung by a bee. On top of all that, he had a receding hairline that perfectly showed the top of his head.

"Lady... Rizza..." the man gulped between words. Standing up nervously, he moved around the desk to greet her.

"What can I help you with?" He was much more accommodating than the last man, which probably had something to do with how often she came down here growing up. He was more used to Rizza's eerie presence than those in the kitchen.

"Hello, Wiles. I need to see the crown princess's personal handmaid. Does she still work here?" Rizza asked, getting straight to the point.

Part of the reason she asked for the princess's servant, and not Pratt's, was because she knew that Pratt's would alert his loser master to her investigation. She could not risk it. She did not want him telling the king she had not dropped her investigation. She was so sick of being locked up.

"Well... yes, she is in attendance of the queen now. Shall I send someone to fetch her?" Wiles was quick to comply. He was calmer now that he knew she was not there to cause trouble for him.

"Please," Rizza answered politely before moving to a couch to sit down and wait patiently for her arrival.
It seemed strange to Rizza that the girl had transferred from the crown princess to the queen. Why would that be the case? Rizza remembered that Drake's marriage had originally been an alliance with another kingdom, which meant that the crowned princess's servants all came from her kingdom.

Rizza only had to wait a quarter of a candlestick before the girl appeared. She looked rather stressed out, but, overall, still pretty healthy. When she saw Rizza, unlike most, she did not flinch. Instead, she smiled. That was odd. It was more off-putting to Rizza than if the girl had flinched. Perhaps she'd already mentally prepared herself.

"Rizza. What can I do for you?" the girl asked curiously. She already knew Rizza hated formalities. That may have made her likable, if it wasn't so strange. Rizza, for her part, wasted no time. She stood up to greet the woman calmly, and nodded. She had no time to worry about why she found the woman odd.

"Actually, I want to know some information. When you were serving the princess... the night they... you know... do you remember what wine you brought them? I know it was a silly little thing, but it's important," Rizza said calmly.

"Well... I brought them the princess's favorite. A rose wine..." She seemed confused. "Why do you ask?" The girl frowned, she was confused, and Rizza could tell, yet, she was still willing to answer.

Rizza nodded. "And... when you were fetching it... did anything strange happen by chance? Like... say, you set it down for a moment, or...?" Rizza was fishing at this point. She couldn't directly tell the girl what she was looking for. If she knew, then Rizza would have problems.

"Oh... well, no, not that I can-..." She paused. It seemed like she remembered something before she continued. "A boy bumped into me. We both fell down and the bottles, thankfully, hit the carpet. Could that be what you mean?"

"Bottles? Plural? As in, more than one?" Rizza confirmed. If she was right... that was when the switch happened. Again, she was met with a frown.

"Well, yes... prince Pratt's servant was also carrying one... he seemed in a rush. I suppose the prince was in a bad mood, since you had so strongly rejected him." She explained calmly. She did not see the point to Rizza's line of questioning. Rizza nodded, that confirmed her suspicions rather nicely.

"Okay... thank you. Sorry for the random questioning." Rizza looked dejected for show. She did not want the others to know she had actually figured out the problem. Prince Pratt's servant switched the bottle... that killed the crown prince and princess.

"If there will be nothing else then, Rizza, I really must get back to the queen." The girl's words were calm and composed, but the aura around her seemed tense, somehow. Rizza almost let her go. Her hand up to dismiss her before she stopped. She looked at the servant girl. She wasn't special in any way. Her features weren't great, and she didn't really stand out all that much, but her eyes held a sort of wisdom one did not always see in a servant.

"Tell me... you came from the kingdom your original lady came from, right?" Rizza asked.

"Yes..." the girl answered, her frown increasing.

"So why are you now serving the queen? That hardly makes any sense." Rizza continued. Her gaze bore into the other woman's. She couldn't tell what the girl was thinking, how rare.

"I... that is... The queen asked for me. I don't know why. Maybe it was because I served her late lady well." The girl's answer was calm and composed. She almost seemed thoughtful. Rizza dropped it with a simple nod.

"That makes sense. The queen is always good to those who work." She smiled at the maid before waving her off. She watched the girl as she curtsied and left.

She now knew how Pratt did it... now to figure out how to prove it. This was a headache and a half.

The Ball

Rizza's gaze went over the bronze mirror in front of her. Her face was bathed in a golden glow as she stared at her reflection, and a soft sigh escaped her. She couldn't help but feel the trepidation that made her heart quiver. Tonight was the first official night of their engagement. From there, the wedding was only a short time away. This was all too fast.

Maids were putting up her hair and putting lavish ribbons and trinkets in it. In the end, her hair looked oddly like a blooming lotus with black strands falling from it. She had no idea how the hell they had managed that with her unkempt, spiky hair, but was quite impressed by the accomplishment.

So many events had gone by since she had entered the capital, good... and bad – mostly bad. Still, so many things came to pass, so many questions were left unanswered, and the looming one was forever nagging at her mind. Yet, tonight, she had to pretend she was fine. She had to pretend she didn't know Pratt murdered his older brother. She had to pretend to be happy and on good terms with the man who made her stomach churn. She wasn't quite sure she could do it.

The dress she'd been forced to wear, one that matched Pratt's suit for the evening, was a deep blue, a royal color that gave her black hair and fair skin a rather gem-like feel to it. She almost wanted to call herself pretty, despite looking like a monster. With her mouth closed, she almost looked normal, even. Her pointed teeth were hidden behind her lips, but nothing could hide the flecks of silver on her face, or the piercing purple of her eyes. Rizza stared. She couldn't see the purple, but knew the color was purple because of what she'd been told, and it didn't look natural.

"Miss Rizza, if I didn't know better, I'd think you were a lady of the court." One Maid commented. The comment earned her an elbow to the ribs by another, and she frowned. Rizza couldn't help the laughter that bubbled in her throat, though it sounded dry to her ears. The ladies were nervous. Not wanting to offend a new royal, they seemed to almost fear retaliation after such a comment was uttered. Not that they were wrong.

"Do I? That's something I never thought I'd hear in this lifetime. Thank you." Rizza could choose to be rude all the time, but the maid meant no harm. Her words were harsh, but not untrue. Rizza never looked like a lady of the court, and she certainly never was one in this life.

"Well... to be fair, you will be a lady of the court soon. That's what the ball is for." The girl tried to amend her previous social faux pas, attempting to make it better. It made it worse, but she was trying.

Rizza stood from her chair, her smile light as she heard a soft knock on the door. She knew who it was even before the door was opened and he was allowed in. His magic permeated the air, and she could feel the bile in her throat surging. She forced it down. Elegance, grace, and not a hint of distaste. She mentally giggled at her own rhyme. She used it as a distraction from her discomfort.

"Rizza, you look.... ." His words were barely audible as he stood by the door.

"Like a lady of the court?" Rizza tossed out the words that the maid had tossed out. She turned to face him and caught the shy blush of the maid. The poor girl couldn't catch a break that night.

"Beautiful. You look beautiful, Rizza." His words eased through his smile, full of pride. His gaze was locked on her dress, but quickly traveled up to her face. There wasn't much to stare at below the neck anyway, she had no real curvature. His hand was extended out in offering.

Rizza bit back the pain in her stomach, ignored the ache in her chest, and took his hand. Her smile was forced, but she was at least trying to pretend she wasn't in pain. She had a sneaking suspicion she looked constipated.

"Thank you... let's go. It wouldn't be proper for the guests of honor to be late for the ball, would it?" She quickly changed the topic. Her tension showed in every action, but he didn't seem to notice. Maybe he didn't care.

"Yes, Let's." He agreed amenably, and walked them both to the door.

The ball was in the castle, so they didn't need a carriage. That being said, they still had armed guards escorting them. It made Rizza feel claustrophobic, though it was supposed to be a sign of recognition and respect. Her gaze lifted from the ground to look at the men towering around her. This didn't seem respectful at all; it seemed more like a prison walk, a walk to the guillotine if nothing else.

Rizza's hand went to her throat subconsciously as she walked. Her discomfort was evident from the way her throat bobbed when she swallowed. Her gaze was dull, and her body language tense. She almost jumped from her skin and blasted the entire group when a hand landed on her shoulder.

Rizza glanced up to see Pratt looking down at her. How had she never noticed he was almost a head taller? He was so tall. The smile on his face was supposed to be reassuring, but she couldn't help but stare into his pitch-black eyes. He looked as much a creature of the night as she did, something that people would consider a nightmare, except his eyes were kind, his smile was light and hid the points of his teeth, and nothing about him seemed aggressive. The outfit he wore was meant to cater to and match hers. His colors were the same as hers, and the black accentuated his outfit nicely. Rizza was mildly impressed by it all.

Rizza hadn't even really thought about it before, but he wasn't imposing. She supposed part of her 'charm' was the fact that she held herself as if she was supposed to be a monster. Was it because that was how people saw her anyway, so she just... met their expectations? Rizza looked away. She could tell Pratt was still watching her, but she didn't care. He would still be a beloved prince, possibly king in the future. As for her? She would be the monster he married. The thought twisted a knot in her stomach. She had to stop this.

"Can I take it... that you've at least begun to take interest in me?" Pratt's words drew her out of her reflection. He had taken her intense gaze as some sort of warm invitation, that perhaps she would consider their union as something other than an act of malice on his family's part.

She blinked several times before looking away from him. She shook her head softly as she did so. "I don't think so, no." He had killed his brother, switched the wine, poisoned him in a very subdued manner that none had caught. How had she not caught it? It was so obvious. She had caught it. She had caught it weeks later, and no one would believe her. If she'd just caught it at the time....

There was no 'what if' in life, only the reality of what was, and that was always hard. She swallowed down the pain. It didn't matter if he was attractive and approachable. He was a murderer. Tonight, she would find a way to prove it.

That was what she told herself, yet, as they entered the ballroom, she was still at a loss for what she could say. What could she do? She had no proof. The maid... perhaps if she called the maid, she would be able to prove it. Rizza nodded, and gave herself a small amount of comfort. She would prove it.

Pratt's arm was gracefully out, and Rizza's hand was gently placed in the crook of it. The two cut a decent figure as they made their way through the swarms of people. The ballroom practically parted like a sea before them as they moved. All eyes were on them, and Rizza's discomfort grew with every moment.

Again, she felt Pratt's hand on her. This time, it was on the hand that rested on his arm. He offered a gentle smile, but she couldn't bring herself to return it. Instead, she continued to walk in silence as the tension ate at her. The only times she ever had this much attention latched onto her was when she was in trouble. This entire event was nothing more than her feeling like she was in trouble.

Before she knew it, Rizza and Pratt were standing ready to greet the queen and king. They sat on a stand at the edge of the ballroom, their chairs were elegant and apart from any other in the room, set aside so they could be the centerpiece of the ball without having to actually take part. It was tasteful. Rizza curtsied as Pratt bowed.

The king and queen were dressed in similar outfits that matched. The queen was in a long, flowing white dress with blue accents and trim. The lacing in it made it almost look like rain was falling down the dress, like a pure canvas of clouds. It was quite beautiful. Matching, the king was in a white suit with a blue undercoat and blue accents. It didn't quite cut the same figure, as he had gained weight over the years, but he looked royal all the same.

"Good, very good." The king's voice was the same as always, a disapproving baritone with a hint of disinterest, though his words were softer. He seemed almost pleased... almost. His face was plastered with disapproval. It seemed to be the only look he knew. Beyond that, he was staring firmly at Rizza, as if he was daring her to cause a problem. She intelligently kept her mouth shut for once. It wasn't time, not yet.

"You two look just adorable together." The queen smiled, but her smile seemed forced. There were bags under her eyes, and she just, overall, looked exhausted. Rizza frowned slightly, but quickly repressed it. She wondered if the shock had finally passed and the queen was finally feeling the loss of her son. It would not be a surprise, she had loved him and doted on him greatly. There were too many eyes on her, so Rizza said nothing. She was worried about the queen, but she wouldn't show it. Perhaps she could find a good spot to talk to her during this charade to check on her.

"Mother, please." Pratt's words were soft, and there was a bit of humor in them. Yet, his face was filled with pleasure. He didn't actually mind what she'd said. He liked being compared to Rizza and placed in her company, it was clear as day.

It was then that Rizza realized she was expected to say something pleasant. Rizza smiled forcefully, and was going to open her mouth, but couldn't think of anything. Instead, she just ended up curtsying again and staying silent.

The king let out a grunt before looking away. He seemed

satisfied enough with her formality. At least she wasn't causing trouble, right? He waved his hand as if to dismiss them.

"Go, dance. We've been waiting on you." The queen spoke softly, and offered a tired smile before opening her hand, palm up, to gesture outward. She offered the floor to them.

As if on cue, the entire court shifted so they were able to get to the center of the dance floor. As they walked toward it, more people cleared. It seemed the first dance of the night would be a solo between them. Rizza resisted the urge to sigh. The music started up at that point. The musicians were hidden away from the crowd but the reverberation of their music through the ballroom was still melodious and beautiful even as they were out of sight.

If it were not for the fact that she had gone through the required court etiquette training for a lady, she wouldn't know how. Dancing was required, along with needlepoint, and other useless things. She hated it, but it came in handy sometimes.

Pratt turned to face her at the same time she turned to face him. Bracing herself, she waited for the music to start as she placed her hand in his. His hands were soft. She figured he'd never known a day of labor in his life. A small smirk crawled over her face at that thought.

His hand touched her hip, and the music started: the waltz. Slow and steady as they moved across the dance floor, somehow, their steps were graceful, and they looked well matched. He led and she followed, and she was swept away by the music. Those on the side watched with avid interest as they danced.

Rizza bit the inside of her lip as she moved. He smelled good, his scent was a soft sandalwood with hints of lavender. It was nice, refreshing and clean. She didn't know how to react to the fact that she liked his scent. Was it bad that after time with him, she'd wished he wasn't a bad guy, that he wasn't a murderer? She had to remind herself that he was one.

Rizza looked up at Pratt, a frown on her face. She almost looked betrayed as she stared up at him.

"What's wrong, Rizza? Your dancing is beautiful... no one

will judge you here." Pratt was worried that she was upset because of the crowds, or because she wasn't a good dancer. How silly, he was trying to calm her fears. He smiled so easily, laughed so calmly.

Rizza couldn't understand how someone could do that. How could someone be so two-faced? How could someone act so well that they had everyone in the court fooled into thinking they were indeed a good person? Rizza couldn't imagine having to put up a front like that, it sounded exhausting just thinking about it.

Her fingers tightened on his as she looked back down towards his chest after a moment.

"The night... of your brother's murder..." Rizza spoke softly. She could feel the Prince tense under her fingers, his arms tensing as his shoulders did, but she didn't stop. "You ordered wine, wine that, for us, isn't a big deal, tastes quite good."

"Yes, I did." Pratt didn't deny it. His words were curt. He didn't like talking about that night. Why did it feel like there was a knife digging into Rizza's chest? She wanted him to deny it, to say it was ordered for him, to say something, but not just own up to it.

"Did you know... your servant ran into another in the hall... and you didn't get your wine?" Rizza asked curiously. She glanced up at him again. This time she locked eyes with him. She studied his face. She wanted to see every expression he had, every inclination.

He frowned, his eyebrows knitting together slightly as he looked down at her before leaning close to her. In doing so, he made it so others wouldn't see his face. All eyes were still on them, after all.

"I didn't get the bottle of wine that I was supposed to. I raised hell in the kitchen. Why do you know of this? Better yet, what are you trying to say, Rizza?" Pratt's words were soft, yet deadly. His voice was suddenly very cold.

That was all Rizza needed. She shoved him away, which caused the music to grind to a halt. Everyone stared at them. They were only halfway through the dance when she did it.

"It was you!" Rizza snarled. The sound echoed through the quiet room. No one said a word as she spoke. Everyone's eyes were wide open. The room grew very quiet as everyone watched them. They had been watching them the entire time, but they had not been expecting a scene of this nature.

"What? What now, Rizza?" Pratt growled back. His fists were balled up as he spoke. The light in the room seemed to dim a bit as he did. Rizza wasn't scared.

"You killed him. YOU KNEW! You knew that wine was poisonous to those who drank holy water! How else would the wine that you ordered that day end up in Drake's room that night if not because of you? Did you plan it, wait 'til he ordered wine before sending your servant to interrupt the crown princess's delivery of their wine, and switch the bottles? If I'd seen the bottle that day, it would have been easier to see." Rizza's voice was filled with disgust, but she made sure everyone in the ballroom could hear her.

You could hear a pin drop in the ballroom with how quiet it was in there. No one said a word as they stared between the two. The temperature in the room seemed to drop several degrees with the tension between Rizza and Pratt. Pratt, for his part, did not back down or flinch. He stared at Rizza with a rage in his eyes. It made her heart sink further as she just used it to assume she was correct.

"Oh... oh, dear..." The queen's voice cut through the silence like butter. Rizza and Pratt turned at the same time to look at her. Tears were streaming down her face as a shaking hand covered her mouth.

"I... I didn't want to see this." The queen's voice was shaking slightly as she slowly stood up. The king was going to get up and rage, but she held him back with a hand before walking down the dais.

She didn't stop until she was right in front of Rizza. Rizza was shocked at seeing the queen cry. She was a strong woman who did not show her emotions in front of others. Even after finding Drake dead she had not shed a tear. But now, she was crying. Her steps were the only thing to be heard as she approached Rizza. The moment she stopped in front of her, a hard smack landed against Rizza's cheek.

Rizza's head stood off to the side as she took in her shock. The queen had slapped her. Why had she slapped her? Rizza was so confused as to what was happening. She had finally figured out Pratt's evil plan. She'd exposed him in front of everyone. He should be the one getting the negative response. Why was she the one being hit?

"I have-" Rizza was going to say 'proof' when another slap landed on her face. Her cheeks burned with the pain of them. Rizza felt heat flood up her face along with tears. "I have proof..." She whispered softly. The room was filled with soft whispering gossip. Her ears burned from the shame of being stared at like a villain even though she was in the right. No one believed her.

"Enough, Rizza. You can't cover up what you've done anymore. You can't pin this on my son. Considering your years of service with the kingdom, not only in this life of yours, but in your past, I was willing to bury it." The queen's words sounded righteous and kind. She seemed to hold the high ground, and Rizza didn't know what she meant. Rizza looked up at her with confusion and tears in her eyes.

"What... what I've done?" Rizza spoke slowly, each word enunciated. What did the queen mean? What did she mean 'what you've done'? What had Rizza done, she found the culprit for the murder, didn't she?

"Come out." The queen spoke softly. She didn't take her gaze off Rizza. Yet, Rizza's gaze traveled to the edge of the room where someone stepped forward. It was the maid that Rizza had spoken with. She almost was happy to see her, but this seemed wrong. Rizza frowned, and looked between her and the queen. When the girl finally approached and bowed before the queen, Rizza's gut instinct was brought to fruition.

"Your Majesty." The maid was soft-spoken and dainty.

"You served the previous crown princess?" the queen asked softly. Her voice was still filled with sorrow, but it was also filled with resolve. She stared Rizza down. The queen had come prepared. Why was the girl already on standby in the ballroom? Rizza was at a loss for words.

"I did, your majesty," she replied softly. Her actions were dignified and graceful. She curtsies to the queen and then knelt obediently to answer any and all questions.

"And the wine, from that night?" The queen continued on. Rizza was getting a worse feeling.

"I went to fetch it, your majesty," she said softly.

"Very good. Relay to the court what you have told me," the queen ordered. Her gaze was getting uglier by the moment, and Rizza really didn't like this. Tension built in her as she started to realize... she'd been tricked.

Rizza turned her gaze to the maid as she began to finally talk.

"That day, I ran into a servant. I had never seen them in the palace before, and they were rushing off, carrying a bottle of wine. It seemed like they were in a hurry. We bumped into each other, and landed on the carpet in the hall. The bottles were mixed up and... and I think I took the wrong wine to the Prince and Princess... My lady, I am so sorry." Her composure shattered in an instant. Tears began to fall onto the floor from the trembling girl. She was still bent over, so one couldn't see her face, but they could see the way she cried and trembled.

"What do you mean 'hadn't seen them in the palace before'? You clearly told me it was..." Rizza was going to talk about her conversation with the girl in the servant's quarters, but she was cut off.

"Continue." The queen said softly, firmly. She didn't even spare Rizza a glance. By now everyone in the court was listening to this maids story. Rizza was also listening, but she was completely baffled.

"I... I had never seen them before." The girl repeated softly. Rizza was starting to feel sick as she saw the girl look up at her with mild fear before pointing a finger at Rizza. "But, later, I saw that same servant accepting money from her! She said, 'well done, this will solve the lineage problem', and then paid them well. I...

was terrified!"

The words caused a wave of gasps to escape the crowd as Rizza took a step back. Her eyes widened at the girl's words. What? She had never paid anyone to... to switch wine bottles. That didn't even make sense. What about the prince?

The queen snapped, and a beaten-up guard was dragged forward. Rizza recognized him, but wasn't allowed to go to him. It was Lance.

"That's him, that guard!" The maid trembled as she whispered the words in an accusatory tone. It was like she was terrified to see him again. Rizza frowned. He was a sweet kid. Wait, when had she ever paid him? She had not even met him or become friends with him until after Drake and his fiance's death. How could this make any sense?

Rizza realized she was being set up and her eyes narrowed dangerously.

"I hadn't even met him 'til long after the Prince was dead... How could I have paid him to switch the bottles?" Rizza turned her gaze on the maid. The girl trembled as she was stared down. "Tell the truth." Rizza cast her magic. The girl trembled more as she began to sob.

"Please! Please, don't kill me! I swear, this is the truth." Rizza's magic wasn't working. Her eyes widened. The girl had drunk holy water, so she wouldn't be able to force the truth. The court stared at Rizza, and Rizza looked at the guard, then looked at the queen. She was being set up, and she had no way of making the others be honest. Was this what it felt like to be helpless? She knew no one would believe her if she couldn't force the girl to tell the truth. Rizza blanched.

"No... no, your majesty... it wasn't me." Rizza spoke softly before her feet trembled. Her legs gave out, and she hit the ground. "I would never! Drake was like my brother! I would never..."

"ENOUGH!" The king finally cut in. He bellowed. His face was beet red, it verged on purple as he looked at the congregation below. He then turned to look at Rizza with pure, unbridled hatred.

"You WITCH! We bring you into our court, our home, and how do you repay our years of kindness?! You murder my son! SOMEONE! Come take her away!" The king waved his hand. Rizza wasn't given a chance to speak.

Everything was suddenly going wrong. Suddenly, everything was turning upside down. Rizza was shouting her innocence as she was dragged away. Her gaze locked on the king, then on the prince. Pratt seemed shocked. He didn't seem to have quite processed it. Before the door was closed, Rizza could see a slight smile on the queen's face. A hint of sadism passed through her gaze before the door was slammed.

The queen... Pain shot through Rizza's temples, and she lost consciousness.

Have you ever seen someone so pathetic?

Rizza's sleep wasn't pleasant. Pain tormented her, and fragmented memories surfaced. They weren't from this life, though, and getting them back felt like razor blades scraping against her mind. If they were full memories, it would have been fine, but no, they were about her death, about what happened. She'd seen something... something happened. Rizza remembered trying to talk something over with the queen. Pain... pain... pain.

She woke up. The first thing she registered was the pain. Iron was wrapped around her wrists, and holy water coated it. It caused her skin to blister where it touched, and she winced as she moved. Each jostle caused more skin to tear and blood to drip like ichor down her arm.

The next thing she noticed was that she was in a jail cell. That was obvious from the chains, and the manacles around her wrists. Rizza glanced around. A bright light was shining on her and she flinched away from it. It was the sun, it was already daytime. How long had she been out? She had no idea. The window was high up in the wall, and set in just a way that the bright light was uncomfortable for her. The stone was bare except where she sat shackled to it and the cell was moderately clean, but nothing in it as well. Rizza couldn't help but think of the dismal situation she'd ended up in. The holy water soaked chains only reinforcing how badly she'd messed up this time.

This was the first time in her life she'd ever been imprisoned, at least, in this life. She didn't remember if she'd ever been in one previously, but she probably had, as a pirate or something. Still, pain was the only thing she felt, and it worsened when she remembered WHY she was in this cell. She had been framed for a murder she hadn't committed. So many questions were burning in her mind, so many things that she wanted answers to.

Disgust and hatred washed over her. How had this happened? She'd caught the murderer... or so she thought. She was ready to present it to the court... or so she thought. Things were supposed to be easy for her. She was going to be the hero. She was going to avoid her marriage, put a murderer to death, and go back to her mountains. Rizza took a deep breath and let it out slowly. She shifted her positioning, wincing at the pain that caused before looking around once more. Thinking, putting herself in her own head, was not fun for her. She had to take a deep breath again and let it out.

Rizza missed her mountains. Bitterness welled up in her. She wished she could be back in her home. She missed the soft babbling brooks, the birds, everything. They were the mountains none dared venture to, all because a monstrous witch lived in them. All because she lived in them.

"A fine mess you've made of coming to the capital this time, Rizza..." Her voice echoed emptily against the stone walls of her cell. Her words were filled with self-loathing. It was a fine mess, indeed. If she hadn't come to the capital, if she hadn't been so naïve, none of this would have happened. At least, not to her. She wouldn't be married; she wouldn't have had to watch her 'brother' die. She wouldn't have had-... Rizza cut off her thoughts, they weren't helping. It was not like she could have ignored the summons anyways. She'd made the stupid oath.

"A fine mess, indeed," a voice echoed, sounding tired and stressed. Rizza couldn't see past the sunlight. Yet she knew, now, that she wasn't alone. The cell was empty, but beyond it was not. Her body shifted against the wall once more, and she winced as she pulled on the chains, which, in turn, caused the shackles to scrape her wrists rawer.

"Who's there?" Rizza's voice sounded awkward to her ears now, scraggly. She didn't care. Who would care? She was framed for the murder.

"Funny, that you're in the situation you tried to put me in," the voice echoed again before the light seemed to dim. Did he dim the sun? No, he used magic to block out the light in the window. It was Pratt.

He sat on a crate by the end of the jail cell. His fingers were steepled together. He had changed clothing. What he wore was still peacock worthy, but less flashy than his usual attire. A white silk shirt with tight black jeans and a pair of leather boots. He just looked exhausted. Like he hadn't slept a wink.

"Why are you here? To gloat? To laugh?" Rizza asked. She doubted he was here to prove her innocent, not after all she'd done to prove him guilty, to insist he was. Now? After seeing how the queen had looked when she was being dragged away? She doubted it. She doubted it vehemently. She had a feeling she'd been tricked, but why?

A mocking laugh echoed across the room. He ran a hand through his hair before looking at her. "You're ridiculous. Even at a time like this, you can't hate me. I'm the only person who believes it wasn't you, and you still find room to make jabs at me. Does it ever get tiring?"

"Tiring? No... considering you tried to use me to up your own magical ability." Rizza responded rather rapidly, then regretted it. He was the only person who was standing up for her. Why would he do that? She couldn't help from attacking him, however. People being nice to her the last few years was not something that really happened. It was easier to just push them away ahead of time.

"Right... and you won't believe that, for the millionth time, it wasn't my idea?" Pratt asked. Self-mockery was now in his voice. He sighed. She felt about as tired as he looked and sounded, but she was hurt, as well.

"I... am sorry. I suppose maybe the murderer... wasn't you, but then, how did your servant mix up the bottle with the other? How did it happen?" Rizza asked, her voice filled with doubt. He still very may well be the murderer, and he could be in league with the queen. Yet, she couldn't determine the motive. What would they have to gain? What did they gain from her death, from Drake's death? Pratt gained the throne, but why use her? What threat did she pose? She was a month away from the capital before being dragged here.

Pratt remained silent as he stared at Rizza. They were locked in another stare off. It was him who broke the silence. "I don't know. But you don't believe me do you?" His voice just sounded tired.

"No. I don't." She thought about lying to him. She was probably going to die again in this life because of him. So maybe she could just once get the upper hand. But she didn't. She looked away from him, no longer wanting to stare at a man who'd outsmarted her.

"Right. The guards are coming to take you to the trial but I doubt that is an accurate word for it. I hope you're prepared." Pratt stood. The light once more burned into her retina's leaving her unable to see his departure. All she heard was the slamming metal door followed by footsteps.

It wasn't long after that before the guards came, and took her to her trial.

The Trial

The court was arranged in an orderly manner, courtiers on the left and the right serving as the witness stands, and the king at the head on a throne next to the queen. Standing off to his left was his son, Pratt.

Rizza was in chains covered in holy water, kneeling on the ground before the thrones. Her head hung low, and her fingers curled into fists. She was still in the same ball gown, her hair was now in a mess around her face, and, overall, she just looked terrible, but that suited Rizza. So much for being a lady of the court someday.

"Good. Very good. First, you murder my son. Second, you blame my second son. Then, you dare try to accuse him of it in front of the entire court on the day of your engagement, all to get out of your wedding." The king's words were cold. Menacing. "What do you have to say, witch?"

He knew she had a name, but he refused to use it, as if a plague would befall him and decimate his kingdom if he uttered it. It was intentionally pointed and cold, dehumanizing her for the sake of it.

No one in the room dared move or talk. There were probably thoughts about how terrible she was, the scornful looks on everyone's faces were enough to say as much. However, Rizza could not use her magic in that state. She'd let them take her, let them chain her. So as of that moment she was helpless. Pain wasn't just what she felt anywhere the holy water touched, it was deep in the pit of her stomach and heart. Betrayal stung worse than any other wound she'd felt.

Rizza didn't answer right away. Silence hung in the air as she slowly raised her head. It was the first time the court had seen her cry, and it wasn't pretty. Dark tears stained her face like black ink, and ran down her cheeks. Her gaze was steady as she quietly let the tears flow.

"I would never have killed Drake." Rizza's voice was quiet, but firm.

"Oh, really? So you had no motive, despite how often you and Drake fought?" The king's voice was mocking now. He sneered down at her. Rizza could tell by the way he looked at her that he was ready to just behead her. This 'trial' was a joke, and the entire court knew it, so they stayed quiet, but silent judgement rained down on Rizza in waves. In their eyes, and in the king's, it was all her fault. The queen shed tears as she quietly held a kerchief to her face.

Rizza looked around the room before letting out a mockin\g laugh. "Oh, please. Arguments between children... isn't that what they were called for all those years? They were just arguments between children. Yet, now I am accused of treason." Rizza shook her head before looking up at the court. "Yet, I can't figure out why. I have done NOTHING but serve this court for two lifetimes. I have helped you all countless times. Yes, I have pulled pranks. Yes, I have been a bit meaner than I should be sometimes, but I have never gone out of my way to be actively malicious. None of that matters to you all, does it? You all want a villain, and I'm convenient. You'd rather just trust that girl's word than look into it." Rizza sneered in disgust.

The king scoffed as she finished talking. He leaned on his armrest, and stared down at her. "We would rather just believe her, much like you wanted us to just believe you when you accused Pratt? Like you wanted us to all jump the sword, and kill my second son, right after the death of my first?" His voice was rising in anger again.

Rizza watched as the queen moved to placate him, her fingers going to gently intertwine with the king's, brushing over him in a loving way, a way that Rizza never realized could be done. She watched in utter fascination and disgust. The queen had lied, but she still didn't know why, and she knew pointing it out here would be no good.

"Maybe... maybe we should investigate it more... maybe someone would have more information. Could we maybe... I don't know... make a plea to the city, and see if anyone has any information?" the queen asked on behalf of Rizza, her gaze going over to Rizza with a look of sadness, as if looking at her own child. Rizza didn't know what to believe at this point. Had she imagined the look on the queen's face at the ball? No, she definitely hadn't, so why was the queen speaking up for her now? That made zero sense.

The king paused, the court remained silent, Rizza remained silent, then, there was a long sigh, and the king rubbed his head. He, too, wanted to know who murdered his son, he didn't want to believe it was Rizza, but nothing pointed to it being anyone else.

"Fine. Guards, send word, if anyone has any knowledge of what happened with my son's murder, if anyone can prove Rizza innocent, or guilty, let them come forward. They have until sunset." The king's words were calm.

Everyone in the court knew this day was going to be long, as no one was allowed to leave the room until everything had been concluded. With all of them remaining, it meant that, at the end of the day, there would be an execution. The only uncertainty now was whose execution it would be.

The guards were quick to follow orders. One left the room immediately while the others closed the doors behind him. There was a loud 'bang' in the hall as the doors shut, and then, silence reigned once more.

It was entirely quiet for a while, no one dared speak, heck, no one dared breathe too loudly. They were scared of upsetting the king, but as the minutes dragged on into half an hour, an hour, and so on, people began to talk. Quietly, and to themselves, people talked, their voices in low, dissonant whispers among themselves.

Rizza could hear bits of conversation, threads of it, speaking of the ingratitude she showed, speaking of how no one would ever step forward for a witch. Her head was bowed, her body slumped, her wrists, ankles, and neck burned. She had cuffs all over her, and worst of all, her chest ached. It felt like there was a hole in it. Yet, she couldn't say anything. She was trapped in a misery of her own making. It felt as if she were at the bottom of a lake, the whispers and chatter in the room echoing around and simply filtering through the waters that were her sorrow.

She sat in silence. The room could talk all it wanted, and Rizza would listen as it did. It would talk, and talk, and talk. That was all people were good for anyway, talking, it was all anyone was ever good for, it seemed. All people ever did was talk, so Rizza would let them talk. That was all she could do, anyway.

There was no point arguing with these people, no point trying to convince them of her innocence, no point trying to say they were wrong about her, that she would never have betrayed the kingdom. When someone pulls as many pranks as she did on a court, they are bound to get some sort of revenge. This was it. This was the moment where Karma bit Rizza in the ass.

Blaming her was probably easier, since she wasn't scared to die, and she would live again. Anyone else would never see another sun rise, would never see another moment of their lives, but Rizza would. She would get another life, she would be re-born anew. Sure, at first, she wouldn't remember this life, or the others, but, over time, memories would come back. The tomes would join her wherever she was, because the kingdoms would be assured to help her with that. So, she would face the punishment, and it would not even matter.

Then, Rizza remembered something. She'd spent so long alive in this life, yet she hadn't categorized her latest work. She hadn't written in any tome or journal since she had gotten to the capital. She wouldn't remember any of this life from the point of getting to the castle this last time, this entire event. It would be gone.

Rizza raised her head slowly, her gaze locked onto the king as she did, and she chewed on her lip. Did she dare? She dared.

"Your Majesty," Rizza called out softly. He had been quietly discussing something with Pratt at that moment. Yet, when Rizza called, he looked over. Hatred still showed in his face. Rizza had to resist the urge to cringe away from it.

"What?" His voice was gruff. He already seemed like he didn't want to talk to her. Hours had passed, and he felt as if his time had been wasted. The sun had already peaked in the sky and it was afternoon. No one had even had food yet here this wretch was, bothering him.

"My tomes, I always write in them. If I am to die today, which I very well may if this is not solved, I need to record the recent events." Rizza spoke softly. She could feel the way the king stared at her in mockery. She knew no one else understood how important those books were. But to her, they were everything. They saved her time and time again from spending countless decades relearning things she'd learned before. Lessons that would be left to discovery once more. And this? This would be a lesson in trust.

"You don't believe you're going to die?" He seemed to laugh darkly at her optimism. Some of the court joined in with his laughter. Rizza didn't laugh, however, and neither did the queen or Pratt.

"Fine. Someone go fetch her book, and a pen and ink. Let her write her last words. It's not like it matters." The king brushed it off. Of course, to him, it did not matter, he wasn't the one who had to spend years remembering past lives. To her, it mattered a lot. It saved so much time if she could just read about her past.

"I will go, father," Pratt volunteered, his words even as he moved from the side of the throne. The king nodded his affirmation before Pratt left. The guards, again, shut the door behind him, and, again, silence took over.

It didn't take Pratt long. He soon returned with a smaller book and writing utensils, a pen and ink, in hand. They were simple, yet well-crafted. He offered them to Rizza, and when he saw how the cuffs would hurt if he made her raise her arms, he slowly set them on the ground in front of her. His hands were gloved so it did not bother him at all to touch them, and even the king did not stop him from doing so. No one assumed her to run and with the other cuffs and such still in place around her body, it was not like she'd be able to.

"Thank you." She said softly. It was ironic that the person being kind to her was the person she loathed the most before, left to cater to his whims because she had messed up, it was just grand.

Rizza picked up the pen and ink. She carefully dipped the nib into the ink before opening the book. It was smaller than her others, because this life hadn't been long yet. Each time she need-ed a new page, she would just conjure one. If she needed the book to be bigger, she would just will it to be bigger, so this one was still small. It seemed it wouldn't get much larger, either.

Rizza set to work. She began carefully detailing her work from the time she arrived at the castle, all the way up till now. From going into the town to pose as a beggar old man, running into Mars – sweet, sweet Mars – to finding the prince dead, accus-ing Pratt, everything that had led up to her seemingly inevitable doom. Yes, that was what this was: doom.

Rizza sighed softly. Her hand hovered over the paper. A bit of ink splattered from her pen onto the paper, and she watched as it dried. Then, she began to write, as if she was already certain to die. For a long while the only thing that was heard in the large room was the scratching of her pen against the page.

I have lived my life until now in a very honest manner, I think. Granted, that was not the most splendid way to live it, but I tried to be honest. I tried to be true to myself. I may have been meaner when I could have been kind, over-the-top where it was not needed. So... to my future self, the self that will read this in another life, or all the other lives: be kinder. Smile more. You're ugly, but you don't have to be ugly on the inside. Yes, that means that even if people ask you stupid questions, you don't have to give them stupid answers. You're immortal. Act your age. I didn't, not this time. Also, don't trust so easily next time. I believe I've been betrayed but I have no proof of it, yet.

Rizza had just finished writing that last bit when the doors opened again. She didn't look up. She waited for the page to dry as the others entered. A soft sigh escaped her. She was waiting for the guards to tell the court that no one would come forward, that Rizza was doomed and life was over. Yet, that did not happen. Rizza was greeted with shock as a man and his son were presented to her upon looking up, the same man and son that she had seen in the market so long ago during the festival. Her gaze turned to them, and the confusion was written all over her face.

The man looked terrified, but the boy, he looked determined. He saw Rizza, and offered a slight smile. Rizza offered one back. She didn't quite know what was going to happen, but that small act of kindness gave her a small glimmer of hope. Perhaps her life was not over after all.

"You come with news?" the king asked, impatience in his voice as he saw the man dawdling. The guard who acted as his escort quickly offered a salute before beginning to explain.

"When I was asking for any who would like to speak on behalf of or against Rizza, I came across this gentleman. He said he may have some information to give regarding the case. So we listened to him and..." The guard turned back to the door.

It seemed the surprises were not over yet as two more blokes were dragged in. Rizza had seen them around the castle before, they were servants, simple boys with no real weight to them, but they wore nice clothing now, crafted of silk and linen, stuff no servant could afford. Rizza's eyebrows furrowed together.

"What's going on?" Rizza asked. Even she was confused by this turn of events. She looked at the man.

He looked at her briefly before a sweat broke out over his brow, and he quickly looked away. He seemed utterly terrified to be in the presence of not only the nobility, but her, as well. Rizza watched as he slowly moved forward before he knelt. His son moved with him and knelt next to Rizza, instead of kneeling before the court. He offered her another smile.

"We are here to help." He said softly. Rizza couldn't help the slightly sad smile that crept up her face. This was so weird.

"Thank you," she whispered back.

"Okay, so, we have a peasant and his son, and two gentle-men?" The king was waiting for an explanation, and it was clear he wasn't very pleased about being kept waiting. "Explain, before I just have everyone's head and call it a day."

"You-... Your majesties, your highnesses, your-" The man stuttered. He turned so he was now facing his ruler rather than the witch who scared the daylights out of him.

"Yes, yes. Get on with it, already." He growled in annoyance. He'd been cooped up in the courtroom all day and there for the king was done with this. It was clear he just wanted to have someone's head, and he wanted Rizza's more than any other's.

"I'm so sorry. My son and I couldn't stay away after hearing about... Lady Rizza's plight. It wasn't our business. We knew of the crown prince, may his and his wife's souls rest in peace, but we didn't realize how bad this was, and we weren't going to get involved, as we are just lowly commoners but..." The man spoke rapidly as he seemed to trip over his words. He seemed utterly terrified just being there.

"But we can't let Rizza go to jail!" The boy called out. He looked at Rizza with determination as he spoke up. He was much bolder than his father, and his father seemed terrified by the idea. "Rizza has helped us before, so we couldn't just let her take the fall! It wasn't Rizza!" The boy shouted bravely in front of the court. Though his words were brave, all he was met with was derision and looks of affronting, as if the mere sight of him was an offense that couldn't be tolerated by the high-class snobs of the court.

"Oh? And what proof do you have of your claim, boy?" The king sat up in his chair, interest in his gaze now as he stared down at the young lad who had the audacity to raise his voice before the king. It truly was astounding, because, so far, the only person brave – and stupid – enough to do that was Rizza. This was a new one.

"I can help with that, your majesty." One of the guards shoved the two servants forward so they landed on their knees, their binding chains clattering against the floor. The guard looked utterly pissed off.

"These two were servants here at the court. I'd recognize them anywhere, because we have been looking for 'em for several weeks now. They disappeared with a bunch of kitchen silver about the time the prince died." The guard was annoyed as hell. "And, now, come to find out, they seem to have a hand in some of this. Go on. Tell the Lord what you dared say at the bar while you bragged to all your chums." The guard gave one of them a kick.

Up until now, the boys had been cowering. It was obvious that they were petrified, and guilty as heck. If nothing else, then for robbing the kitchen of its silver. This 'crime' was becoming a mockery, and Rizza had no words or way to begin. Her gaze swept over the two as they coward away. Yet, surprisingly, they spoke. No criminal would be that complacent when terrified. Rizza was expecting yet another scheme.

"We were bragging about the money we made... when we were paid to switch the wine out. We figured it was a sweet gig, you know, a quick cash grab. We didn't know the prince was gonna die, we swear! When he did, we got scared, so we took the silver and ran." One of the boys broke down sobbing. "We swear we didn't mean nuthin' by it. We didn't mean 'is highness no harm, we just thought we was giving him a different wine, something that was a prank, that's all." The boy quietly shook as he explained what happened. Both of them cowered as they began to beg for forgiveness.

The father and son duo knelt quietly on the floor, the boy maintained his determined look but there was also a gleam of pride and heroism in his eyes now. Rizza couldn't help but admire the young con artist's gallantry at that moment.

The king rubbed his eyebrows as he looked between the two before waving his hand. Instant silence fell over the hall once more, and the king glared down at them. His gaze was piercing as his words were spoken syllable by syllable. "Who? Who paid you to switch the wine?" The two shook softly and began to shake their heads as if they didn't dare tell. The king slammed his hands down on the armrests of his chair as he bellowed down at them.

"WHO PAID YOU TWO TO SWITCH THE WINES?!" The king's voice echoed in the hall, and no one dared to even breathe. His anger was palpable.

Rizza sat off to the side, wide-eyed at this turn of events. It was so easy? Two people come forward with this, and, suddenly, it's their fault? How could she begin to deal with this... She had spent weeks trying to figure it out, and, all along, all she had to do was locate these two? She wasn't even the one to solve the mystery?

One of them, the braver of the two – or the stupider, who knew – pointed at the dais where the king sat. Yet, he wasn't pointing at the king. All eyes drew to Pratt as the boy pointed. Tears streaming down his face as he did. The courtroom grew very, very silent at that exact moment. Pratt stood stunned as the finger of accusation was now pointed at him. Rather than looking guilty, he looked shocked.

"They did, they paid us." The boy sobbed quietly. The entire audience gasped, yet again. It was like a terrible play.

Rizza spends weeks playing detective, telling everyone the bad guy is Pratt and now they believe her? Now, someone comes forward, right as she is about to lose her head?

Rizza began to laugh, tears streaming down her face as she did. Everyone else in the court was shocked and horrified while she alone was laughing at the situation.

"NOW, DO YOU BELIEVE ME?!" she shouted, laughter escaping her before she forced it down. She looked at the court. Maybe death wasn't all that was left for her. Though, this felt too early to say that for certain. Things were like a twilight zone and she had no idea exactly how to process it all, so she was laughing. The court was now looking at Pratt, and even for as pale as he was, he was looking really pale. He took a step away from the king as everyone watched.

"You? You did this?" The king was at a loss. His voice was broken as he stared at Pratt. "Why?" His voice was looking for a reason. And for once. Everyone watched, as the king began to cry. Tears poured out of his eyes. Sorrow was obvious as he questioned his second eldest son. "Why would you do this? Drake... he looked after you, he protected you. How could you do this to the family, to the country? All for the throne? Is that what this is about, the throne?" The king looked utterly disgusted at the idea. The tears were replaced with rage again. He could not have brought himself to believe in the backstabbing one child of his given to another until it was forced in front of his face in such a brutal way. Now that he was forced to face it, he didn't have the strength.

Then, Pratt sneered, his shock overcome as he looked around the court. He shook his head. Rizza was still wrapping her mind around the fact that she'd been right. I mean, she'd blamed him, but, in the end, even she'd had her doubts. Yet, here it was, all laid out in front of her. He was the murderer, and she was right. But, why didn't that feel good?

"Oh, don't lecture me about the lengths people go to for the throne. Whose legendary might was it that slew his own older brothers with the help of a powerful wizard to take the throne? None other than yours, father." Pratt's voice was filled with mockery and ridicule, the same as what everyone had been using towards Rizza a while ago.

Rizza watched from the side. One minute, the courtroom was in silent shock, the next, chaos. The guards lunged to try and grab Pratt, they wanted to protect the king. Yet, Pratt didn't give them a chance. His hand shot out, and the guards flung back.

"I will be back, and justice will be had." The prince snarled. Just like that, a black puff of smoke, and he was gone. The court was in an uproar. It was him, there was no denying it anymore.

The Aftermath

Everyone was frantic to find him, everyone was checking every nook and cranny of the castle, and while all that was going on, Rizza sat in the throne room with the king, the queen, and the two peasants who saved her. The courtiers had scrambled, and the two servants had been sent to jail. That left only the five of them and a couple of guards to protect the royals.

All was silent in the throne room for a while, no one dared to speak as everyone processed what happened. Then, the boy looked over at Rizza, triumph on his face as he stared at her.

"Does this make us even for you making the gems real?" The boy asked. Rizza looked up at him, then, she began to laugh slightly. Her fingers reached out to pull him into an awkward, chained-up hug as she ruffled his hair. Of course his father looked horrified as Rizza hugged the boy. He was still half expecting her to hurt them in some way. The king and queen sat in silence, observing with a very large lack of actual interest considering the news they'd just heard.

"Yes, I'd say this does. Also, I didn't make them real, I just made them look real for a couple of days. I'm sure the spell has worn off by now, but they'll never notice." Rizza laughed softly and the boy laughed with her. Yet, it was a tense laughter, the kind of laughter that is bred from not knowing what else to do. It wasn't as if those two were immune to the tension in the room. They felt it the same as everyone else. With how many times the tables had turned it was hard not to be tense and stressed about the situation. Rizza was still certain that things weren't fully solved. For all the hell she'd been through, somehow it seemed too easy.

Finally, Rizza got herself together. She looked over at the king. The two made eye contact, and held it for a long time.

"You know... he's not-" Rizza was going to say 'wrong', when a curt 'shut up' was barked by the king. He knew what she was going to say. He didn't want to hear about how Rizza, in her past life, had helped him take over the kingdom, but, in his defense, his brothers were all mad with power. Only he retained some semblance of sanity, so she had helped him.

"Okay... then... can I be unchained now? These really hurt." Rizza spoke softly, changing the subject. Naturally, she wouldn't expect the king to apologize, and he didn't, but he waved his hand to signal a guard to undo the chains that bound her.

The queen stood at that point, a sad smile on her face as she took the keys from the guard and undid the chains herself. After that, she pulled Rizza into a tight hug. Rizza didn't know what to make of it. She stood shell-shocked for a moment, before finally leaning in and hugging the woman back. Images of the look on the queen's face in several instances that mattered replayed in Rizza's mind.

The queen felt nice, but something still nagged at Rizza. She wouldn't say it aloud, learning, finally, to hold her thoughts inward a bit. The queen's face after the ball still haunted her. Yet, Rizza couldn't comment on it. She could only begin to guess what the queen was thinking at the time, and that alone frightened her. She needed to find out what happened to her in her past life, and why the queen had lied about Rizza being involved in Drake's murder.

"I'm sorry, Rizza. None of this would have been pinned on you if not for me." The queen spoke softly. Her voice was tender and apologetic. Rizza offered her a smile as she pulled free of the hug. She could feel the wounds slowly beginning to heal on her form.

"Hey, I still have my head, so I consider that a win." She brushed off the incident before looking at the king. There was tension between them both before she turned to look at the peasant. He wasn't looking at her. He wasn't even looking up. He was staring at the ground, still kneeling there. Rizza slowly moved towards him. She had talked to his son this time, but not him. He'd been so adamantly afraid of her before that it was strange to see him here now.

"Why? Why did you help me? I... I thought you hated me," Rizza questioned. Her gaze was filled with confusion as she stared at the man kneeling on the ground. He slowly looked up at her before looking away again. His hand went to the back of his neck nervously, and the boy tugged on his arm as if to get him to fess up.

"Come on, papa, just tell her. She's not evil." He seemed to be standing up for Rizza and the effort made her smile a little.

"Alright... alright. We helped because... well, you helped us. You scare me, witch, but you aren't bad people. You did me a good deed, I can feed my family now. It wouldn't sit right if I didn't help you." He finally spoke. He slowly stood up and dusted his knees off before pointing a finger at her. "But don't think this changes anything. I still don't want to see you again. We aren't friends, you hear? You stay away from my family. I don't want you meddling around in my affairs and getting me in trouble." Rizza listened to him speak and the smile that was tugging at her lip turned into a grin.

"I wouldn't dream of it. Consider us even. I helped you, you helped me, no more." Rizza offered him a quick curtsy. "Thank you."

The man paused for a moment before nodding. He then looked at the queen and king. He gave them a brief moment of recognition with a bow before he quickly left the palace. He didn't want to stay any longer than necessary. The boy followed after him. He offered one last wave to Rizza before disappearing out the door after his father.

Silence once again overtook the hall. It only lasted a moment this time, though, as Rizza turned to look at the royalty. She offered a brief smile before frowning.

"If... it's all the same to you... I'd just like to go back to my mountains, your majesties." Rizza quietly requested. She was tired, and nothing sounded more appealing at that moment than just heading back to her home.

"After we find Pratt, and get his sentence carried out, then you can leave, Rizza. For now... go wash up." The king didn't dismiss her from court. Instead, he just dismissed her from the room. He looked utterly exhausted. There were times to pick battles, but Rizza decided that was not a battle to pick.

Rizza nodded. She picked up the book, and headed for the door. That was a fight for another day.

Rizza pushed open the door to her room in the royal wing. She supposed they would let her stay here, since she was already here. It would be nice, at least. Rizza let out a sigh as she shut the door behind her.

Her feet slowly dragged her forward towards the rest of the room. Exhaustion washed over her as she made her way over towards the bathtub.

"Someone... can you... oh." Rizza was going to call for a bath. Yet, it seemed someone had beaten her to it. There was steaming water in the bathtub already, and she didn't need to worry about waiting for someone to draw it for her. A sigh of thanks escaped her towards whichever thoughtful servant pulled that off.

Rizza slowly moved towards the bath, her fingers pulling the clothing from her form as she moved. Hairpins hit the floor along with clothing and jewelry as she slowly slipped free of her garments until she stood in the buff. Only then did she move into the water.

Dipping a toe into the water Rizza slowly put her foot into it. It was warm, not too scolding hot, but not too cold either. The heating stone was at the bottom, keeping it at the right temperature, and Rizza could feel the water relax her muscles. A sigh of bliss escaped her. She slipped fully into the water until only her upper face was exposed, her nose barely breaking the surface as she sat there, eyes closed.

She needed a bath. She doubted she had ever craved a bath so much in her life. At that moment, it was very needed. As she thought about what had just happened, she realized there was very little that could make her as happy as she felt right now, at least in this life. Being found innocent by someone she'd helped on a whim was an amazing feeling.

Maybe, Rizza mused to herself, just maybe there was a god, and maybe they didn't hate her. The idea of it amused her to no end as she lounged about.

Her peace wasn't going to last, though. When Rizza finally bothered to open her eyes. The first thing she saw was Pratt. He was leaning against the wall near the bathing area with his hands folded across his chest. His gaze locked on her as she sat in the water, and he looked pissed.

"Rizza." His voice was cold as he spoke. His fists balled up as he stood there. Rizza stared at him. She was still in the water up to her nose so only her eyes really peaked out over the surface and she was very much aware that nothing in the tub was covering her nudity from his view. The idea that he'd been standing there and she'd let her guard down... she wanted to scream, to announce he was there, but she was bathing. She narrowed her eyes at him.

"I take it the bath was your doing?" she asked curiously after lifting her head out of the water enough to speak without inhaling it. She didn't yell, not yet. She was the stronger magic wielder, so she was in no danger. At that point she was more worried about how damaged her pride had become. If she killed him it would be preserved but that... she still had a nagging feeling that something wasn't right about the murder.

"It was. I figured you wouldn't call the guards if you were naked," he responded promptly: smart man. Rizza knew he was smart though. He had gotten this far in life without being hated.

"Okay, so why are you here?" She decided to play the game, mostly because some things still didn't add up: the queen, the ending of it all. Something was off. All the stories mixed, and nothing really seemed solid. First, she had what she'd been told originally, then the maid came forward and changed the story. Then the story changed again when the servants showed up. None of it made sense, so she was at least willing to hear him out.

"Do you, uh... want something to cover yourself with?" he asked, his gaze seeming to leave the tub as a hint of color-tinted his cheeks. It seemed he was trying to play hardball but her lack of reaction to him seeing her naked unnerved him. She had won that round. Small bouts of satisfaction filled Rizza.

However, her victory was shor- lived for only then did Rizza realize she was still naked, very, very painfully, obviously so. Her gaze went down and her face heated up. She quickly clouded the water with a wave of her hand before looking back at him.

"Your plan is... a pain. You know that, right?" Rizza grumbled, annoyed.

"Yes, I seem to have found the flaw." The prince replied. He only looked back after she was covered enough to reveal nothing to him. He stared at her before letting out an elongated sigh, his hand running through his hair as he began to pace. "I didn't know where else to go. Everyone else is sure to turn me in, and, oddly enough, despite all you've done to convince them I'm the criminal, I didn't think you would," he spoke. His words were filled with open distress.

Rizza lifted an eyebrow. "You didn't think the single person who's been against you this entire time wouldn't turn you in?" That didn't make sense, though his gamble had paid off. She wouldn't just hand him over like that, not when some things were so off, needing explanations, and she had been treated the way she had by the king and queen.

"Yes, I figured you of all people would realize there are holes in this story. With how eager you were to see me pinned for the murder, you spent time investigating it, you actually looked for proof. Granted, you wouldn't have if everyone had just believed you... but... still... Rizza... I need your help," the prince sighed. He looked defeated. He knelt on the ground and clasped his hands together in an overexaggerated begging gesture. "I have nowhere else to turn, and I fear I've been set up. Still, I don't know why. I need help finding out who did this, and why they did this. If we could just figure it out– no, you – if you could just figure it out, it would be amazing."

"Me? You want me to solve this? Why do you think I even believe you?" Rizza sounded affronted. All she wanted to do was go home. The mountains flashed in her mind again, she could turn him in and go to the mountains, the beautiful, beautiful mountains. If she did that, life would be so much easier for her. She wouldn't have to worry about any of this anymore. All she wanted was to go to the mountains. It was not as if she even liked Pratt. From the moment she met him she'd found his pompous attitude intolerable and she really didn't see a point in joining him in anything including his own rescue. Plus, he had basically just watched her get unjustly locked up and proceeded to just... let it happen. What right did he have to beg her for help?

"Because I saw how you were staring at my mother as they dragged you away, and I saw that look on her face. You're not the only one with doubts about her." Pratt's voice was dead serious. Rizza knew she hadn't dreamed it, hadn't been wrong. Her head snapped up to stare at him as he said that and she narrowed her eyes. She still did not want to help him, but that nagging feeling was back as soon as he said that.

He had seen it too? She wasn't wrong. The queen had looked off. Even when Prince Drake had died, she had... now that Rizza thought of it. She stared at Pratt. Silence stood between them for a while.

Then, there was a loud knock at the door. Pratt froze, ready to teleport the second Rizza called out.

"Rizza?" A servant called out. This one was familiar with the fact that Rizza hated being called 'lady' and being disturbed by sudden intrusions. That was Pratt's only saving grace, if she'd just barged in they would have both been condemned as conspiring against the crown.

"The king requests your presence... when you're fit to see him." The words were clear. The king wanted her to clean up before going back to the throne room. She sighed softly.
Silence sat between Pratt and Rizza as they stared at each other. It would do Rizza no good to call out now, she was afraid of being

incriminated again.

"I'll be there in a while, tell the king that, no need to come in." She replied firmly. She heard an affirmation before footsteps headed down the hall. The maid was gone and silence was returned. Pratt stared at her.

"So... will you help me?" he asked softly. He didn't speak until he was certain they were alone again. Rizza mulled it over. She could turn him in, use him as a scapegoat, but there was something off with all of this, with her past life. The more she thought of it being tied to her previous death, the more her head hurt. Her head hurting usually meant she had a memory missing that she needed. Even if she did it for selfish reasons, she knew she had to at least look into the case further.

"Fine. I will help you, on one condition." Rizza agreed after a while, her gaze going to look at the prince, who looked noticeably elated.

"Anything, name it," he quickly agreed.

"Never... ever... come into my room while I'm bathing again. Now, hide, or something, I have an audience with your father. I doubt they will check my room for you, since it's obvious I'm stronger than you, and I accused you to begin with." Rizza waved her hand as if to shoo him away from her.

You called?

Rizza re-entered the court rather quickly after leaving it. Her gaze went around the grand hall as she entered. Only an hour ago, she was chained to the floor, and now, again, she was walking freely about, as if none of it had happened.

The courtiers had been regathered, and the place was more or less in a semblance of peace. There was unease spread throughout the room, but that wasn't really a surprise. When a magical man gets called a criminal, everyone tends to panic. They don't know what he's capable of, and it all seems rather... fishy.

That being the case, everyone seemed utterly terrified at the idea of having to deal with all of this any longer than they needed to. Their gazes went to Rizza as she entered, and everyone went quiet.

People usually fell silent when she entered a room, there was nothing new there, no change, and that was good, at least. No one had started giving her special treatment because of all of this, and, certainly, no one was bothering to try and apologize for wrongly accusing her. There was a clear lack of niceties and remorse, but her name was cleared, at least, and that much was nice.

She ignored the courtiers that milled about, for the most part, as she made her way up to where the king sat. The queen was missing, probably exhausted from all the events, so that left his highness on the thrones by himself. Rizza was careful to curtsy when she saw him.

Usually, this was where she would say some stupid smart-mouth remark and make him livid, but, for once, she decided that wasn't in her best interest. Instead, she focused on trying to remain polite. That seemed to gain her some respect as he began to speak.

"Rizza. This kingdom owes you an apology. Though it was only briefly, you have suffered a great deal at our hands. None of us believed that Pratt would have the capability to harm his own brother, and, now, you are proven correct. Not only did we not believe you, we even tried to throw you in jail for the crimes he committed, and we tried to wed you to him." The king paused after all that. He seemed slightly put out that he was having to admit his fault, poor man. He loathed apologizing for being rude to her after all she'd done to cause hell for the last few days. Her childish actions had caused panic on more than one occasion and, according to the conversation she'd had with that peasant she probably scammed several nobles as well. The idea that he was apologizing was completely ridiculous to him. However, for the sake of maintaining face and dignity, he still did so.

Rizza waited patiently for him to continue, and, slowly, he began to. "I, on behalf of everyone here, including myself, would like to apologize to you. Your engagement to Pratt is hereby called off, and you are absolved of all crimes and allegations against you." His words were calm and reassuring as he spoke, very fitting for a king.

Rizza bowed softly to him for a moment before standing up straight. She opened her mouth slightly before shutting it again. Then, she frowned.

"May I speak, your highness?" Rizza decided to not start off their 'on the right foot' talk with more blatant disrespect, so she started being a bit formal, just a bit. He was treating her with dignity, and all things considering she felt that she should give him that courtesy as well.

"Granted," the king replied calmly. He was tired, and he no longer had the energy to deal with all of this. Yet, he needed to show Rizza some face, and he did, he let Rizza speak.

"Thank you. First, thank you for your apology, and the absolvement of guilt, the marriage, and all of that, and... now, this is the part you won't like..." Rizza smiled apologetically as she began to pace in front of the throne. She truly was sorry for the words she was about to say. Especially considering that the king had lowered his ego enough to be kind to her and apologize. She knew her wishy-washy attitude was about to get her into a load of trouble.

All the nobles in the room were avidly watching the inter-action. Most of them had never seen Rizza apologize for a single thing she did nor had they seen her be polite. Seeing her act so formally now was very shocking to them. They had been waiting for the other shoe to drop.

"What?" The king seemed utterly put out that she was doing this. He sat up on his throne. His posture somehow became even more perfect than it already was. There was something almost intimidatingly powerful about this new stance he took in his chair. He knew she was going to say something he didn't like. This wasn't good.

"Well... Isn't this entire thing just fishy?" Rizza started off. Her stance shifted from foot to foot as she fidgeted in place. "I mean... that palace maid... first, she tells me Pratt's ser-vant switched the bottles, then, she tells everyone my servant switched the bottles, then, two more servants come up, and say they switched the bottles. Two of the three stories, admittedly, point towards Pratt, but something seems wrong. None of this adds up. It almost feels like... I don't know... someone wants us to believe it is Pratt's fault. Like... there is something else going on." Rizza explained her reasoning. She didn't give all the details for why she thought what she thought. Her hands were used to point out each point. As she listed off the in-continuity in the different stories she ticked them off on her fingers.

Still, the king's face slowly grew more and more exhaust-ed the more he listened. All he wanted was to be done with all of this. He had dropped all charges against Rizza, cleared her name, and even apologized. Yet, here she was, arguing with him, yet again. She wouldn't drop it, wouldn't let it go. He didn't even be-gin to know how to deal with this.

"You-... Do you just like going against the world?" The king's voice was soft, so soft that even Rizza had a hard time catching it.

"I'm sorry?" Rizza turned to face him fully once more. Her hands were clasped behind her back, and her head was tilted to the side in confusion. She had no idea what he meant.

"Do you just like being at odds with the world? Is that what it is? Even when people finally see things your way, you immediately turn around and see them differently? What, because you have been proven right, now you have to question it? You can't just accept that you were right, and we were wrong? The second it all comes to light, you have to just... turn around and say he's innocent? Are you daft, or just trying to piss me off?" His voice rose with each additional question. If the king had been holding something in his hand at that moment, Rizza had no doubt he'd have thrown it at her head. The man was utterly enraged by her.

Rizza frowned as she stared at the king. His words made sense. She did seem to be very fickle about this. After all, she had been claiming it was all Pratt's doing this entire time, up until the very moment that he'd been proven to be the one at fault by others. Then, she just turned around and planted the seed of doubt back in.

Rizza was very self-centered, but even she could tell how silly it looked. She offered up an apologetic smile as she shrugged softly. She had already known this was going to irritate him and the court.

"All I'm saying is that... if there is a chance – just a chance – that it was not him, would you be willing to listen to that chance, or are you going to condemn your son to death no matter what? You were dead set against it being him before... what if it really isn't him? Isn't that a good thing? I mean I don't like him and here I stand advocating for him." Rizza pressed on. She was good at going forward when others knew better, even though she had probably just walked off a cliff.

The king stared at her. There was obvious anger in his gaze as he watched her with a twitching eyelid. Pure rage showed on his face while he did. It was like he didn't have the words to describe how mad he was at that moment. How could one find the words to describe that kind of rage? She was literally pitting him against his son as if he was the bad father that was giving up on him.

His mouth opened, then it closed a few times. He didn't know where to begin, where to start his rant, how he wanted to express his rage at Rizza. Every time something seemed like it was settled, every time something seemed like it was wrong, or that everyone was stressed and just wanted to be done with it – every time – Rizza got involved, she mucked it up, and she went against everyone. Why couldn't Rizza just... sit down, sit one out, take one for the team, and shut the hell up?

The king wanted to yell all of this, he wanted to shake her, Rizza could tell. She didn't have to read his mind to know what he was thinking. The more he fumed, the more amused she was. She couldn't laugh, though. If she laughed, she had a feeling he'd behead her for the fun of it. That wouldn't be good. She bit the inside of her lip to keep her expression straight. However, doing so only caused her to wince and make it look like she was mildly scared because her needle-like teeth literally dug a chunk out of her flesh. Why would anyone ever do that to control their smile? That hurt.

"Get... out." The king finally spat out two words. Only two. The entire court froze when they heard them. They were said so softly, it almost seemed like they hadn't been said at all, until they were repeated. "Get out!" He bellowed, his voice hoarse. He pointed at the door. Rizza was really glad he had nothing in his hands to throw at her at that moment. He very well may have thrown something at her if he could. Rizza knew damn well he would have.

He didn't, however, so she was safe. Rizza offered a small smile before she curtsied. "I can see you are stressed. I'll just... go, then," she said softly. She didn't tell him she was off to go plot with the very son he was looking for. That wouldn't be good. He'd probably charge her with conspiracy. No, scratch the proba- bly. He would charge her with conspiracy.

Before she left, Rizza paused and looked at him. "Before I go... what of the guard that was detained? I had only met him after…"

"He's been released, and paid well for his grievances. Now, get out." The king demanded once more. He was so enraged, he had no patience to talk to her. Rizza offered a brief smile.

After dropping into a curtsy, she quickly left the throne room, her feet carrying her down the hall, and back towards her room. At least the guard that had been assigned to her during castle arrest hadn't been killed. That poor boy was probably terrified of her now that he'd been implicated. Ah… so much for making a friend.

Rizza had many things she needed to get done, and only a short amount of time to do them. If Pratt was discovered, she would be at risk. She needed to quickly figure out what was going on. If she could just get to the bottom of all of this, then her life would be far better off.

Let's Chat

Rizza sat in her parlor across from Pratt. They stared at each other quietly for some time. Neither one of them started the conversation, or broke the awkward tension between them. Rizza had put up wards around the room and on the door, so no one could get in or listen at the door. This made it easier to make it seem like Pratt wasn't here. Even if someone did enter, though, it wouldn't be hard to make him invisible.

Pratt had proven rather obviously that he could disappear easily if he wanted to, so, there they sat, quietly, uninterrupted, as the entire castle looked for him, having a staring contest. Rizza watched him silently, analyzing his features, analyzing every expression that crossed his face. She wanted to know what was going on in that head of his. Something had to be off for him to come looking for her. It was ridiculous. Why would he think she would help him, when she was the one who suspected him all along, the one who accused him in front of everyone??

Rizza was dumbstruck by the idea, still, he had a point, there was common ground and lots of unanswered questions. Rizza let out a sigh. He perked up, and something flashed in his face, maybe victory or something. Why, she had no idea, she'd already agreed to help him.

"We need to talk... about this..." Pratt finally broke the silence, the first to cave. Rizza was gleeful over her victory, but tried to play it all off like she didn't care one bit. She sat back in her chair calmly, and stared over at him with a quirked brow.

"Yes. Yes, we do," she agreed. He was right, talking was important. "Let's start with the obvious holes in the stories. As I mentioned to your father earlier-"

"You brought this up to him?" Pratt's eyes widened. "Just now? When you were in the throne room?" He confirmed his suspicions. He didn't seem thrilled by the idea that she'd done that.

Rizza let out a sigh. "Yes. Now, if you would let me continue." She glared at him. He shut up, and she nodded.

"As I was saying. As I brought up to your father earlier, there are several loose ends in all of this. The first one being the maid with her double stories. She told me your servant switched the wine, then turned around and said that I had it switched, then, two more people came and said they switched the wine. I am wondering if the wine was even the cause of death at this point. I mean, yes, it could have killed them, and probably did, but I don't know who's lying. Not only that, but when I tried to compel the girl to tell the truth, I found she'd drank holy water, I couldn't compel her." Rizza grumbled in utter annoyance. Who drinks holy water anyway? That was so annoying. The royal family had a lot of answering to do because of that little stunt of theirs.

"Yes, that's true. I didn't know about what all the maid had said, Mother had cut you off when you had been talking about it. Still, I wonder why that maid drank holy water, only a select few people know of the effect it has on you. We intentionally don't let that get out, so, that must mean-" Rizza and Pratt met eyes.

"-That whoever did this had to have been a royal." They said simultaneously. "The queen." They added after a short pause.

Talking at the same time made Rizza cringe, but she couldn't deny that they both had the same thought, and now, they had a primary suspect.

"Of course, our guesses are literally based on the fact that the queen looked weird as I was being dragged out. It could have just been a slip." Rizza pointed out the obvious, her hand moving to massage her temples as she spoke. This entire thing was just a pain to even think about. Yet, here they were, sitting and thinking about it.

"Right, but didn't it seem odd? Think about how my mother acted when Drake had died, even after all that went down. She did look tired, but she didn't look sad, and did you even see her cry over him?" Pratt pointed out. Rizza thought back, and had to shake her head. "Exactly. Everything about this is strange. The thing I can't figure out is... why? Why would she be bent on killing Drake, what does she have to gain? More so... why does she have to blame me?" Pratt seemed hurt as he voiced that last thought. The way his voice cracked, it almost sounded... lonely, like he wasn't expecting that sort of betrayal. His hands folded into his lap and he looked at them for a moment, and then it was gone. He looked back up and his expression was normal again.

Rizza assumed having parents was like that, one didn't expect to be betrayed, so, when one did, it was quite the shock. Rizza shook her head softly before moving past the thought. Now was not the time to wallow in emotions. If they were going to clear his name, and possibly prove her benefactor to be a murderer, the thought pained her, then they had to be efficient. If the queen suspected they were on to her, this would be a problem.

Rizza ran her hand through her hair as she thought about things. "Something else doesn't add up, either. When I saw her face... the creepy smile she was doing as I was being taken... my head started hurting, then I got fragmented memories back from my past life." Rizza said softly, her fingers going over her temple to rub it as she thought about it once more. The idea of it was causing her pain already.

Pratt sat up at that. He seemed interested in what she had to say, and even leaned forward a bit, his gaze studying her expression. "You said you don't remember how you died, right? The castle talks about that mystery, how the great wizard was murdered, but no one could figure out how. Then, you were found not even a year later on a doorstep."

Rizza nodded in agreement. Yes, that was how it happened. "I have no memories of how I died, or why. If I could access those... maybe – just maybe – we could find a clue as to what the hell happened." Rizza looked at Pratt.

Pratt nodded in agreement. "So... we need your tome. Maybe it will tell us something about what happened in that life. Maybe you offended someone, or maybe there is a puppeteer in this court, someone pulling the strings."

Rizza smiled softly and nodded. "Never in my life did I

think I'd be solving my own murder, and your brother's, at the same time," she joked, a small laugh escaping her.

"Trust me, this is not how I saw my life going, either." He added. Then, he nodded at her, and she flicked her wrist. He was made invisible to the naked eye, but she could still easily sense him because of his magic.

"To the library, we go," Rizza said softly. She grabbed her cloak, and headed for the door. The hood was up, and as she entered the hall, she looked around calmly. Seeing no one around, she left. Pratt was close at her heels.

So Much Research

Rizza stepped into her wing of the library. She called it 'her wing' because it was where all of her tomes were kept, perfectly preserved throughout the years to suit her needs when she needed them, each one bound in leather and looking similar to the last. It truly was a beautiful collection.

It was too bad that no one but her could read the writing in them, or she may have enjoyed sharing them with others. After all, some of them could have been made into really funny books, with how she had lived out her life. It was too bad that she was too lazy to transcribe them into a common language that could then be made into a book to be shared with the world. Plus, others of the books looked like a five-year-old had scribbled them. Her writing did not always remain refined, her writing was rather bland.

Rizza wasted no time going to the shelf where her latest entries were stored. The latest book was easy to find, and she quickly plucked it off the shelf. The book from this life was kept with her almost at all times, so this recent book was the one from the life before.

"I don't know how much good looking through this will do. The funny thing about being murdered is that it really doesn't leave much time to make journal entries." Rizza pointed out, a small, amused smile on her face as she grabbed the book. She could feel Pratt hovering near her.

"Maybe not," he responded quickly. "But it may give us some clues as to who wanted you dead. If we can get those clues, perhaps we can solve this, as well." It seemed like a logical solution. Part of Rizza felt like they were taking the long way about this.

"You know, if this is all the queen's fault... we could literally just trade out her holy water with regular water for a week, let the stuff drain from her system, then make her tell the truth." Rizza pointed out the obvious once again.

There was silence between them for a moment, the book hovering in Rizza's hand before it was pushed towards her chest by an invisible hand.

"That is true, but, then, we wouldn't solve your murder." He pointed out calmly. Why was he so invested in solving her murder? Rizza was confused. Why did that matter? Was it...? Rizza glanced at the air where he was supposed to be. Was it because he was trying to help her? She couldn't help wondering as it crossed her mind. Yet, the idea seemed ridiculous. Why would he help her that way? What did he have to gain from helping her figure out who killed her in a previous life?

Rizza clutched the book a bit tighter for a brief moment, then moved over to an empty studying table and flipped open the tome. There were plenty of journal entries. She knew he couldn't read the writing, so she was stuck flipping through pages while he sat off to the side and waited.

She was meticulous, though she really didn't have to be so thorough. She had seen this book a million and ten times, and she knew every inch of it well. It wasn't the first time she had gone looking through it for clues.

Today, life has been rather mundane. The king has taken the throne as expected. My magic was hardly needed, and the council succeeded their votes to him with ease after the other princes mysteriously vanished. Shame, really. Soon, the king will wed the new queen. That is something to behold unto itself, but we shall see how it goes. She is a beautiful woman. I was there for her upbringing, after all. Yet, I can't help but wonder if this is the right alliance for her. Still, she asked me to help him, so I did.

I can't help but wonder, now that the wedding is fast approaching, if I did the right thing. The king seems well enough on the throne, he has a strong head on his shoulders, but he never smiles, and the queen seems so unhappy. I love it when she smiles. I can't help but feel like my heart breaks when she loses the joy in her heart that so clearly shines on her face.

The king should make her happy, though, right? That is how this works, is it not?

Rizza cringed as she read the pages. She was such a loser in her past life, such a goody-goody trying to help everyone out, especially the queen, though she had to give him props for helping the queen. Rizza looked down at the pages.

"What did it say?" Pratt questioned. His voice was low, as there were servants walking around, cleaning the area. Rizza glanced up to see if any of them were giving them the time of day. They weren't.

She quickly responded, reading out loud and translating the words in the tome. A snort escaped her yet again as she read over her words about the queen's smile. "You'd think I was a poet, or in love, or both. It is truly just-"

"In love... Maybe that was it, maybe you were in love. Keep reading." Pratt urged on. He didn't seem as put out at the idea of her in love with his mother as she did. Rizza cringed at the idea. She was not in love, especially not with the queen, that was ridiculous.

It's a happy day here in the kingdom, the king and queen finally have an heir. They have been trying vigorously for two years, now. I will never tell them that the king was impotent until I performed some magic, some things don't need to be said. Drake has been born, and he is very healthy. I carefully gifted him resilience in battle in case he is to go to war in the future. That child is well-blessed... and looks just like his mother.

Prince Drake is growing up strong. He's only a year old, and he is already up and walking, and trying to talk. His parents are very proud, and, I must say, so am I. I have not been able to have much interaction with the royal family lately. The king has become rather territorial over his wife and child, not that I can blame him, of course. There have been recent attempts of assassination, and wives are the easiest targets. At least I can tell that the queen is well-loved in that sense. Still, I can't help but see her frowning every now and again. She never used to frown. I wish I could help.

"You really didn't seem to like my father much before this." Pratt pointed out. Only then did Rizza realize she'd still been reading aloud. She snorted softly.

"Yes, well, the man is a stick in the mud. It seems no matter what life I live in, I hate that kind of person." She pointed out casually. She didn't think much of it, and simply shrugged instead.

Still, something was eating at her. "Why do I keep talking about the queen's smile? Could you be right? Could I have been in love with her?" Rizza frowned. That would be weird. Love was such a foreign concept to Rizza in this life, she couldn't imagine it in another.

"It's not impossible, right? I mean, weren't you married in past lives?" Pratt asked practically. Rizza thought about it, then nodded.

"Yes, I suppose in a couple of them I was married. I had never thought of that before. Weird." Rizza hummed softly to herself. "So, supposing I was in love with the queen, what would that mean? Did your father kill me, then, find out about some tryst we had, or something?" She briefly paused. "Oh, god, are you my son?" The thought appalled her, and she could hear Pratt gagging, as well. There was some shuffling then the bookshelf moved as if someone was using it for support rather quickly to avoid falling over from shock. Poor man. The idea clearly wasn't pleasant to either of them.

"Still, that would explain the magic in you... I mean, your magic is so much stronger than any other wizard that has existed, except my own." Rizza pointed out. "Maybe it's because of me..." She couldn't help but wonder.

"Oh, god... please tell me that's not the case, but if it was,

would your death be a mystery, and why would my father raise
you again? Obviously, if he knew, you and Mother would be in a
whole lot of trouble. It's not like he'd raise me at that point, either, so that doesn't seem very likely." Pratt quickly dismissed it
with a whole bunch of sound logic. He really didn't want to think
about being her child. Especially not after literally having been
shoved into an engagement with her.

Rizza didn't know why, but hearing him dismiss the idea
was rather delightful. She was very glad that he wasn't her son,
that would have been creepy as heck, and knowing he wasn't was
better for her.

Rizza let out a sigh, and at about that moment, the door
to the library opened. Rizza glanced up. The library was a place
few came to unless they truly needed to, such as the servants who
maintained the place, so seeing another soul here was strange.
What was even more strange, was that it was the queen who entered.

Rizza watched as she pushed open the door. She seemed to
be holding her head in one hand as she walked, not paying attention to where she was going. As she moved, Rizza tensed. Rizza
wasn't hard to spot, though, and the queen noticed her almost
immediately.

"Rizza... oh, Rizza..." Her voice was soft, but something
flashed in her eyes that Rizza couldn't quite place. Was there
anything behind her eyes, or did Rizza imagine it? She couldn't
tell. Rizza had really never been on guard with the queen before,
this was the first time she was looking at the woman in a way that
was different from normal. Yet, her expression remained carefully
neutral.

"Yes, your highness?" Rizza asked quietly. She was careful
to show respect to the woman, but she wasn't about to cozy up to
her anymore, especially not after being slapped twice like that,
it hurt. She had been wrongly accused of something that she was
pretty sure the queen did, and it was just messed up.

Another part of her, however, wanted to know what her
past life had seen in this woman. Was it her eyes? Her smile?

What? Rizza studied her face carefully. Meanwhile, the queen moved close enough to glance at what Rizza was reading.

"Are you looking over your past lives again?" she asked casually. There wasn't anything pressing in her tone, she just seemed like she was making casual conversation. Still, Rizza felt uneasy, and ended up shutting the tome, not that it changed anything. The queen couldn't read the language she wrote in, which was why she wrote in that language to begin with.

"I am, yes. I figured I would reminisce about a time when people actually trusted me." Rizza couldn't keep the hurt out of her voice. The queen looked at her, mildly shocked, before her face filled with grief.

"Rizza, I am so sorry... I am so sorry I slapped you and blamed you. I was deceived, and I..." The queen looked as if Rizza had wronged her somehow. Rizza had simply pointed out how things had gone, and yet the queen looked as if she was the one who had been wronged. How strange was that?

"What about the maid, the one who lied?" Rizza asked carefully. She had a feeling if the girl had lied, it was on the queen's orders. It may be easier to get to the girl than it was to get to the queen.

"She has been executed for accusing you unjustly," the queen answered immediately. Her face contorted in anger at the mere mention of the girl. "I can't believe she would deceive me like that. I wonder if she held some grudge against you or maybe some small grievance... it doesn't matter. I got revenge for you. How dare she-... just thinking about it makes me so angry," the queen ranted. Her fingers twisted at the fabric of her dress as she spoke.

Rizza sighed softly at the mention that the girl had been killed. "Damn... If she was still alive, maybe I could have asked her a few questions about why, or even gotten her to spill the truth after the holy water had left her system." Rizza glanced at the queen.

There was an obvious moment of hesitation as the queen heard about the holy water before her brows furrowed together.

"What do you mean about the holy water?" she asked, very carefully.

"The holy water that was in her system. She had drunk holy water, or she wouldn't have been able to lie while compelled," Rizza replied. Her gaze locked onto the queen. "Though, what bothers me is that I don't know how she knew." The queen looked at Rizza, and surprise washed over her face. She had no words for a moment, then, when she did speak, it was with obvious uncertainty.

"Well... that's a good question. Only a select few know of the effects holy water has against you. Maybe she drank some on accident or something, mistook it for regular water?" The queen offered.

Rizza shrugged before looking back down at her tome. There was a feeling in the pit of her stomach that she really didn't like at that moment, the feeling of betrayal, of having someone lie right to your face, and act like you didn't know it.

Did everyone in the castle think of her as a complete joke? Did they think that she didn't know what was going on around there? Rizza stared down at the book before an idea sprung into her mind.

"You know... I guess I really was in love with you in my past life." Rizza laughed slightly, trying to make it sound like she was amused with herself. Bile bit into the back of her throat, and she forced it down.

"In love... with me?" The queen seemed shocked by the notion. "What do you mean?" she continued on before looking at the tome. An obvious look flashed across her face, one of discomfort and... that sadistic look from before.

"Yeah, I wrote about you a lot in this tome, constantly talking about your wishes, your life. It really makes it hard to figure out what went on in mine. I guess I was lovestruck, so, thanks for taking care of me in this one, and sorry if I made things hard for you before," Rizza offered. She was carefully watching the queen's expressions. The queen seemed mostly confused. Rizza didn't want to give up, though. She didn't want the queen to get away with this crime of framing her son, but now it seemed like she may. Rizza was worried this went deeper, she just didn't want to admit it to herself.

"You weren't a trouble to me, Rizza. In your past life, you were my support, my pillar, my strength." She offered a slight smile, as if the memory brought her joy. "You were my closest ally, so of course I would raise you now that you have been reborn. I just wish we had found whoever had murdered you." There was pity in her voice as she spoke of the murder. Rizza sighed and nodded before changing topics.

"So, why did you come to the library? Looking for anything in particular?" she asked curiously. Rizza didn't know what else to change the topic to, so she questioned why the queen had interrupted her. The queen looked rather sheepish as she heard the question, almost as if she'd been caught doing something she wasn't supposed to. Rizza waited.

"Well... to be honest... I was looking for Pratt." The queen seemed slightly upset about the idea. "I just-... I can't believe he would-... my baby boys." Rizza watched as the queen seemed to almost crumple. Yet, tears didn't spill. If a mother was upset about her son's fighting, especially to this extent, wouldn't she cry? Actually cry? Why wasn't the queen crying? Rizza couldn't explain it, she just knew that the more she watched this, the more she didn't trust the queen. She couldn't shake it.

"Why would Pratt be in the library?" Rizza chuckled softly. "Seems a bit too obvious, doesn't it?"

The queen seemed surprised at that idea before nodding. "I suppose you're right. It's just... I know he loved it here, and I already checked the burnt part of the garden. He wasn't there, either. I was just hoping that maybe if I got to him first... I could... I don't know, talk to him? Save him? I'm a mother, after all..." The queen sighed. She seemed to have aged ten years during all of this. Rizza couldn't help but feel that this was superficial. Is it because she already knew the truth? Why did this feel different then when she had dealt with Pratt? Was it because, with Pratt, she had only been mostly certain it was his fault? Now, with the queen, Rizza didn't know what to say. She was truly at a loss.

"Well... maybe you'll get to him first. If I run into him, he won't be able to run anymore. It's too bad I was in chains the last time, or I would have stopped him," Rizza replied earnestly. She would have stopped him. He would have had a chance to flee. Now? They were working together to prove his mother was the murderer, not him.

Rizza wondered how weird it must be to hear two people talking about him as if he wasn't right there. Granted, the queen didn't know he was there, but she did. She knew very well he was still off to her left, listening to everything they said. A mischievous smile crept up her face at the thought.

"You know... even if we can't find him, one good thing would come of this. There won't be an ugly king on the throne." Rizza snickered until she felt a jolt of pain in her calf. She winced.

"Rizza!" the queen scolded her. "You look no different than he, you shouldn't tease his looks. That isn't nice." The queen was quick to chastise her, and Rizza did feel slightly bad. After all, the queen was right, she looked similar to him. How could she go around making fun of his looks when her looks weren't to die for, either?

Rizza shrugged before picking the tome up, and putting it back on the shelf. She let out a small laugh. She could just tell Pratt what it said line for line back in the room. This trip was a waste of time.

"Well, I think I've done enough reading for today. Good luck with looking for your son. If I see him, I'll be sure to let you know," Rizza lied through her teeth as she looked back at the queen.

The queen gave her a weak smile before sending her off. She nodded calmly, and headed for the door. She could feel Pratt close on her heels. This trip to the library wasn't a complete bust, at least. They got the chance to talk to the queen. Would she suspect them because of all of this?

Them? Rizza. She would suspect Rizza because of that questioning, Pratt wasn't even visible. Rizza sighed. She needed to go back to her room, and they needed to regroup. There had to be a way to get this done more efficiently, and the two of them would figure it out.

Is it Really That Easy?

Rizza shut the door behind the both of them, and threw back up the ward before dropping the illusionary spell that hid Pratt. When she turned to see his face, it wasn't pretty. He looked like he'd been fighting nightmares and, overall, just looked upset. Was it because of his mother, even though she had said nice things? Perhaps... she didn't know.

Rizza glanced at Pratt. She waited for him to say something. While waiting, she moved over to her chair in the lounge, and sat down. Her fingers went to rub her temples softly as she thought about all that was going on. There had to be a way to solve her murder.

She wasn't really worried about proving the queen guilty when everyone thought it was Pratt. She wouldn't tell Pratt, but that was easy. All she had to do there was have someone replace her holy water for about a week. After that, she could just make her tell the truth. Being magical had its means. She could probably get Pratt to-... no, he couldn't touch the holy water, so they'd need someone they could trust. Huh, maybe this would be more difficult than it seemed. Especially considering no one liked Rizza for her past transgressions and now, more recently, her wishy-washy disposition on whom the culprit was.

Rizza frowned softly as she thought about that. Finding someone the two of them could trust? They needed to at least set that part of the plan in motion. Once the queen was discovered as the one who framed Pratt for who knows what reason, this would all be over. Pratt could go back to his life, and Rizza? She could go back to her mountains.

Rizza nodded at the idea. That was a solid plan. She liked her mountains, far away from people, far away from prying eyes and loud noises, away from those who would condemn her for her looks among other things.

"Why-... How could she do that?" Pratt asked aloud. It drew Rizza out of her self-pondering, and prompted her to look up at him. Her eyebrow arched slightly as she did, confusion written all over her face.

"How could she... do what?" Rizza finally asked, her confusion no less obvious. What were they talking about? Had they been talking? Could he read minds? Rizza flashed through her consciousness and didn't detect another soul. No, so what was he talking about?

"How could she... act like she cared about me? Was she even looking for me? My mother can't be so naïve as to think I'd return to my favorite places after being labeled a criminal, could she? So, then, what was she doing?" Pratt seemed confused and upset. He paced through the hallway, his feet making soft noises on the carpet as he shuffled across it. This was all out of place, all so very strange to begin with.

"Wait, your favorite places... the library... and the garden?" Rizza asked softly. How had they never run into each other before? Those were her favorite places, as well.

"And the windows that look out on the gardens." Pratt added absentmindedly.

"So... you like the places I like?" Rizza inquired. She lost track again. The prince was before her, looking rather decent and supposedly not a murderer, so she wondered... Rizza tilted her head softly and watched him.

"Yes... Wait... what?" Pratt seemed to come out of his daze for a moment to turn his head and look at Rizza. His eyebrows were drawn together as if questioning something before they rose, and a look of mockery crossed his face. The realization seemed to have struck him at the same time that they both liked the places the other visited frequently. Though, the way he looked at that moment argued that he was not doing it on purpose to stalk her, rather a harmless coincidence.

"You can't be serious." He said softly before scoffing. He ran a hand through his hair and shot her another look before shaking his head. "I spend weeks trying to court you, trying to get us to get along, so that maybe this marriage bullshit wouldn't be so bad, and now you have taken an interest in me? Now you are thinking that we may be similar? Seriously, Rizza?" Pratt couldn't help the laughter that bubbled up from his throat. He ended up laughing and shaking his head, but it wasn't a laughter of joy. It sounded more distressed.

Rizza frowned as he laughed at her. She looked away from Pratt as she felt her cheeks heating up. "No. I wasn't taking interest in you... get your head out of the gutter. I was merely wondering how we could share so many common places, and never bump into one another." Rizza explained the interest away quickly. She buried her thoughts that they could have similarities. They were clearly just good places to visit, anyone with half a brain would visit where they did often.

Pratt stared at her. He seemed dubious about the whole thought before snorting and shaking his head again. "We wouldn't have run into each other. If you forget, I'm about two years younger than you. Beyond that, I didn't start going to the library and those areas 'til after you left."

Pratt's words made sense. If they were never in those areas at the same time, then of course she would never have run into him. Even knowing the other royal children were about, Rizza didn't really 'run into' them at all. They were usually kept secluded to study and learn, away from prying eyes and annoying adults, but mostly away from those that they could annoy or offend.

The court didn't seem to have a lot of welcoming environments for children. In fact, it seemed to almost loathe their existence. Rizza couldn't imagine growing up adhering to that strict social custom. She had always been a part of the court. They may not have enjoyed it, but she was always a part of it. In fact, Rizza was always a part of it because no one could really stop her from being so. No one could tell her no; she had the power. They just had the titles.

"Wait... did you say... bullshit wedding? So you didn't want to be married, either? Then why the HELL were you pushing it so hard!?" Rizza suddenly got mad. If he didn't want to marry her, either, why was he punishing them both? What good did that do for anyone? All it did was force two people who weren't compatible to be together. There was something fundamentally wrong with that idea. Pratt stared at her as if she had two heads. His look of absolute abjuration was obvious, and it made Rizza bristle. Why was he looking at her like she was an idiot? She was no idiot, not in her mind, anyway.

"Are you serious? Of course I didn't want to marry you!" he snapped, his tension showing as he did so. "Why would I want to marry you? You literally ruin everything you touch, you attack anyone with zero provocation, and you treat human lives like a game. All because... what? You get to live again? I'm so glad none of us matter to you, but we only get one life. We only get one chance. If you fuck up, you can do it all again, so, no, I didn't want to marry some god-complex child with an over-inflated ego." Pratt looked as if he'd heard the greatest joke ever, the idea that he'd actually liked her. The idea was inconceivable to him.

His words cut deep into her. Her gaze widened as she listened to him speak. No one had ever talked to her like that before, and, hearing it, Rizza hurt. Rizza bit the inside of her lip. She could feel blood pooling into her mouth as she bit a little too hard and caused the points of her teeth to dig into her flesh. No one had ever said... anything... that cruel to her before. They only ever dared speak behind her back in a way she could ignore and pin them on fear and cowardice.

Rizza looked away from him. A small laugh escaping her. Why was she laughing? That wasn't funny. That was downright cruel and mean. How could she laugh at something like that? Rizza couldn't even really believe her ears. He was... so straightforward.

"I see... well if you felt that way... then why? Why bother?" Rizza's voice was hoarse as she asked. There was tension between them now. It had been there since they met, but it seemed more tense now. It seemed more painful now. Right when they were about to get along, it got blown to hell again.

"Because, as a prince, I don't decide my marriage. I just thought I could make it a little less painful, maybe fix some of your nastier habits." He replied calmly. She could hear clothing rustle as if he was fixing himself up, as if he was straightening his clothing to get rid of the dirt he had just thrown all over the room.

Rizza continued to notice the coppery taste of blood in her mouth. The bitter tinge to it grounded her, in a way, but it hurt. His words hurt. His actions hurt. It all hurt. Rizza let out a small, self-mocking laugh.

"Right... because the monster needs to be trained... get out," Rizza said softly. The wards around the room dropped. The air in the place took a sharp change as Rizza processed her emotions. She could not help the fact that he was right, nor could she deny that he was. However, she was not going to let someone treat her like that. She knew she deserved the punishments she'd gotten in the past and she was now working to right some of her wrongs by at least absolving him of guilt. However, he took his emotional moment with his mommy problems out on her and made her feel as miserable as he felt. That was wrong. She could feel Pratt's panic as he realized that she was mad, but she didn't care. The pain she felt was too much at that moment.

One thing Rizza knew, beyond a shadow of a doubt, was that she was really, really bad at dealing with her feelings. She didn't like being in pain, and knew if he didn't leave, she'd lash out at him.

"I beg your pardon?" the prince asked. "I was merely telling the truth. You have been pushing it for so long, I... suppose I blew up a bit." He defended his word choice, defended his actions. Some part of Rizza felt that maybe he had the right to say those things to her. Maybe he did get the chance to be that jerk, all because she couldn't be nice to start with. Part of her felt that maybe that was the case. The other part of her was feeling really low, like someone had just tread all over her, and then kicked her for good measure.

"Get... out.. I will solve my own murder. You want to free yourself of guilt? Get someone to switch out the queen's holy water with regular water for a week. After that, just make her tell the truth. I don't give a damn. Just leave, I want nothing more to do with you." Rizza's voice was soft. She sounded eerily calm, and the silence of the room only punctuated that fact.

Yet, Rizza felt empty inside. She felt hurt, and emotional, and all sorts of things. Pain radiated through her like nothing she could describe. Why did it feel so wrong to be called out like that? Was he not the same as her? Maybe he wasn't. They looked the same, they had the same interests, but they weren't the same. He didn't have a god complex, as he said, he wasn't self-centered, he put the kingdom before himself. That was why he had the right to claim himself better than her. The reasons he... Rizza felt more flesh tear as she bit her lip. She noticed something past her lips beyond the taste of blood, though. It was salty, and watery.

Rizza reached up to touch her face. Tears? Why was she crying? She hadn't been hurt, no one had been murdered... or, maybe she had been hurt. His words had cut her like a knife, and it had caused tears. Rizza rubbed at her cheeks to get rid of them.

She realized Pratt was still standing there. Her gaze went over to him for a moment. He looked shocked. She was bleeding slightly and crying. The want for self-destruction was obvious within her. She didn't deal well with his words at all. She'd already given him the solution to his stupid problem so seeing him standing there only hurt her more. Especially because the way he looked right now, as if she'd wronged him by being hurt only made it worse. She hated the feeling of being the villain, even if she was one.

"Rizza I..." He caught himself on his words. Tripping himself over what to say as his brain raced. Was he sorry? Who knew? Maybe in some part, some way, he was, but he sure as hell didn't seem like it. What did one say after totally wrecking someone that way?

"You have one more chance. Leave, or I call the palace guards." She said softly. Her voice was muffled as she tried to conceal the wreck she had made of her face. She carefully stood up, and moved away from the lounge, towards the bedroom.

"Rizza, please..." Pratt's voice was broken at this point. He seemed to have realized his mistake, but it was already made. He could only watch as she walked away from him. The sound of the bedroom door clicking shut behind her was all that was heard in the room.

When Rizza did bother to come out of the room, wounds healed, and tired of feeling sorry for herself in this life, he was gone. That didn't matter, she told herself. She wanted him gone. She wanted him to leave. She pushed away all the bitterness of the current moment, and focused on something else.

Rizza needed to regain her memories. Was she going to help the prince with his problem? No, he could solve that on his own. She thought she was going to, but he was a jerk, so that was out. Of course Rizza had her flaws. Everyone had their flaws. That wasn't really a surprise. It wasn't a shock that Rizza wasn't perfect, so why did he have to call her out?

Rizza summoned Kit, and got some new clothing. She changed out of what she'd been wearing earlier, and began to walk the halls of the castle. There were fragments of her memory that she had gotten back, small things that gave her clues to unlock the rest of the memories. One of them was a room, at the end of one of the halls. She had a feeling it was her old room.

Memories

Rizza moved through the halls. She didn't waste time greeting people as they passed her by, or anything. Life seemed... colorless... to her at the moment, but she had a mission. She had a plan, and she would see it through. Though, she couldn't help but listen for the sounds of guards. If Pratt was caught... they'd all be running.

Rizza never heard anything of the sort, so she didn't have to worry or ponder on it too long. Instead, she focused on the task at hand: finding her memories. Rizza rounded a corner, heading for the room, when she almost slammed into Lance, the guard who had been so nice to her all that time. The boy who had stood by her when everyone else turned their back.

"I-... Oh, I'm sorry..." Lance said softly. His voice was nervous as he saw her. Rizza could see he still had bruises and cuts on him from being beaten senseless. The poor boy was lucky to still be alive after all that had gone down. Rizza wondered if he hated her for it. Pratt's words about not caring about the lives of those who only lived once hit her again. She stared at Lance and suddenly the wounds he'd received because of her seemed that much more painful to look at. They were her fault.

"No, I am sorry. I wasn't watching where I was going... are you... uhm... okay?" Rizza decided to inquire of his wellbeing. The poor boy had been through hell. She wondered, truly wondered, if he would hate her for it. It was obvious that he should, right? Rizza held out hope that, maybe, she wasn't alone.

Lance flinched away from her slightly. That gave Rizza the thought that she needed. She nodded her head softly, and moved to move past him. If he was scared of her again, it was better that she get out of his presence.

A soft hand landed on her shoulder. Granted, it wasn't

literally very soft because it was covered in armor, but the gesture behind it was very soft. She turned back to look at Lance, and he offered her a wry smile.

"You... didn't just abandon me to die. I heard the king say that you asked about me. I'm sure that was partly why they remembered to let me go. So... thank you, Rizza." He said softly. His words were firm.

Rizza couldn't help but wonder how such a boy could have ended up in such trouble with someone like her, how silly it was. Though, he did seem to know she didn't just abandon him. That was good, at least.

She watched him steadily for a moment before reaching out to put a hand on his. Magic surged between the two of them, and his wounds slowly faded. She could feel cracked ribs setting and bruises fading as she worked her magic. When she was done, he was as good as new, probably a little bit better. She fixed the elbow that had been bothering him for a couple of years, as well.

"I am sorry, for the part I played in getting you involved. I am sorry you ever had to deal with those accusations or those assaults. If it had been up to me, you never would have been involved. so I am sorry," Rizza said softly. She offered him a light smile that didn't quite reach her eyes. She couldn't bring herself to be happy that he still liked her. As Pratt had pointed out, she ruined everything she touched. Lance had almost died because of her.

"I-... Wow, I feel good... did you heal my elbow?" Lance seemed to disregard her distress. He moved his arm before offering a broad smile. All the fear, once again, washed away from his face. He no longer seemed to care as he looked at Rizza with a charming smile. This little seamstress's son was quite the character. "Don't you fret about it, Rizza. Where are you off to? Maybe I can help you out a bit. I know Prince Pratt is still on the loose, wouldn't want to run into him by myself." Lance offered up his services to her almost immediately. His hidden meaning being the fact that he, perhaps, did not want beaten up again, this time with magic. Since he'd gotten involved with Rizza he'd already gotten hurt. The easiest protection he could find was the most powerful witch in the realm which he was beginning to realize was unorthodox but not technically a bad person.

Rizza watched him for a moment. He seemed eager to help out, and Rizza really didn't think being alone with her thoughts at that moment was a good idea. She hesitated for a brief second before nodding her head.

"Alright, you can come along. I don't see what harm it would do to have you along with me, anyway. I think it may even be... well, fun." Rizza smiled softly before she offered out her arm.

He linked arms with her, and they headed down the hall together. Some of the weight that had been holding her back seemed to lift away as he did. She had at least one friend among all this chaos, one person who did not resent her in the entire world. That was more amazing than anything she'd felt in a while.

She filled him in on what she was doing as they walked, talking of how the matter was of dire need to be solved. It was part of the reason she was okay with coming back to the castle. Now that she had so many of her memories back, and so much of her power, it was easier to solve this murder. She had been waiting for a good time. This seemed as good as any.

Lance didn't really seem surprised, he'd heard of the great Wizard she was in her past life. Even he couldn't help but point out how much more likeable she was as a guy. Was that something to do with the gender, she wondered, or was it just that her personality was different when she was male? Or was it just in that life that she was compassionate and likeable? Rizza couldn't be certain. Regardless, Rizza couldn't help but jab Lance in the ribs. Too bad it wasn't painful for him because of his armor. For her, on the other hand, it had hurt her finger. Metal didn't work well for making jabs.

Lance laughed as he watched her pout while comforting her poor finger by cradling it against her torso. At least she could count on him to be her friend. The thought gave her consolation as they finally reached the wing and the room that Rizza had been looking for. She usually got lost in the castle. Yet, this time, she knew exactly where she was.

"Isn't this the door you led us to the first day we met?" Lance asked curiously when he saw where they were at. He seemed to have a good memory, as well. Rizza only realized he was right after he pointed it out. She looked up at the door. It had been the one they had gone to originally.

"Would you look at that... maybe my past self was trying to tell me something," Rizza said casually. A small laugh escaped her before she shook her head. Perhaps she should learn to just blindly wander around from now on. Who knew what her past selves were trying to get her to remember?

Rizza touched the door lightly, magic surging through the room. She realized, as she cast her magic out to scan the area, that not only was the room not occupied, it couldn't be. There was a magical seal on the door that prevented someone from getting in. She could tell that the seal was strong enough that only she could break it or even examine the room with her magic. If anyone else tried this they would probably wind up with a nasty surprise.

Rizza frowned. "Why would I lock my own door before my death...?" she wondered softly. Her gaze went to the door as she slowly broke the seal on it. Lance stood to the side and watched, and a myriad of rainbow-like colors danced across the hard wooden door.

Finally, after quite some time, Rizza got the door to unlock. A satisfying click could be heard as the door swung open for them. What greeted them? Over twenty years of dust.

Rizza coughed as the dust flooded out of the room. There were no windows in the place, so it was totally dark until Lance found a candle to light and lit the lamps in the place. Rizza couldn't help but wave a hand in front of her face as she walked into the room.

"Remind me to make a note in my tomes that if I ever spell-seal a room... to make sure dust can't enter the damn thing either." Rizza grumbled. She was utterly annoyed by the idea that there was so much dust around.

"Hey, make a note in your tomes to..." Lance immediately began to remind her.

"Shut the hell up." Rizza laughed slightly, and Lance gave her a cheeky grin.

After that, they turned back to the task at hand. Rizza carefully sealed the door shut behind them once more before she looked around her room. The place seemed more or less normal, there was a writing desk, a basic bed, some clothing, nothing really out of the ordinary. There were even some cute figurines sitting on a shelf above her bed, and plenty of books.

Rizza frowned as she looked around. On a cursory glance, there wasn't anything too interesting about it, so why had she sealed it off? Obviously, she was hiding something. Rizza moved into the room. The first thing she did was to look under her bed. Her fingers roamed through the dust as she looked for something.

"What are you doing?" Lance asked curiously.

"I am looking for a hidden panel or something. I usually put them under my bed. At least, in this life, I do, I don't know about previous lives," Rizza offered her explanation. She continued her search. There was usually a hole or something that gave away the hidden panel. She wasn't finding anything, though.

From behind her, after about five minutes of searching, Rizza heard a distinct click. She turned her head to see Lance pulling open a wall panel above the writing desk that had, at first glance, looked like just a painting.

Rizza paused, and then stood up. She was covered in dust. A soft cough escaped her as she moved towards him and towards the wall panel. By this point, they were both beginning to look like beggars off the street rather than a noble witch and her guard companion.

"Right, well... good work... you're better at this detective stuff than I am. By the way, how did they implicate you in my supposed crime?" Rizza asked as she moved to look through the contents of the wall. At least she had properly warded that cubby. Rizza paused in her actions to look a t the door. It was still open. Without much thought she used a small wave of magic to pull it shut and lock it once more. She didn't want someone unsavory seeing what they were about to look at, no matter what it was.

"How did they implicate me? Oh, some maid randomly came at me with two guards, pointed at me and said 'that's him, he's the one Rizza paid'. The next thing I knew, I was getting my ass kicked and dragged off to the dungeon. I don't really know how to explain it." Lance rubbed the back of his neck as he moved out of Rizza's way so she could get to the hatch. He had seen the door shut on its own but decided not to comment on the eerie, silent action. "Either way... I don't blame you. It sounds like you didn't get treated much better than I did." He had heard about the use of chains that left her raw and bleeding. Though he didn't know how it happened or how it worked, he'd heard about it.

That was another thing that bothered Rizza. Which royal took the time to put holy water on her chains? She knew it was a royal because no one else really knew about that problem. It was a headache to think about.

Rizza pushed the thought aside. She let out a soft 'mm' of recognition before digging into the cubby. She found all sorts of different things in it: little trinkets she had kept, a really pretty pocket watch, and then, something she didn't expect.

Rizza carefully pulled the small booklet out from the other stacks of paper that were there. The poems, she didn't even want to read, as she had a feeling that they would be lovey. God, she was such a sap in her past life. Rizza carefully examined the book in her hand. It wasn't big, it was actually quite small, but it seemed to look the same as the tomes she wrote. She frowned.

"What's that?" Lance asked. He looked at the book in her hand curiously. Nothing about it seemed abnormal for him. He didn't understand what would be so special about a book. Of course, he had probably never seen her wing of the library with all her tomes in it. He wouldn't put those things together without that knowledge.

Rizza glanced up at him for a moment before looking back at the book. "A tome... that was hidden away from the royals. Odd, I wonder if... I was hoping I'd be reborn or something..."

Rizza said softly.

She was hoping that coming into this room, beyond finding clues for what happened, she'd be able to gain memories back. The book jogged something; a small headache was starting, but it wasn't a completed memory, not yet.

Rizza sat on the bed, ignoring the dirt that was there, and flipped open the tome. Lance stood off to the side. The place he positioned himself was between Rizza and the door; once a guard, always a guard.

The queen is beautiful. Of course, I cannot write about this in my normal books, I can never let the king know of the love I hold for his wife, such things could prove dire. What would he think? I am ridiculous, and he can never learn of this.

Soon, Prince Drake will be two. It truly is amazing how time flies, he has gotten so big already. He has shown an interest in swordplay, playing with his wooden practice sword every chance he gets. He even cries if it's not by his side.

Reading about baby Drake was weird, especially because she could almost see what Drake was doing. It was as if the memories were aiding the mental picture the notes were giving. She ran her fingers across the page with a small smile. How ironic, yet wonderful. Though the idea that he was already two before she was even reborn made her remember that was several years older than her as well. Why was she allowed to play with him but Pratt had not been allowed to play with them? She had a feeling it had nothing to do with age and more to do with the fact that the royal family probably thought no one but Drake could be fit to be her playmate... or maybe they were shielding their other children.

Rizza skipped forward into the book, flipping forward a couple of pages until something new caught her eye.

Something has been off lately. The queen has seemed... on edge, as if she is hiding something, but I cannot tell what. She won't talk to me, and it doesn't seem like the king knows, either.

I will have to try and talk to her again. I doubt I'll get very far, but if I can't talk to her, who will she have to talk to? I am her confidant, her best friend, I am the one who is always there for her. I have to try.

Rizza's eyebrows drew together as pain assailed her head. This was the brink of a memory, and she knew it. She pushed on, skipping forward a bit more even as Lance's voice echoed in the background with concern.

I spoke with the queen. Rather, I tried to, but all she did was get angry. Why? What is so unscrupulous about her confidant checking in on her? The days have been getting progressively worse as the queen grows more anxious. I fear it won't be long 'till I find out what happened, and... I doubt it will be good.

Well, I was right, it wasn't good. I do not have much time to write, as I fear that I have been discovered. Yet, I need my next life to know about this. Should I find this tome, should this room be found by me, I need my future self to realize that I ran out of time. Some things are not meant to be discovered. It seems that the queen was not faithful. Not only am I not the only sorcerer she has kept around... it seems the other fool fell in love, as well.

Rizza's head began to split from the pain she was feeling while reading. There was no more in the journal, but the room began to spin for her. Rizza cringed as she felt herself blacking out. The tome tumbled from her fingers onto the stone floor as she hit the bed.

Lance felt his heart drop as he watched the witch convulse and fall back onto the bed. He moved towards her as her eyes rolled back and she passed out. However, all he could do was wait. No one knew they were there and he knew Rizza wanted to keep it that way since the door was firmly shut. So, he stood guard and waited.

A Taste of the Past

Rizza's memories swam at her all at once, her vision blurry as if she was in a dark tunnel, yet she could hear and see things just fine. Then, the room cleared, it looked as if she was actually there. She watched as a man approached the queen.

The setting was ambiguous, though, it was late at night, and only dim candles lit the hall. Rizza could tell they were in an obscure part of the castle that hardly any but the servants went to, but why? What was here? Why was she here?

Rizza could see the queen in the distance. Her hood was up, but Rizza knew on instinct that it was her, but she didn't know who the man with her was. They seemed to be having a heated discussion, and when Rizza cast a bit of magic to listen in, she could tell why.

"Why do I have to remain a secret? Why can't you just tell them?" the man asked. His voice was a terse whisper, and he seemed extremely upset. His body language showed nervousness and anxiety, but also a bit of force and anger, as if he was really fed up with whatever had been going on lately.

"I am married, that's why. What good will it do to tell them about you? You will just lose your head. I am the queen. What, did you expect to be part of some harem or something?" The queen whispered back. Her voice was also terse, but she sounded more stressed than anything. It was as if she had her back in a corner.

Rizza could remember how she had felt then, the feeling of dread crept up as she realized the reason the queen was here so late: she must be having an affair. It was Rizza's misfortune to spot her in the hall that night. Rizza watched her walk, and wondered where she had been going. She remembered now, she'd seen what had happened.

The next part didn't shock her, Rizza had seen this all

before, this was nothing more than a memory. The man grabbed the queen. She didn't do much to resist as she was pulled into his embrace.

"I just want you. You alone are enough for me. I just wish... you would see me the same." The man responded, his fangs flashing in the light. Fangs? That's right... he's a wizard, just like Rizza had been.

Rizza remembered the way his teeth glittered in the light. She couldn't see his hair or his eyes, but she knew he had black hair, she knew he had gold flecks along his face, and she had a very strong suspicion that he would look remarkably like an older Pratt.

Rizza's vision swam.

I Remember

Rizza gasped as she woke up. Lance was standing over her, worried, as he held smelling salts under her nose. She looked down at them before pushing them away. They smelled god awful. Why did humans use those stupid things?

They were good for one thing, though: they definitely woke Rizza up. Rizza could feel the pain in her head, the memory now pulled together fully, yet forcefully. It felt as if someone had literally stitched it together, then stapled it into her head. She remembered it all: why she had written so quickly, why things had happened. She had written just enough to trigger her own memory. That was... quite the feat, and the gamble. If she hadn't remembered it, she never would have solved her own murder, since it was the only evidence left behind of the damn crime.

Rizza groaned as she held her head, and Lance was quick to help her sit up as she did so.

"Lady Rizza? Are you alright? What happened? You blacked out and I-... I didn't know what to do." Lance seemed utterly worried. His face was pale in the dim yellow lighting, and he looked utterly beside himself with worry. He had been calling her name as she read, but she had not answered. When she collapsed, he almost had a heart attack.

Rizza couldn't help but smile as she reached out delicately to pat his head. He was such a good boy, he worked so hard on being there for her, how could she not appreciate his efforts? This entire time spent in the castle felt like such a waste, though. If she had just found the room years ago, just looked in the journal... or maybe it hadn't been time. She did start out life not knowing how to properly use her magic. Perhaps it was a self-defense not to go to the room, a subconscious action to preserve her life.

"I got my memories from my past life back. Not all of

them... but I have the crucial ones. Lance... this kingdom could be in danger, or, rather, the royal family." Her gaze shot up as she looked at the guard. "Will you help me?"

Lance looked at her. His words were caught in his throat. He didn't know what to say, suddenly being asked to help someone, without being given a reason why. Lance's mouth parted like a gaping fish for a moment before he closed it and swiftly nodded his head.

"Good, because we have a lot of things to do. First things first, I need you to find out if someone has begun switching the queen's holy water out for regular water. If they haven't, start doing so. If they have... leave it be, and just report back. This is important. We only have so much time. If Pratt is killed before we succeed, it will just add to the king's guilt."

"Of course. I will do whatever you ask." Lance was quick to agree. He was on his feet in a second. However, he hesitated soon after as he turned back to her. "Wait... don't we want Pratt dead?"

"No, he's just a simple idiot with a shitty mother." Rizza replied swiftly, and waved off Lance's new series of questions. "No time for that."

Rizza realized how things all tied in now. Rizza had known too much, she had died for knowing too much. The queen had realized Rizza knew of the newborn prince's origins and had silenced her. She could have easily proven Pratt to not be the king's, his existence alone was proof, but why had the queen let Pratt live, and, better yet, where was that other mage?

Rizza knew something was wrong. She knew something was terribly wrong as she got to her feet. Lance was faster than her, though. He was already moving towards the door because of her instructions and lack of will to explain things to him in detail.

"No!" Rizza snapped. Her gaze went to the door as she quickly grabbed him. He wasn't able to touch the door handle before she was on him. Thank god. Rizza quickly cast out her magic to test the area. As she had suspected, there was a trap waiting for them when they opened that damned door, and he'd know the second they touched it.

Rizza snorted. "Some two-bit mage thinks he can fight me, and with the same trick, no doubt. Watch this," Rizza grumbled, her hand splayed out with her palm facing the ground. Her words were punctuated with a soft thud followed by a muffled cry of surprise. Then, she glanced at Lance again, giving him a soft nod as Lance opened the door.

On the other side of the door was a series of cross bolts hovering in midair, as if they had been launched, but then frozen. Behind them stood a mage, frozen in place and fading from his invisibility as he did.

Rizza stepped forward, out of the door, and sneered softly.

"Have we kept you waiting long? I'm sure twenty years of not being able to break my spell on that door has been quite the problem for you, but, honestly, twenty years, and you couldn't come up with a new trap? I'm truly disappointed," Rizza said softly. She pulled down the man's cloak, and was greeted with a very familiar face.

"Prince Pratt?" Lance asked immediately. His eyes widened as he almost called for help. He was so confused now, because Rizza had just said he was not the enemy, but now he was standing there trying to kill them. Rizza silenced him softly and shook her head.

"No, this is not Pratt, this is his father, Carl, a low-life mage who never could stand being in my shadow," Rizza responded earnestly. There was enough freedom for Carl to exhibit a sneer on his face, but his vocal cords were muted. "And, this will be fun." Rizza looked over at Carl. She didn't need him to confess. She pondered just killing him straight out, but that seemed like too good of an end for a man who destroyed a family with his greed, got an innocent boy killed, and almost got his own son murdered as well. All for what? Love? A trifling thing, especially when this so-called love was for a woman who was just using him for better bedroom prowess than what she got in her own marriage.

Rizza stared at him, contemplating her options. She could just kill him, or... Rizza smiled. "Go get rope... and douse it in holy water, Lance. It's the only thing that dampens a witch's magic, and then, meet me in my room."

Rizza had a plan. Her finger lifted into the air, and she made a zipper motion. Suddenly, Carl was standing as still as a plank, both feet together, hands at either side, and head stiffly in place, as if he had been put in a body bag. Rizza smiled.

"Who-... Isn't Pratt the king's son?" Lance asked. He was totally confused at this point. He was still a stage behind where Rizza was in the planning and had not yet caught up to what she'd asked him to do. How was there suddenly another man that looked just like Pratt? Now that Lance looked closer, he could tell the obvious differences between the two, but, still, Pratt was a prince. The Queen had...

"No. The queen cheated on the king. Now, hurry up. We have things to do. Go get the rope." Rizza glanced at Lance again. He finally registered what she had requested of him, and quickly nodded his head. He really needed to stop asking questions. This was too far above his pay grade, and way too dangerous for his liking.

Lance left without further delay, which left Rizza and Carl alone. She snorted as she looked at him, before carefully taking control of the magic that bound him, and using it to not only levitate him behind her, but also turn him invisible so no one would see that she had company.

Rizza grinned. He was trying to take her on, what a fool's errand, and with the same trick, no less. Over twenty years ago, she had died once by that exact trick. She had only lived just long enough to place a ward on the door. No wonder the place was dingy inside. After that? Darkness, and a new life.

The queen had probably kept her close to keep an eye on her. If she discovered anything, Carl, and the queen herself, would know about it. Perhaps they were hoping Rizza would have unlocked the door at a younger age, one where she couldn't fight back as easily, silly, hopeful fools that they were. They should have known better than to think that Rizza would be so compliant even in her ignorance.

Rizza was grinning gleefully. It was amazing what all this chaos had caused. She had found the murderer and even solved a two-decade old case. Rizza couldn't be happier with herself, but, at the same time, it was bittersweet. The cost of discovering all of this was, of course, the feelings resurfacing. She had loved the queen, without reserve. If the queen had just given her the time of day... No, that was a villainous thought. She knew better. She still would have given the queen away, and her little partner, too.

Rizza just could not fathom why the queen would fall for this bloke instead of herself. Her features had been much better in the previous life. Granted, Pratt and his father cut a nice figure, but still. Rizza would like to believe that being taller than him, and a bit more muscular was a bonus. Oh, and the fact that her magic was way stronger also helped.

One nice thing about this, though? Rizza was now certain that Pratt was not her son. That was a slow relief for her. She had been certain he was at one point. At another point she wasn't sure. Now, she was certain again, and it felt good. That left a whole cabaret of feelings she wasn't ready to confront when it came to him, such as why he was the only one who had stood on her side, despite everything. Dang him and his ability to make one overlook his faults.

Rizza's feet carried her to her bedroom door, and only after Lance was inside, the room was defended so those outside couldn't hear inside, the door was firmly locked, and Carl delightfully tied up with ropes that bit into him, did Rizza undo the magic on the man.

"You horse's ass!" Carl shouted. His first words were spitting venom as he tried his best to get a reaction out of Rizza while also trying to get out of the ropes around him. Rizza leaned against a doorway without a single word for a moment before she shook her head. He was clearly in pain as the ropes tightened with his struggles and holy water seeped into his clothing, burning his skin.

"Carl, you used the same trick twice. Of course I'm not going to fall for it the second time. Even if you're stupid, did you really have to be that dumb?" Rizza replied honestly to her earlier assessment of his wasted twenty years resurfacing, her eyeballs rolling around in her head as she did so.

"Fuck you, witch. You're still just jealous that she loves me. Maybe you should have stayed in your grave. Everything would have been easier, then." The man snorted before spitting a loogie at her feet. Rizza glanced at it before flinging it back in his face with a burst of magic. She sneered.

"Keep your spittle to yourself, this room is rather nice. No, I do not envy you for the love of the queen. As, frankly, she has been proven to be, without a doubt, evil. Killing two of her children? That's just fucked up. I mean, okay, she only succeeded at killing one, but still." Rizza shuddered in disgust at the idea.

"You don't know what you're talking about! You don't know how close Drake was to finding out. He had to go. They couldn't let him jeopardize the entire family. You don't even understand!" Carl ranted and raved. Rizza had thought she'd have to pull information out of him. Yet here he was, spilling his guts like a moron. She leaned back in the chair she was in, and stared at him while he went off.

"Of course... you wanted Drake dead because he-... Oh, never mind, this will all be revealed later on, anyways," Rizza grumbled.

Lance was still confused, and he looked over at Rizza like a puppy whose owner was giving commands it didn't understand. Rizza pitied him.

"I am planning on showing this asinine fool off to the court, and proving the Queen's guilt without a shadow of a doubt, especially when I use my honesty spell on her ass and make her spill." Rizza smirked.

"Oh, so that's why you wanted me to make sure her holy water wasn't holy water." Lance came to the realization, his fist landing in the palm of his other hand with an 'aha' expression. Rizza really wanted to smile but this was serious business. He was finally catching up to what was going on. He still wasn't sure why holy water had such an effect but if Rizza said so he was inclined to believe it.

Carl, again, tried spitting at her, only to have it land in his face. He let out a snarl as he struggled in his bindings. "Augh! Stop doing that!" he shouted.

"Then stop spitting on my floor," Rizza replied tartly. She was utterly aggravated. Rizza rubbed her temple before shaking her head softly.

"Did you have a chance to go and do what I asked, to get the holy water switched out?" Rizza asked curiously. She had a feeling she knew what all the puzzle pieces were now, she just needed to fit them together. Pratt could thank her later.

"Yes, yes, I did. Someone has already done it," Lance said quickly. He nodded vigorously and smiled. Rizza nodded in return before suddenly turning to him.

"This is going to hurt a bit." Before he could ask what, Rizza started. Her magic began realigning his image and changing his outward appearance to that of Carl's. The subtle sound of bones realigning, breaking and reforming and things changing could be heard. Lance gasped in pain. He ended up looking exactly like the man in a matter of minutes, and when he was done, he whimpered.

"What did you do?" He asked. Rizza offered him a mirror and he gasped in shock and mild horror as he saw himself. "I... I... look like a... a..." He was stuttering, trying to come up with the right words, words that wouldn't offend Rizza, since she was actually rather nice to him all things considered.

"A monster," Rizza finished for him. She was used to being called one enough that she didn't really care.

"Hey, I have feelings, you know?" Carl chimed in from the side. He was clearly not as used to the comments as she was. Rizza glanced at him before suddenly reaching out and plucking at his throat. His spit covered face was ghastly to look at as it was, and he was annoying enough that this was a double bonus for her.

She didn't actually touch his throat, but the action seemed to have drawn something out of him. He suddenly couldn't speak, no matter how hard he tried. Then, Rizza looked at Lance. If she were to just give him Carl's voice, he'd lose his own, so, instead, she grabbed a random pendant off the nightstand, and put the voice inside the gem before handing it back to Lance.

"Take this. As long as you wear it, you'll sound like him." Rizza said firmly.

Lance took the pendant, and slipped it on. He tried out his new voice a couple of times and seemed utterly creeped out. The poor boy looked ready to faint as he looked over at Rizza. Magic and extreme plotting was not his idea of a good time.

"Why... am I like this?" Lance finally asked.

"Because you are going to pretend to be Carl in front of the queen, so she won't suspect anything. Oh, also, take these." Rizza made a pluck at Carl's head this time, and the man seemed to slump in the chair for a moment before glaring silently at Rizza. Rizza smiled. It of course hurt to lose memories, just like it hurt to regain them. Carl probably felt like he'd been shot with how quickly she'd done it. She didn't care.

She took the memories, and placed them in a different amulet before handing it to Lance. Once he had it, Lance had a splitting headache. Pain shot through his temples as memories invaded his brain that weren't his own. He gritted his teeth against the pain until it subsided.

When it did, Rizza nodded. "You'll need those to fool the queen into believing you're the real deal. I think we are about done with the disguise. You should be able to pull this off nicely for about a week. After that, I'll turn you back." Rizza smiled.

"Why don't we just take Carl to the king and prove Pratt's innocence and expose the queen?" Lance asked, he seemed dejected at having to deal with all of this rigmarole to get things done.

"Because that would be no fun. I want her to confess, in her own voice, the things she did," Rizza grumbled in annoyance. If one wanted to mess with the most powerful being in the world, fine. Rizza would mess right back.

After that, a week passed.

Precursor

A week had gone by, and Rizza had kept Carl carefully secluded in her room. With a bit of magic, the maids who came and went didn't even know he was there. Meanwhile, Lance was pretending to be Carl. The poor boy didn't know what to do when the queen wanted to do that with him, so he found this or that excuse to leave. He also spent every moment that he was able to escape from the queen bitching about how she tried to sleep with him, as if having to bed a beautiful woman was such a tragedy. Then again, it could get his head taken off. So... better he complained instead of letting nature take its course. Plus, she was old enough to be the boy's mother.

No one had seen Pratt during that week. The king was utterly furious that he could not be found, but Rizza assured him that he would be. She also spent time buttering up to the queen. She had accepted the apology from her, and they had begun to get close once more. Overall, it was a pretty easy week.

Rizza had kept her eyes out for Pratt. The man had hurt her, badly, but they were still working towards the same goal. Granted, he didn't know that. He had no idea Rizza had figured everything out already, all the little clues, everything. She hadn't even told Lance what happened in full yet.

He had been trying to figure things out on his own, but the boy wasn't the sharpest tool in the shed, and was having a small problem with it. Still he was trying, and it was admirable. He gave up after three days of asking Rizza what happened. She had been bent on not doing any reveal until the big reveal.

Rizza was all about the show, about the style and the flare, and she would get them all. A show with style, flare, and finesse? That was her cup of tea. Rizza would not give any of those things up, not to Lance or anyone else, so he was left to wait, like the rest of the unsuspecting castle.

The daily lives of the castle seemed to settle into a mundane drawl. Everything was going well, and Rizza finally found Pratt.

Or rather, Pratt found Rizza.

'Twas the night before Rizza was going to do her grand reveal. She had set it all up so that at morning court the next day, the queen would spill her guts, the real Carl would be revealed, and everything would be cleared up. The king would, of course, have to execute his wife, but that was small potatoes in the grand scheme of things.

Rizza was relaxed in her bathtub when she felt a change in the air. Her gaze shifted up and she spotted Pratt as he blinked into existence. A sigh escaped her as once more she clouded the bathwater she was sitting in. At least this time, he didn't get a sneak peek.

Of course, she had wanted him to come out eventually despite their quarrel, but while she was bathing, it was just rude. She would have settled for him revealing himself gratefully after she had unveiled his mother as the treacherous woman she was and cleared his good name. That way, he could forget about all the nasty things she said about him to his face as well as behind his back.

"You just really like spying on a girl in the bath, don't you? I never knew the Prince had such a bad habit," Rizza chided, annoyance in her voice. Carl was kept carefully on the other side of the screen, away from prying eyes. She had no interest in showing off her female form to her love rival of a past life, that was just disgusting.

"You know, my timing is pretty bad." Pratt admitted. Then, he stared at her warily for a moment. "Are you still mad at me?" he finally asked, trepidation in his voice. He looked ready to leave the moment she said anything of the affirmative variety. He was not ready to die for something he had not done.

"No, not particularly. The things you said were harsh, but they weren't untrue," Rizza said calmly. Her fingers dipped into the water and she splashed it around a bit absent-mindedly. She had already put a ward up around the room so their conversation wouldn't be overheard. "Though, an apology wouldn't make me mad, either," she tossed out as an afterthought.

"Rizza... I'm sorry..." Pratt grumbled after a moment. He meant it, but it was still hard to say. Rizza wasn't going to complain, though. It was more than most would do for her.

Then, a devious light flickered in her eyes. She debated on telling Pratt then and there about his father, the man sitting in the corner of the room, invisible to the naked eye. She debated watching him break down before anyone else had the chance to, but she didn't think that would be fun.

"I have been switching out the holy water," Pratt said calmly.

"You have been?" Rizza's eyebrow arched. She looked up at Pratt once more. He was leaning against the wall. She had a feeling it had been him helping with the water, but it was hard to tell with how many backstabbing liars there were in this castle.

"Well, my servant has. The man is only loyal to me. The water should be fully out of her system by tomorrow, and her maid's, too." Pratt explained calmly. It seemed he had more trusted allies than she did. That was good, at least.

"Ah, I know that already. I have been keeping tabs on her. I was actually planning to do a grand reveal of all of her heinous acts tomorrow. Did you want to come watch?" Rizza offered. Her fingers splashed in the bath a bit more. Then, a thought emerged in her head, and she made a rubber ducky appear in the water. She began to play with it, amusing herself with whimsical things as they talked.

"Come watch? Wait, you already have a plan? I was going to come beg you to do something." Pratt furrowed his eyebrows. He'd already mentally prepped himself to get on his knees and grovel. Yet, it seemed pointless now. It wasn't like Rizza to be so... prepared... for anything.

"Yes, yes, I have a plan. You see, she killed me. It was her. Well, not directly, but I'll get into the nitty-gritty of it tomorrow. Please do make an appearance. It will be so much better that way." Rizza grinned maniacally as she played with her duck.

"You-... That poor rubber ducky, what are you doing to it?"

Pratt was going to comment on her plan, but caught himself staring at Rizza as she pried at the bottom of it.

"Why, I'm turning it inside out, or... trying to... I feel if I keep pulling on this hole, it will just cause the duck to rip." Rizza sighed and gave up on her efforts. The poor rubber duck, as Pratt had called it, was left alone as she flicked it and caused it to sail across the water towards her feet. "Anything else? Or did you just want to reconvene tomorrow after I prove you innocent?" Rizza asked. Obviously, Pratt needed Rizza to do it, because if he tried, he'd be killed.

"No... no, that was..." Pratt seemed to notice something as he looked out into her room. He could sense a magical presence, and, after a moment, cast a dispel of illusion. He spotted the man in the corner and stared at him with wide eyes. Staring back at him were two very angry ones that looked... similar.

"Oh... you weren't supposed to see him, yet," Rizza grumbled. "Pratt, meet your father, Carl."

She took the chance of him looking away from her to climb free of the water and put on a robe. She carefully tied it so she was decently covered before stepping out into the room. She glanced between Carl and Pratt before nodding.

"So glad you've met each other. He can't talk right now, Lance has his voice." Rizza explained easily enough. The two men were staring each other down. One as if he'd seen a ghost, and the other pissed beyond all belief.

"Lance... has his ... What do you mean Lance has his voice? Where the hell did he come from, and what do you mean, he's my father? Why does he look like me?" Pratt had to take a moment to recompose himself. He had to give it to Rizza, she really did know how to make everyone question what the hell was going on. He didn't even know where to begin with this bit of news. Rizza, on the other hand, was highly amused. She couldn't help but laugh slightly as Pratt got upset about this discovery.

"Lance has his voice. I took Carl's voice and gave it to Lance, so Lance could pretend to be Carl for the week, and your mother wouldn't realize I had caught him. Honestly, catch up,

Pratt. What have you been doing this entire week, just sitting around waiting for the holy water to be out of her system?" Rizza knew she hit the nail on the head when Pratt flinched and looked away awkwardly. She let out a soft laughing sigh as she shook her head.

"Beautiful. Yes, he is your father. Your mother mated with this poor fellow, and conceived you. I will explain this whole dramatic, bull crap play tomorrow at the grand finale." Rizza shook her head. "For now, get out. I promise I will answer everything, I just don't want to have to answer the same questions five times. Lance has also been asking these questions." Rizza shooed Pratt towards the door.

He didn't leave right away. Instead, he stared at his father a moment longer. After that, he looked at Rizza. He looked like he had a lot he wanted to say, but in the end, he kept it to himself as he vanished from sight.

Rizza waited until he was gone before looking over at Carl. She frowned, and snapped her fingers, reapplying the illusionary magic that made him invisible. Though he was invisible, Rizza knew he could still see her. She let out a sigh, and grabbed the sheet she'd been using before tossing it over his head. It, too, went invisible after coming into contact with him.

Satisfied that he wouldn't be spying on her in her sleep, she changed into a nightgown and crawled under the covers. Tomorrow was going to be a very, very big day for them all. Rizza was so excited.

The Grand Finale

Lance rubbed his jaw after the illusionary magic was removed from him. He carefully handed back both of the amulets that had been given to him, and Rizza casually tossed the memories and the voice back at Carl. Both Lance and Carl reeled as the memories were pulled from one head and thrown casually into the other.

It was early morning still, court would be going on in the main chambers. It was the perfect time to prepare and present her little performance. Rizza was busy getting ready and helping Lance to do the same.

The room seemed to be dense with anticipation and trepidation. Unease on what was about to happen was clear on the faces of Lance and Carl, even while Rizza looked calm and composed herself.

"You bitch, what are you planning to do now?" Carl hadn't been privy to the goings-on any more than anyone else had, so he, too, was curious. Rizza glanced at him before snorting out a laugh. The man was arrogant and cocky. His magic was stilted and required a surprise attack. That meant he was basically cannon fodder to her. As if she was going to tell him a single thing.

"You are so much more likeable when you're quiet…" She immediately muted him once more. Rizza didn't even look at him as she busied herself getting ready.

There were many things still yet to prepare. Mainly, what would she wear? She had three cloaks laid out on the bed before her. one was a dark purple, another a burgundy and then there was her typical red. Was she going to stay traditional, or was she going to spice things up? Decisions. Rizza stared down at her cloaks for a bit before finally seeming to settle on the red one. Traditional wouldn't give as much away as quickly as the other ostentatious cloaks would.

After Rizza was done straightening her cloak she looked over at Carl again. Casually, Rizza moved over toward him. She patted his cheek as a smile blossomed on her face.

"No fear, Carl. You'll get to see the Grand Finale of all of this scheming, same as everyone else. " Rizza wasn't going to spoil things for Carl, either. An entire week, she had waited an entire boring week of sucking up to the villain to make this beautiful drama play out well.

A week to brood over the fact that... she hadn't been important. The events that had led up to her untimely demise, the events that led to Drake's demise and the stupid engagement... none of it had been about her. That had been festering in her soul for an entire week. Well, now it was about her. Or at least, it was about to be.

As they were getting ready, there was a flash of magic, and Pratt appeared in the room. Rizza turned to look at him. He still looked shell-shocked, and when he saw Carl, his face contorted once more. Rizza couldn't help but admire the beginning of the drama. This was already fun, and it had barely begun.

"Hello, Pratt, following along invisibly?" She asked curiously. She didn't even try to comfort the man who had found out his mother was a scheming, treacherous, snake. Rather she jumped right into the meat of things. She wanted to get this show on the road.

He removed his eyes from his father for long enough to look at her and give her a firm nod. She nodded in return, and let him use his own magic to conceal him. After all, who would reveal him? The only two who could were herself and Carl, and Carl was a little bit... useless, as usual.

"Are you ready, Lance?" Lance, for his part, was still staring at himself in the mirror. He was so happy to be back to who he actually was. He'd been using his fingers to push at his cheeks and feel his skin now that it was back to normal. He was glad he had his own appearance, to him he suddenly looked dashing after spending a week looking like a wizard. Rizza doubted the boy would ever hate his own appearance again. Another kind deed done, boosting a boy's moral and confidence in his own visage. Wonderful.

He turned and gave her a nod, and she summoned Carl. He lifted off the ground into the air with the move of her hand, and was carted after them as they walked down the hall to morning court. It was going to be so much fun.

Rizza was so excited for this event. Even though Rizza was covered in her cloak she still couldn't help the smile that peaked out from under it. The only thing that was visible under her cloak was the slow curl up of her lip as she did. And so, they proceeded to the stage.

As they made their way to the massive double doors that made up the throne room of the court, Rizza smiled. Lance, of course, went to entreat the guards to open it, but Rizza didn't give him time. With a wave of her hand and a blemish of magic, she threw the doors open. They slammed into the walls on either side, causing quite the commotion.

The room was filled with courtiers and peasants alike, people there to be heard by the king, and those there to advise him and listen to the commoners of their regions so as to better serve them. All processions halted, however, as Rizza blew open the doors. Several commoners were seen cowering in fear at her action, and the king's face... Well, wasn't he pissed at her antics?

The commoners had clearly been in the middle of explaining their current problems to him when she interrupted. One knelt on the ground before the throne and even as Rizza's gaze swept over him, he cowered into the floor. His actions made it seem as if he were trying to become the carpet itself, or the marble under it.

Rizza was quick to look up onto the throne as she saw the king. He was notably pissed off. His mouth opened, his fingers clenched into fists and he slammed his hand down on his chair, ready to yell at her.

"Rizza this..." His first reaction was to bellow about her interrupting court, until he saw the man suspended in the air behind her. Rizza could tell what he was thinking, and she shook her head. The others also noticed who she had behind her, and there was a round of gasps and amazement.

"Pratt... She actually caught Pratt... How did she do it... I thought-..." Whispers flooded the room as everyone began to speculate about how the useless witch-... useless? Rizza bristled at that comment. Her gaze darted over to the person who said it. Instantly the courtier cowered behind his companions. The entire group looked ready to flee at that moment as they all took a step back and away. That part of the room became silent.

Rizza had to draw her angry gaze. She had a mission, a purpose, a point to this shallow little performance she'd started. She straightened her hood with a snort before turning back to the king and queen. Moving forward into the room, Carl floating behind and Lance on her side she moved until she was the center of it. In the middle of everyone's gazes and everyone's attention.

"No, this isn't Pratt. Your highness, please sit down. This will be fun." Rizza smiled under her hood. Her teeth showed little needles in her mouth. The guards that had initially risen to alert as Rizza entered in such an aggressive manner backed off a tad but kept their weapons drawn.

The queen saw Carl, and immediately tried to find an excuse to leave the room, but when she tried to speak, she found she could not. Furthermore, when she tried to stand, she felt as if she were suddenly tied to the chair. Then, the magic intensified until she was looking directly into Rizza's eyes, which were filled with barely-repressed mirth and amusement at the queen's distress. Rizza had cast magic as the queen began to put things together. She'd even made it so the Queen, and only the Queen, could see her eyes under her hood as she peeked from under it. There was a very obvious understanding between the two. It wasn't about Rizza before, but it is now.

The king's face was filled with confusion. Everyone in the court began to whisper among themselves once more as Rizza brought the man forward and made him kneel. Carl's face was ghastly as he sneered. He strained against the silencing spell that held him, but it did no good for him. He was trapped.

"I am sure you have questions, and I will address them all at the end, but first, let me take some time to enlighten you all as to what's been going on." Rizza's face was contorted into a malicious grin. She loved this part, the part where she got to look like the victor who saved the day. Granted, she was the idiot who got murdered in her previous life, but, today, she could be the hero who saved the day.

Rizza got started. She left Carl where he knelt as she moved to a spot that put her at dead center of all the attention, just where she wanted to be.

"So, as most of you know, over twenty years ago, my glorious self was murdered." Rizza spoke softly. Her smile was obvious on her face, as if she didn't care about it at all.

"Rizza…" The king's voice held an edge of warning. He did not understand why she would bring that up now, when she was busy showing off a man who looked just like his son. The king was no fool, and he shot a side-eye at his wife. He wanted to stop her, but at the same time he wanted to know what was going on. Though Rizza chose a public place to dredge out his family's dirty laundry… it was needed.

The queen was spellbound and unable to speak. Fear had already begun to permeate her existence, because she realized her holy water was not working. That meant… Rizza had figured it out a week ago… then why hadn't Carl tipped her off? Rizza saw the panic in the queen's gaze and knew what she must be thinking.

"Sorry, my queen, Carl couldn't tell you about this ahead of time, he was already taken care of. You were spending time with Lance this week." Rizza watched as her eyes widened in terror. Her gaze shot to the king and his gaze narrowed. Oh, this really was too fun for Rizza. It took all her self-control to keep from cackling.

The restlessness of the room grew and while all attention was on Rizza and Carl, the man who'd been on the floor before was taking his chance to flee. He crawled away among the feet and legs of the nobles around him as he tried his best to get away from the limelight. No one even tried to stop him. Rather, many moved aside, understanding the fear he felt.

"Your highness, let me tell the story, I promise this is the fun part. Well, for me, anyways." She drew focus back to herself like an expert storyteller leading the audience into the beginning of a magnificent and enchanting tale.

The king's brows furrowed, but he didn't interrupt. When Rizza knew he was going to let her speak, she smiled. She'd already silenced the queen, so she couldn't interrupt. That was for the best.

"Many of you knew me in my past life. Suave, charming, handsome... amazing wizard that I was, not to pat my own back. Many of you were my friends then, unlike now, where I terrify the daylights out of you." The court seemed to nervously chuckle at that, and Rizza nodded.

"Yet, alas, someone had the audacity to rob you all of my presence and service then, leaving you with the disgrace of a magician I am now, trapped in the body of a brat with the mind of a five-year-old. Truly, it's tragic. At least, that's how all of you would depict it." She paused to stare at them all. No one dared to meet her gaze. She knew what they thought of her. She was not so blind as to miss it.

"And we have whom to blame for THAT, as well? Why, the queen, of course. Why would she take me in? Was it the debt she owed to the previous me, the me who put her ass on the throne? No, of course not. Such a vile woman would not be so kind." Rizza began to pace the floor. She was setting the stage for herself, and making herself look grand and imposing. The big reveal was the best.

"I can't blame her fully, though. Her taking me in gave me time to get familiar with the castle once more. During my years here, I'd always wanted to explore the reason for my previous death. What had I done that was so mean, so heinous, someone would actually feel the need to end my life then, but not now, when I have tortured you all so?" Rizza put on a sorrowful expression as she covered her face with the back of her hand as if tortured herself.

"Rizza…" The king's voice was a terse warning. He did not like the dramatics as much as she did, did not like how she dragged out the story, and did not like her alluding so much to his wife: the wife he was beginning to get very, very angry with. His hands curled against his throne and the courtiers who got wrapped up in Rizza's recanting of the past quickly schooled their expressions as they did not want to end up on his bad side.

Rizza smiled sheepishly, and cleared her throat for a bit. "So, anyway, skipping forward, I was banished, then brought back, and forcibly engaged to the endearing prince Pratt, who looks JUST like his father, but we'll get to that." Rizza glanced back at Carl very obviously before staring at the queen with a soft 'tsk'. The king's temper shot through the roof at this point, so Rizza quickly rushed forward. She could see his face turning red and the vein on his forehead threatened to burst if she did not.

"But, yes… then, the late prince Drake and his wonderful fiancée were assassinated, and I was the first to point fingers at Pratt. How wrong I was, I led you all down a terrible path, and set it up perfectly for the real culprit to frame him. So, how does all of this tie together, you may be asking?" Rizza spoke a bit faster, because the king was reaching for his scepter, and she had a feeling he was going to throw it at her if she didn't.

"I spent time trying to learn of the awful things he did, and, finally, I realized the wine in the prince's room was not deadly. It wouldn't be deadly until someone mixed it with holy water. Who convinced the court to drink holy water, I wonder? Who convinced the royals? The Irredelum in the wine is what killed Prince Drake and his beautiful wife." Rizza took a moment to breathe. The memory hurt. Then, she stared directly at the queen, already having a feeling she knew whose idea it was to take holy water into their systems. Her suspicions were confirmed when the entire court, and the king, once more stared at the queen. Of course it had been her doing, probably at Carl's recommendation.

"No, I wasn't the target. This entire tragedy, my death, the crown prince's death, every death that has happened to this court has been related to this incident. I was nothing more than a tragic pawn in this like everyone else. This was never about me... and that hurts." Her gaze went to the queen, and then to Carl with a look of horror and absolute disappointment. "After all I did for you two. You could have made it about me a little."

Carl stared back at her like she was a daft idiot before letting out a silent laugh. Rizza put a hand to her chest as she stared around the room. "Damn it... It didn't even matter... I was just part of this shit because I figured out in my past life that these two were making a cuckold of the king... Can you all believe that?" Rizza gestured to the queen and Carl, clearly baffled by it all. No one else seemed as shocked. Not everyone cared about Rizza as much as she did. She knew that but it still hurt.

While she was having her minor breakdown, all the tension in the court cracked and everyone wanted to smack their foreheads. Such a huge crime was being laid at the queen's feet, and Rizza was only upset because she didn't matter?

Rizza forced herself to regain her own composure after the king slammed his hand down onto his throne. His glare was intense.

"Right... Anyways, it's about me now. Take that, you jerks. You thought you'd get the last laugh after murdering me, but HA, it is I who gets to laugh." Rizza pointed at both the queen and Carl as she spoke. Then, she turned back to the king. "AS I WAS SAYING! Yes, everything, even my pitiful death, was because of the queen... she orchestrated-..." Rizza was cut off mid-sentence.

"Even Sir Edgar's death?" Someone in the council spoke up. Rizza frowned. Who was Sir Edgar? She had no idea. She waved her hand off at him.

"Er... no. I didn't even know he died." Rizza answered awkwardly. Who the hell was Sir Edgar? The others seemed disappointed by that.

"Anyways, no. This all came about because the queen, who fell deeply in love, did not fall in love with the king. She fell in love with power and authority. She fell in lust with a two-bit mage named Carl, and she didn't fall in love with him until after marrying the king and realizing he under-performed at night– sorry, your highness, her words, not mine." Rizza bowed slightly to the king before looking back at the crowd. She could see the scarlet color on the king's face turn from one of rage to embarrassment as she spoke those words aloud. There were several courtiers who hid their faces behind their fans or hands to avoid getting yelled at for laughing. This morning's court session had become a mockery and any seriousness of the situation was hard to have with such convoluted problems arising.

"What proof do you have?" The king asked, his face a scarlet red after what Rizza just said. He was staring at his wife, but his voice was filled with doubt, as if he could not believe his ears. He was trying to keep on track because he had none of the humor of the situation.

"What proof? Your highness, the proof sits at your feet. This is Carl. Tell me who you thought he looked like when I brought him in." Rizza smiled faintly. The king's gaze dropped to the man on the ground. The queen was looking very pale at this point. Though the king had not joined in on announcing that Rizza had caught Pratt, everyone had heard the words spoken by those in the masses. Even the king had the same reaction at first.

"That's... truly not Prince Pratt?" The king asked. His voice still held doubt. He did not want to believe that among all the things that had gone wrong that his son... was not his.

"How can that be me, when I am right here?" Pratt asked, his form appearing with a shimmer. His form was graceful, and he was obviously standing next to Rizza this entire time. He bowed to his father. He looked very shaken, but he kept it to a minimum as he tried to keep courteous.

"I am sorry I did not come forward sooner. I did not want to be killed for a crime I didn't commit." He said softly. He then looked up at the king with a bit of regret. "I am sorry for failing you, Father."

The king's face at this point was changing colors dramatically. Rizza could tell he was about to explode in a fit of rage, but she was quick to stop him.

"Wait, before you blow up, let me finish." Rizza held up her hands.

The king almost asked what more there could be, but he still wanted to know how all of this tied together, so he sat down. His face was blank as he waited for the rest.

"So, to recap, this is Pratt, this is Pratt's father, and, of course, the queen is his mother. I was wondering how you ended up with a magical son, until I put this together. You see, In my past life, I had discovered this betrayal of your wife's, so I was going to tell you. Little did I realize that I'd grown soft. I let my guard down. The second I stepped from my bedroom after writing in my tome that detailed all of what I knew, I was killed. I only had enough remaining life force to seal off the room so that Carl here could not destroy the evidence. Carl had shot me dead with crossbow bolts, and then gone into hiding once more. No one could solve the murder, because no one in the castle knew he was in the castle." Rizza explained patiently. She glanced around, then looked at Pratt. Pratt met her gaze, his own filled with mixed emotions ranging from curiosity, hurt, to dread.

"This is where the hard part comes in. Your mother, the queen, raised me, in hopes I'd open the door that I had sealed with my final breath. She was hoping to burn the evidence of her crime before anyone, including myself, found out. Then, after that, she was planning to get rid of me. How? By framing me for killing Drake, of course." Rizza turned to look at the queen, a sneer on her face.

"I'm sure that was not her original plan, since Drake was a beloved son of hers, at least, I'd hope no mother would be that brutal. However, when Drake started to suspect his brother's origins, and started having doubts about weird things happening in the castle, the queen and Carl knew he must go, and so, the plot was born. She convinced his highness to invite me to the castle once more under the pretense of marrying Pratt and strengthening his magic. After that, it was a cinch to switch the wine in the bedroom to something that would react with the holy water, like Rivelum, a wine that Pratt enjoyed well, and no one would be the wiser. Even I missed it, at first. Then, she just had to frame me."

Rizza went on to explain in detail while pacing the room like a detective.

"Ah. We will let the queen tell her own story shortly." Rizza then looked back at the dais where the king and queen sat.

"Wait, if the queen was framing, you... then what about the two servants who framed Pratt?" The king was no fool. He was starting to put the dots together. Rizza nodded her head along.

"I, too, was wondering about that. I didn't realize it, until I got my memories back, and saw Carl once more." Rizza snorted softly before laughing.

"The servants were paid by Carl. They were so blinded by their greed that they didn't realize he wasn't the prince, so they honestly thought it was Pratt who paid them. They weren't lying, they were just dumb, like everyone else here was when I originally brought him in. The resemblance really is uncanny." Rizza shook her head. "Such a stupid oversight, really. You'd think with all the murder, the queen would have had the sense to murder those two as well."

Rizza shrugged softly before continuing. "So, on a fluke, I was proven innocent, and Pratt was now to blame. The queen would have continued her affair in silence and gotten away with it, if not for that fluke." Rizza tsk'd softly.

"Wait... so me being involved... was also a fluke?" Pratt realized what was going on, and he looked at Rizza. Rizza looked across the room. Everyone was in a mixed state of shock, awe, and horror at the understanding. She then looked back at the prince.

"You were, yes. You weren't supposed to be born. You were the result of a night of drunk sex that resulted in pregnancy, and against the queen's better judgement, she didn't kill you. So, you lived on, and would have continued to be blissfully unaware if I hadn't figured all this out." Rizza said calmly. "The only reason the queen suggested we get married was so she had an excuse to drag me out of the mountains and make me her scapegoat when Drake started to discover things." Rizza said calmly. "This entire play was not about either of us, it was about this adulterous couple right here."

Rizza turned her gaze back to the queen, and back to Carl. She stared at them both before chuckling as the king's face got darker. Pratt, in comparison, paled. He looked like he was going to be sick with how blunt Rizza was about his lack of importance.

"I've heard enough." The king said. His voice lacked its usual thunder. He was devastated by the news and had no way of coming to terms with it. So much killing, so many lies right under his nose. All of which had been solved by a bit of dumb luck.

"But, wait, hold on. Don't you want to hear it from the horse's mouth?" Rizza asked curiously. She looked at the queen and lifted the muting spell she had placed. She replaced it with a spell of truth and willingness. It made her compliant to speak.

"Yes, god damn it! It was me!" The queen shouted. She wished she could shut up but she couldn't, the spell wouldn't allow it. Her nails bit into the armrests of her chair as she sat there. "I killed Rizza in her past life, I had an affair, I killed my own son when he was on the verge of figuring it out, I did it all. I framed Rizza, and I planned to kill Pratt, too, using Rizza's hand, all to protect my crown. It was me! If it weren't for Drake's meddling, none of this would have happened, if Rizza hadn't followed me that night all those years ago, I wouldn't have had to do this!" She shouted the words, and the court was stunned into silence. Tears streamed down her face from mixed anger and guilt. She had, after all, killed her son.

The queen was breathing hard at that point. Her chest heaving. She looked like a woman who'd gone stark raving mad. The tears on her face ruined her makeup and made it slide down. No one knew what to say.

Even Rizza was slightly stunned by the ferocity of her admittance to her crime. Rizza whistled softly. "Dang, that was a quick summary. Maybe I should have just let you talk from the start."

"Why didn't you? Wait, if you could have solved all of this so easily, then why wait the week to have her tell it in the first place? It was clear that you didn't need her to." Pratt stared down at Rizza after he came out of his own moment of sorrow at everything that had transpired. He was utterly confused about her logic of waiting so long just to prove him innocent, when she clearly could have done it a long time ago.

"Oh, that?" Rizza questioned softly. She scratched the bridge of her nose sheepishly before grinning ear to ear. "I really just wanted to put on a show. Look at how much more fun this was."

If it was possible for people's jaws to fall off, they probably would have. The entire crowd was stumped into silence as they heard her words. This dramatic, traumatic event came to a head in such a climactic way, all because Rizza was bored. Rizza... was bored, and she wanted attention, so she solved the murder and waited a week to reveal it, just for drama.

The king stared at her for a moment. The court stared at her. Then, the rage finally overwhelmed him.

"Someone! Take the queen away. The execution is tomorrow. Take this low-life, as well. I don't ever want to see these two again. They will both be under the guillotine at sunrise!" He slammed his fists into the wood on his chair, breaking it apart with the force he exerted as his heart began to race.

Shortly after, he fainted from the amount of rage he was exhibiting. The entire court was in an uproar. People raced to his side only to be shoved back by his guards. Rizza and Pratt exchanged looks of horror and surprise. Quickly they both dashed up to help him.

Rizza used her magic to part the sea of people and they rushed to get him to his room.

Now What?

Three days had passed since the big reveal. The court was still in shock and the place had been tipped on its head. All for what, so Rizza could be amused? No, that wasn't the case, not at all.

The king was left in a state of exhaustion. He only woke up a few hours ago, and Rizza and Pratt were by his bedside. The other Prince and the two Princesses were also there. Rizza still hadn't bothered to learn their names. Pratt was carefully holding the king's hand as he slowly came to. He was groggy and out of it.

"Pratt? Lizzy... Becca... Carter..." His voice was horse as he called out to his children. Then, his gaze finally landed on Rizza. He paused. "Rizza." There was a distinct sense of remorse in his voice. He did not quite know how to feel about the witch now that he knew the things he did.

"Your highness." Rizza replied softly. She carefully took his other hand, and channeled some healing magic into it. He slowly sat up in bed, feeling revitalized as Rizza helped him.

He stared at his hands for a moment before letting out a long, drawn-out sigh.

"Well, this wasn't what I expected." He said [illegible]tly. The quiet thunder was gone from his voice. All he so[illegible]ike at this point was a frail, old man. The love of his li[illegible]ayed him, killed his son, and tried to kill the witch. He[illegible]w what to do, what to say. Another son wasn't even h[illegible]gh he had raised him, and he had almost died, as well. Wh[illegible]ness.

"Father..." Pratt called softly.

"No... I'm not... am I? I'm not your father." The king sounded hurt by that fact. He had cared for Pratt this entire time, all of the boy's life, helped him learn swordplay, got the best books for magic, and it was to raise someone else's son.

"Why? Why does my boy have to die... and his gets to live?" the king asked softly, the grief showing on his face. Losing Drake was probably the hardest thing ever for the king. He swallowed his pain as he tried not to cry. Pratt closed his mouth and moved away from the bed slightly. The other of the king's children did not speak. They watched with saddened eyes because in the month that Rizza had been back at the castle their family had quietly fallen apart.

Rizza stared at him for a moment before shrugging. "Because the queen was a psychotic bitch?" Rizza offered up. Everyone turned to stare at her like she had two heads. She scratched the back of her neck slightly. "What? We were all thinking about it."

There was silence in the room for a moment before there was laughter. Everyone needed to laugh after the tension. Rizza, however, didn't know what she had said that was so funny. She was just being honest. Still, they laughed. Everyone seemed to have relaxed a bit.

After the relaxation was over. The king finally looked up at Pratt, his gaze focused on him, uncertainty written all over his face as to what to do now.

"Well... I can't be crown prince, I'm not even yours." Pratt offered up. That seemed to ease some of the tension in the king's shoulders. He didn't want to say it, but it needed to be said. It was easier that Pratt did it himself.

"No... no, you can't. Which makes Carter the only heir to the throne n... unless someone else comes along and tells me they slept w... wife." The king laughed slightly, a bit of dark humor, but n... d him for that one. It was all a bit too fresh.

There... ...ain silence in the room for a bit. No one really knew how to de... with the fact that Pratt was barely a prince anymore. Sure, he was a prince because he was the son of the queen, but that was all, and she'd been deposed, so that... that didn't work.

"Well, I don't know about you all, but I want to go home." Rizza finally spoke up. She didn't care what happened to the kingdom from this point on. They had made her life hell lately, and she was more or less done with it. She just wanted to go back to her mountains.

The king looked at Rizza for a moment. He nodded. Rizza stood up, and dusted herself off. She smiled at the group before heading for the door. Part of her wanted to say 'it's been fun' but it hadn't been, not at all.

"Rizza." The king called out, right as she reached the door. She turned back. "I release you from your vow of fealty." He spoke firmly.

Rizza could feel a sense of magic wash over her. It was like bathing in a cool stream before a weight was lifted from her chest. Like a lock being opened, the binding was removed, and Rizza no longer had to adhere to the royal summons.

The room stared at her and she stared at the king. He offered her as close as he could get to a smile. There was a silent understanding between them that there would be no next time. She would not be returning to the capital ever.

She opened her mouth, and then closed it. After a second, she gave a brief nod and walked out.

Rizza was outside of the city shortly after packing her things. She didn't say goodbye to Lance, or Mars, or anyone. Instead, she just left. In her eyes, it was better that way.

She doubted she'd have much to say to them even if she did say goodbye, and even if she did, Mars would probably be pissed at her for not coming by more often to begin with. It was really for the best.

Rizza carefully patted the side of her horse as she trotted down the trail. She wasn't moving very fast, no reason to rush home now that all this was done. Instead, she enjoyed the sun on her skin and reflected on the past month in the castle. So much had happened. Her firsthand experience with backstabbers at court would be something she'd have a hard time forgetting.

Rizza let out a self-mocking laugh at the idea. She ran her fingers through the mane under them as she thought about it. Kit had been out and about bobbing around her for a while. However, as they rounded a corner, he disappeared.

Rizza arched a brow as she looked up the road. Ahead of her, sitting on a pure white mount, with nothing but a simple bag tossed over his shoulder, was Pratt.

"Off on a journey of your own?" Rizza asked as she approached him. He offered her a small smile and shrugged.

"I'm not much of a prince anymore, so I figured... maybe I'd come join you in the mountains." He spoke softly. There was a hint of hope in his voice.

Rizza glared dubiously at him as he mentioned joining her in the mountains. Company? She lived in the mountains to avoid company. Why would she want company? "No. Sorry, not enough room. Find your own mountain range." Rizza quickly dismissed him as she kicked her horse up into a faster trot.

Pratt let out a distressed laugh as he made his horse go after hers. "Oh, come on. Don't be like that. You may even enjoy my company!"

"I despise company!" Rizza shouted back. Realizing he wasn't giving up, she kicked her horse into a gallop. He just chased after her, and away they went, into the mountains.

The End

Shine

www.powderriverpublishing.com